Indecent Suggestion

ELIZABETH BEVARLY

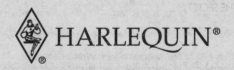

HARLEQUIN®

TORONTO • NEW YORK • LONDON
AMSTERDAM • PARIS • SYDNEY • HAMBURG
STOCKHOLM • ATHENS • TOKYO • MILAN • MADRID
PRAGUE • WARSAW • BUDAPEST • AUCKLAND

For David,
who set the blaze
and keeps it going.

ISBN 0-373-79193-3

INDECENT SUGGESTION

This edition published by arrangement with Harlequin Books S.A.

® and TM are trademarks of the publisher. Trademarks indicated with
® are registered in the United States Patent and Trademark Office, the
Canadian Trade Marks Office and in other countries.

www.eHarlequin.com

Printed in U.S.A.

Turner did a double take to be sure he wasn't seeing things

And when he realized he was seeing what he thought he saw, he could only sit staring openmouthed at the vision.

Becca had emerged from his bedroom wearing nothing but his old college football jersey and a pair of kneesocks.

Never mind that the jersey fell to midthigh on her and covered everything that needed to be covered. That was beside the point. The point was that the outfit his best friend had on was the one she always wore in his second-favorite sexual fantasy about her, the one where she got stranded at his apartment in a snowstorm, and all she had to wear was the very thing she had on now.

"I hope you don't mind me borrowing some clothes," Becca said. "This is the only thing you have that's big enough to cover my, um...my assets," she added with a sheepish grin.

The minute she said it, Turner was helpless to do anything but look at her...assets. And as his gaze roved over her from the top of the silky hair he longed to run his fingers through to the tips of the kneesock-clad toes he wanted to suck, he was nearly overcome with a sexual urge unlike any he had ever experienced before.

Dear Reader,

I once overheard two women talking (oh, all right, I was *eavesdropping* on them) and one said to the other, "I was making love with him, and all of a sudden I wanted to burst out laughing. I was horrified!" To which I responded by thinking, *You're not supposed to laugh while you're having sex? Uh-oh...* I just don't see why sex and laughter have to be mutually exclusive.

So with *Indecent Suggestion,* I tried to show how much *fun* sexual attractions can be. Yeah, there's steam and heat and all that stuff when that certain someone revs your motor, but there should be laughter, too.

I hope Turner and Becca bring you a chuckle as you read about them (and a little steam and heat, too).

Have fun!

Elizabeth Bevarly

Books by Elizabeth Bevarly

HARLEQUIN FLIPSIDE
25—UNDERCOVER WITH THE MOB

SILHOUETTE DESIRE
1363—THE TEMPTATION OF RORY MONAHAN
1389—WHEN JAYNE MET ERIK
1406—THE SECRET LIFE OF CONNOR MONAHAN
1474—TAMING THE PRINCE
1501—TAMING THE BEASTLY MD

Don't miss any of our special offers. Write to us at the following address for information on our newest releases.

Harlequin Reader Service
U.S.: 3010 Walden Ave., P.O. Box 1325, Buffalo, NY 14269
Canadian: P.O. Box 609, Fort Erie, Ont. L2A 5X3

1

"WE HAVE TO STOP THIS, Turner."

Becca Mercer whispered the warning inside the dark storage closet where she and her co-worker had escaped from the drudgery of their jobs to enjoy their dirty little secret in private. But even as they basked in the afterglow of their illicit act, she knew what she was saying was pointless. It wouldn't be long before their sordid desires roared to life again. Those desires—nay, those *needs*—seemed to have lives of their own. For now, though, she lay back and relaxed, closing her eyes to better enjoy the pure satisfaction that curled through her.

She wouldn't trade anything for these stolen moments with Turner. And she was so lucky to have someone like him, someone whose appetite for such forbidden behavior were as relentless as her own. With his blue, blue eyes and unruly black hair, he was wanted by many women. Leisurely, sensuously, she ran a hand through her own shoulder-length, tawny tresses, loving how the scent of their recent act still lingered there.

They often met in the tiny, cramped closet at the end of the hall, whenever the pull of their shared passion was too much to resist. Out of nowhere, the two of them would glance up from their cubicles opposite each other in the offices of Englund Advertising, and their gazes would meet, and they'd know they had to get in a quickie *now*. Sometimes, especially if they were working under the strains of a deadline, they'd have to escape to this closet three, four, even five times a day. That was how desperate they became.

"We have to stop sneaking around this way," she added softly, knowing it was true, even if she dreaded putting a halt to their workday trysts. "What if someone catches us? What if someone finds out what we've been doing?"

"What if someone does?" Turner whispered in reply. "I'm tired of hiding it, anyway. We're consenting adults, Becca. We're responding to a natural impulse, that's all."

"It's not natural," she countered. "Not when it's as strong as this. And we're not responding to it, we're... we're *succumbing* to it. What happens to us is way too powerful to be a simple response."

He murmured a satisfied sound and nudged her knowingly. "Yeah, and that's just the way I like it, baby."

"But we have to *stop*," she insisted again. "It could cost us our jobs. And it could hurt us both in our personal lives. It's getting dangerous."

"It may be getting dangerous," he agreed, "but you can't stop any more than I can. We've tried, Becca. You know we have. But we always end up doing it again. It's consumed us ever since that first time when we were teenagers. There's no way we can stop. We're both insatiable."

True enough, she thought. Because she knew Turner McCloud as well as she knew herself. They'd become friends in first grade, when their shared last initial had landed them close together in classroom seating arrangements. And they'd discovered an immediate connection when both brought peanut butter and banana samwidges in their identical *Star Wars* lunch boxes. Year after year, thanks to the popularity and convenience of alphabetization, they'd ended up together, and over the years, their friendship grew.

Frustrated as teenagers by the restraints and conventions of small-town Indiana life, they'd experienced the usual adolescent flirtations with wild behavior. But one behavior in particular captured and enraptured them, and they'd enjoyed it as often as they could. Knowing they shouldn't, they'd nevertheless been unable to resist. But they'd told no one about it, fearful others would try to make them stop. After high school, they'd attended Indiana University together and, away from parental supervision, discovered their compulsion only grew. As adults, they'd found work in Indianapolis just so they could stay together, and in an urban environment more tolerant of such things, they'd found innumerable ways and places to indulge their desires.

Unfortunately, their workplace wasn't one of them.

However, that didn't keep them from indulging here.

"Remember the first time?" Turner asked now, his voice slicing through the darkness the way it had that first night they'd been so overcome as teenagers. His voice became more rushed, more agitated as he added, "It was so forbidden, and we knew we shouldn't. Everybody warned us about the dangers, told us we were too young, and we wouldn't be able to handle it. But we more than handled it, didn't we, Becca?" he murmured enthusiastically. "And it was so *good* that first time, we had to do it again right away. Hell, you were even more anxious to do it than I was. Remember?"

Her eyes still closed, she let the memories of that first time wash over her. They'd been juniors in high school, and had wanted to escape the goody-two-shoes punch and cookies and pop music at the homecoming dance. After driving around for an hour, they'd parked on the banks of the Ohio River and climbed into the back seat of Turner's red Camaro. A full moon had glistened on the water, a cool breeze had rushed through the open windows and they'd both been edgy and eager. One thing had led to another, and then, suddenly… Well, suddenly, they'd been caught in the throes of the most pleasurable sensations either had ever experienced.

"You bet I remember," she whispered. "It *was* good, wasn't it? Most people say that first time isn't enjoyable. A lot of people have trouble with it. But you and me…"

She didn't have to finish. She knew Turner would remember as well as she did. Everything had worked like a well-oiled machine that night. They'd been naturals.

"I remember when you took it out that first time and how I ran my fingers over it," she continued reverently. "I was afraid to touch it at first, but when I took it in my hand, it felt so good to just hold it and look at it. I'd never seen one up close like that before. It was so long and smooth. So…forbidden. And then, when you told me to put it in my mouth, it was so exciting. So arousing. I *wanted* it in my mouth. I couldn't wait to close my lips over it. And I loved it when I started sucking it. I kept sucking it harder and harder, and it tasted so good, felt so good, and I just filled my mouth with—"

"I remember," he said thickly, cutting her off. "It was incredible that night." He inhaled deeply, releasing the breath in a long, lusty sigh. "Again, Becca," he said roughly. "Just one more time, before we go back to work. That'll get me through the rest of the day. I *need* it."

"Okay," she immediately conceded…yielded…succumbed…whatever. "I need it, too, Turner. I need it so bad."

"C'mon, baby," he crooned, "light my fire."

Becca's heartbeat quickened as she reached toward him, a thrill of exhilaration racing through her. But just as she closed her fingers over his long, smooth rod and drew it into her mouth, just as she was indeed about to light his fire, the door to the closet was thrown open wide, and the harsh light of day—or, rather, the nasty glare of fluorescent lighting, which never did anybody's complexion any good—poured into their cloistered little grotto.

"What the devil is going on in here?" a booming voice exclaimed.

And not just any booming voice, either. Robert Englund's booming voice. And not just any Robert Englund, either. The Robert Englund who'd lent his name to the company Becca and Turner worked for. And she knew that if there were three words to describe her boss, they would be *puritanical, puritanical* and *puritanical*. No way would he approve of what he'd caught them doing.

She squinted in the bright light, able to make out only her employer's rounded silhouette. The booming voice, though—not to mention that puritanical business—went a *long* way toward letting her know just how angry he was.

"Oh, for Pete's sake," he thundered. "Are you two doing it *again?* You're going to burn down the building the way you go at it. How many times do I have to tell you? There's *no smoking on the premises!* Now put out that cigarette."

With that, he stalked off, leaving Becca and Turner crouched in the closet with a still unlit cigarette and a completely unquenched desire. It was just like the song said. They couldn't get no satisfaction.

"OKAY, TURNER, NOW are you convinced we have to quit? Or would you rather we lose our jobs?"

Becca picked at a piece of nonexistent lint on her snug, black wool skirt, tugged down the sleeves of her claret lamb's wool sweater and watched her friend and co-worker pace restlessly the length of the Englund Advertising boardroom. Although neither of them much cared for the dress code of their workplace, finding it a bit too conservative for their tastes, Turner was decidedly less business-like in his business attire than she was.

His charcoal Dockers weren't quite in keeping with the suits their employer demanded, especially since she'd seen his houndstooth jacket slung carelessly over the chair in his cubicle. And instead of the white dress shirts Englund dictated, Turner wore a creamy button-down oxford. He had, however, conceded to the necktie requirement. Of course, the necktie in question had a scantily clad hula dancer painted on it.

Then again, Becca's suit jacket hung on a peg in her own cubicle, and her sweater wasn't a dress shirt, either, so maybe she still had a bit of the rebel in her, too. Sorta. Kinda. In a way.

Outside the windows enclosed the boardroom on two sides; a light snow was sprinkling the Indianapolis skyline, even though November was barely half over and it was too early for any accumulation. Twenty minutes had passed since Englund had caught them smoking in the closet, long enough for him to summon them to this very boardroom, where he'd given them a good dressing-down.

He had said, among other things, that he intended to keep a close eye on both of them, and if he ever caught them smoking at work again, he would fire them. Period.

And Becca would just as soon not have to look for another job. She liked this one in spite of its conservative dress code and shortsighted no-smoking policy. And its unwillingness to explore brave new advertising frontiers. And its archaic mission statement. And its choke hold on creativity. And its lousy health care plan. And its abrasive receptionist. And its appallingly bad coffee.

All right, all right, so maybe she wasn't all that crazy about her job. But she didn't relish looking for a new one, especially with the holidays looming on the horizon.

"Turner?" she echoed when he offered no response. "Did you hear what I said?"

"Yeah, I heard." He reached the far side of the room and spun around to pace back again. "I just don't like it," he added irritably. "Becca, it's not fair that he can make a rule like that."

"Maybe not to you, but it's his business," she pointed out. "He can make all the rules he wants. And he'll fire us if we don't quit smoking."

"We don't have to quit completely," Turner countered, halting in midpace. "We just have to quit doing it at work."

"Oh, yeah, and that's going to be *so* easy," she said. "When was the last time we made it through an entire workday without lighting up two or three times at least?"

"Then we'll just go outside to smoke," he said, crossing his arms over his broad chest in the internationally recognized body language for "I'm right, so there."

Becca dipped her head toward the window behind him. "I don't know if you've noticed, Turner, but we're eighteen stories up. Englund takes up the entire floor, and the businesses beneath us are almost all smoke-free, too. We'd have to go down to the street to smoke, and half the time it takes us ten minutes just to get there, because the elevators run so slow. Unless you think we can slip out unnoticed for a half hour here and there, going outside to smoke isn't doable."

He opened his mouth to argue, but she quickly cut him off.

"And it's snowing today," she added. "If memories of third-grade science serve—which they may not, because most of what I remember from third-grade science is you grossing me out with bug statistics—that means the season of winter is upon us. And I don't want to stand outside in the bitter cold just to have a cigarette. I'll end up spending even more on Chap Stick than I already do on cigarettes."

Turner expelled an impatient breath of air but said nothing.

"And we've got that big account we're trying to win," she further reminded him.

"That big account we're *going* to win," he corrected her.

She nodded. They would win it, she knew. Because the pitch they were working on was nothing short of brilliant. She and Turner had been at Englund for five years now, long enough to have won some small seniority as account reps, but they still weren't in line for any major promotions. At this rate, they'd be stuck in Cubicleville until retirement. Winning this account for Englund would speed them much more quickly up the corporate ladder. They'd be headed straight to Officetown.

"And once we win the account, we'll be stressed to the max," she pointed out. "Whenever we have to work that hard, we smoke like a pit barbecue for a Kennedy family reunion."

This time, in reply, Turner only studied her in silence and thrust out his lower lip like a pouty child.

Becca had to hide the smile she felt threatening. Not that she would ever tell him, of course, but there were times when Turner was just so damn cute. Sexy, even, if you went for the tall, dark and saucy type, which Becca most certainly did *not*. She'd always been drawn to the shy, tame and bookish type, and Turner was none of those things. Of course, the sex with such men had always been rather shy and tame, too—and bookish, she couldn't help thinking, since her last boyfriend had insisted that if they were going to consult the *Kama Sutra* as Becca wanted, then it must only be from a literary standpoint, because he abhorred people who only looked at books for the pictures. So maybe she ought to alter her outlook on the opposite sex....

At any rate, she didn't think of Turner McCloud in any way other than as a friend.

Okay, okay, so maybe they *did* do a little sexual experimenting as teenagers once or twice. But that was to be expected, since they'd grown up in a small Midwestern town and were overcome by hormones at the time, and besides, nothing ever came of it, since Turner never got past second base. And he'd barely made it there.

And okay, okay, so maybe once, a couple of years ago, they *did* imbibe a little too much at the office Christmas party and ended up almost horizontal. But that wasn't so unusual because everyone that night had been feeling festive, and lots of people ended up almost horizontal, and besides, nothing ever came of it. Turner never got past third base. And he'd barely made it there.

And okay, okay, so maybe she *did* sort of have dreams about Turner from time to time. And okay, okay, so maybe they were, um, naked dreams. And okay, okay, so maybe he made it all the way home—and then some—in those dreams. Like the one she'd had a couple of nights ago, for instance, where Turner was bathing in a moonlit desert hot spring, with steam rising up all around his—naked—body, and water was sluicing over his brawny—naked—shoulders and arms, winding through the dark hair on his muscular—naked—chest and sparkling like diamonds in the black hair slicked back from his face. And then suddenly, she'd been in the hot spring with him, and she'd been naked, as well, tracing with her fingertips the little rivulets of water as they wound down his—naked—arms, licking away a drop that clung precariously to his lip, then reaching slowly, slowly, oh…so slowly beneath the water to drag a finger along his strong—naked—thigh before closing her hand over his—very naked, very large—

Uh, where was she? Becca suddenly wondered. She seemed to have gotten off track….

Oh, yeah. Now she remembered. She'd been thinking of Turner as just a friend and nothing more. Which was how she always thought of him. Always. Really. She did. Honest. It was true. Hey, why would she think of him any other way?

But not all women thought of him as a friend, she knew. For instance, that brazen redhead Englund had hired just last month. Lucy somebody. Yeah, that was an appropriate name, all right. Except that it should have been spelled *Loosey*. Talk about hot to trot. And obvious? Please. She was all over Turner like white on rice. The tart. Honestly. What some women would do to attract a man's attention. Not that Becca cared, of course. Or even noticed, for that matter.

Um, where was she? She seemed to have gotten off track again….

Oh, yeah. Now she remembered. She'd been thinking about her good buddy Turner. Yep, that was all he was to her. Her good buddy. And at the moment, he was her agitated good buddy.

"I'm tellin' ya, Becca," he said as he began pacing again, "we need to go into business for ourselves. Just you and me. A partnership. This place isn't suited to us at all."

"Maybe not," she agreed. "But we were lucky to both get hired here. The pay and benefits are good. Well, except for the lousy health care plan. And this isn't exactly a good time to be looking for work somewhere else. The economy sucks. The holidays are coming. It's an even worse time to try and start up a business of our own. I mean, where would we get the capital?"

"Small business loan," he said readily.

Becca shook her head. "It's not a good time to start a business," she reiterated. "But it *is* a good time to quit smoking."

"Becca…"

They'd had this discussion before, a million times, in fact, about how they needed to quit smoking if for no other reason than that it was unhealthy. True, they were only twenty-seven and feeling immortal, but they'd both be better off if they quit. And now, with their jobs at stake, they finally had the motivation. If they took the vow to quit smoking together, maybe they'd be successful this time. They could do like in those twelve-step programs and call each other whenever they were at risk of falling off the wagon. Lighting up the wagon. Whatever.

"Turner, this is a sign that's it's finally time for us to

quit," she said. "The habit is unhealthy, it's expensive, it's socially unacceptable these days, and now it's about to cost us our jobs. We have nothing to lose by quitting, and everything to gain. And if we both make a pact to do it together, we can succeed this time. I know we can."

"We've tried before without success," Turner reminded her. "We've tried going cold turkey, we've tried the patch, we've tried the gum. Hell, we've even tried smacking each other upside the head every time we saw each other light up. But none of it has worked, Becca."

"We haven't tried hypnosis," she said tentatively.

He gaped at her and for a moment said nothing. Wow. She'd never seen him speechless before. But maybe this meant he was at least considering it.

Then, "Oh, no," he said. He shook his head forcefully, settling his hands on his hips. "No, no, no, no, no. No way. No how. Nuh-uh. *Nein. Nyet. Non.*"

Okay, so maybe he wasn't at least considering it.

"I am *not* going to let someone hypnotize me," he added unnecessarily. "That's a load of crap."

"It could work," Becca said, a bit less tentatively this time. "It's worked for other people. My aunt Louise stopped biting her nails after she was hypnotized."

Of course, what Becca didn't add was that Aunt Louise went in to be hypnotized for her phobia of eggplant, and these days she still broke into a sweat whenever she saw ratatouille. Even as a side dish. Hypnosis *had* been beneficial for her aunt in one way. Just, you know, not the right way.

Becca repeated, "It could work for us. We won't know unless we try."

Turner covered the short distance between them in three long strides and dropped into the chair beside hers. He sat the same way now that he had in high school, all sprawling limbs and masculine confidence. These days, though, he took up considerably more room than he had back then. Funny how he'd gone through that second puberty while they were in college at IU. He'd always been so skinny as a kid. Now he was solid rock.

Becca shook off the observation, almost literally. "We could at least try it," she said more softly.

He met her gaze levelly for a moment, and Becca thought again what nice blue eyes he had. Maybe she couldn't blame Loosey for being such a tart around him. The tart.

"Right," he said tersely. "We let ourselves be hypnotized, and the next thing you know, we're on a stage in Vegas with some guy in a red, crushed-velvet blazer, named the Amazing Mesmiro, and he's making us bark like a dog and flap our arms like a chicken. Is that what you really want?" Turner dipped his head lower, smiled a seductive little smile and gazed at her through hooded eyes. He dropped his voice an octave or two as he added, "Because ya know, Becca, *I* can make you bark like a dog if I use the right words and touch you a certain way…."

His voice held just a hint of sexual innuendo, enough to bring that wet, naked-dream business rushing to the fore, and she made herself ignore the tremor of heat that splashed through her midsection. It always made her uncomfortable when Turner acted as though he wanted sex, even when she knew he was only joking. Those few occasions when the two of them had kissed and stroked and groped had ended awkwardly, and it had taken days, sometimes weeks, for the two of them to feel comfortable together again. Turner, especially, had seemed to have trouble getting back to normal. But because of their reactions to each other after getting even remotely sexual, they knew they weren't suited to it. They were much better as friends than lovers. And Becca didn't want to risk losing that friendship.

So she ignored the last part of what he'd said to focus on the first part, something that had her biting back both the sarcastic retort and the smack upside the head she felt threatening. There. That was better. That was more in keeping with the way she wanted to feel about Turner.

"Not that kind of hypnosis," she patiently corrected him. "Hypnotherapy hypnosis."

He eyed her blankly. "And the difference would be...?"

"Hypnotherapists are better dressed, for one thing," she quipped. "They have white jackets and name tags and stuff."

He rolled his eyes.

"And licenses," she quickly added. "They're licensed to do this kind of thing. They go through a lot of training and education, whereas the Amazing Mesmiro probably got his training from the Johnson Smith catalog. Not to mention his license."

Turner's expression remained impassive. "Hypnotherapists are licensed and trained to make people bark like dogs and flap their wings like chickens? Wow. And here I wasted my time with an MBA and a bachelor's degree in marketing."

"They're licensed to help people," Becca told him through gritted teeth. Oh, yeah. That smack upside the head was really close now.

"It won't work," he said.

She studied him through slitted eyes, nibbling the edge

of her lower lip in thought. Turner's gaze seemed to zero in on the movement, and his pupils widened to nearly eclipse the blue irises. She figured he recognized it meant she was lost in thought—he'd be correct about that—and that he was probably dreading what she was going to say next.

And he was correct there, too, she thought. Because what she said next was, "I'll make a bet with you."

It was the perfect way to respond. Turner was just arrogant enough in his masculinity to never, ever, back down from a challenge. But he was also just arrogant enough in his masculinity to hardly ever win a bet he made with her.

"What kind of bet?" he asked.

Bingo, she thought with satisfaction. Aloud, however, she kept her smugness under control and told him, "Tomorrow's Saturday. If you can make it through the entire day tomorrow—from the minute you wake up until the minute you go to sleep—without once having to light up, then I won't say another word about quitting, and we can take our habit outside whenever we feel the need at work. But if you break down and light even one cigarette tomorrow," she quickly continued, "then you have to go with me to a hypnotherapist ASAP."

He grinned, clearly thinking he would have no trouble sticking to such a challenge. "Piece. Of. Cake," he said.

Becca grinned back. Yeah, it would be a piece of cake, all right, she thought. And she made a mental note to go ahead and check the Yellow Pages, under *H* for *Hypnotherapist,* as soon as she got home. No sense waiting until the last minute.

2

TURNER WAS DRAPED ACROSS his couch, dozing off despite the fact that it was barely ten o'clock, and the TV was blaring the closing credits of *The Zombies of Mora Tau,* when he heard the ungodly thunder of what he suspected, in his half-coherent state, must be the pounding of one of those very Mora Tauian zombies. Even though Ray Milland had taken them all out with an angry, torch-bearing mob in the final scene, which Turner had witnessed at least a half-dozen times. And it occurred to him as he struggled to a sitting position and knuckled his eyes that he really should find some other way to spend his Friday nights besides feeding bad B-movie monsters into his DVD player.

The zombie pounding at his front door kicked up again, and he wondered where was an angry, torch-bearing mob when you needed one? Not so much to take care of the zombie at his front door, but because at least a few members of the mob also might be bearing cigarettes, which, coupled with the torches to light them, would set Turner up for the rest of the weekend. Then he remembered Becca's bet. So much for the weekend. Or at least tomorrow. And even though it wasn't Saturday morning yet, he ignored the half-full pack on the end table and went to see who the zombie knocking at his front door was.

But as he rose to standing and his heart began pumping blood into his bleary brain, he decided that the knocking probably wasn't coming from anything as lame as a zombie. If what Turner suspected was true, his visitor was way more dangerous than that. More dangerous, even, than the Magma Creature from Milwaukee. Or the Lizard Man from La Jolla. Or the Wasp Woman from Walla Walla.

Stumbling barefoot across the living room, he mentally cued the *Twilight Zone* music, tugged down his T-shirt that read Vinnie's House of Hubcaps, and made sure the drawstrings of his faded black sweatpants were suitably tied. Couldn't go meeting one's destiny with doom looking like a slob, after all. Well, not *too* much like a slob. Peeking through the peephole, he saw that he had been correct in his suspicions. Because the beast lurking on the other side of his front door was indeed the scariest, most perilous creature known to mankind.

Or at least to this man, kind of.

With a sigh of resignation, Turner curled his fingers over the doorknob and swiveled it, then pulled the door toward himself with an ominous *creeeeeeak*. And even though it probably would have been more appropriate for him to say, in his best Boris Karloff voice, "Gooood ee-eeveniiiing," he instead only smiled and said, "Hi, Becca," to the woman who stood on the other side.

She smiled brightly, a response more dangerous than the heat lasers shooting out of the eye sockets of the Evil Ectoplasm from Encino. Well, more dangerous to Turner, at any rate. The residents of Encino might beg to differ.

"Hiya," she replied cheerfully, in a voice more menacing than the fireballs exhaled by the Fiend from Fresno. Well, more menacing to Turner, anyway. The residents of

Fresno… Oh, never mind. "Thought you might like a little company," she added easily.

He glanced over his shoulder at the clock on his mantelpiece, the one shaped like a minuscule slot machine, with the glowing red numbers of the hour, minutes and seconds where the three cherries would have been had he just hit a jackpot. The clock had a purple lava lamp sitting on one side of it, and a framed, eight-by-ten, black-and-white glossy of Wayne Newton—though it had been autographed to someone named "Buddy," unfortunately—sitting on the other side. But tacky as they were, the things on the mantelpiece went with the lounge look Turner had striven so hard to achieve throughout his apartment.

Of course, the main reason he had striven to achieve a lounge look was because he'd found a lot of stuff appropriate for a lounge theme at local garage sales when he'd moved out of his parents' basement ten years ago, but that was beside the point.

"At ten in the evening?" he asked, turning to look at Becca again.

She lifted one shoulder and let it drop in what he supposed was meant to be a negligent shrug. However, if there was one thing Turner knew about Becca Mercer, it was that she was anything but negligent. No, what Becca Mercer was was…

He expelled a mental sigh of frustration. Gorgeous, that was what she was, he thought as he took in the dark-blond hair that fell just past her shoulders, and the coffee-colored eyes that made his heart pound faster and more furiously than all the caffeine in the world could. And she was built, too—like a brick shit house, as a matter of fact. He dropped his gaze—discreetly, so she wouldn't know what he was doing—and ogled the snug, faded jeans that hugged her curvy hips, and the brief black sweater that molded her full breasts. Oh, yeah. Becca was curvy and full in all the places a man liked to see a woman curvy and full, all the places a man liked to touch and caress and taste and—

And she was intelligent, too, he knew, stopping his errant thoughts before they could get away from him—because they *would* get away from him if he let them, not to mention leave him feeling frustrated as hell, the way they always did where Becca was concerned. And she was funny, too, he continued, still cataloging her positive traits. And she was witty. And sweet. And kind. And hot. And amazing. And a million other things he could spend the rest of the night listing. Above all else, though, she was his best friend in the whole wide world.

Dammit.

Because although Turner cherished his friendship with Becca and had for two decades, what he felt for her deep down—what he'd felt for a long time—went way beyond friendly. As much as he hated to admit it—and God knew he never would admit it to anyone but himself—what he felt for Becca might very well be the big *L*.

No, not lust, though there was certainly plenty of that in the mix. And not licentiousness, either, though that was definitely in there, too. As were lechery, lasciviousness, lubricity and libido. And maybe even a little lewdness, too. But it was that *other* *L*-word that had him so worried. The *big L.* Love. If Turner let himself think about it long enough, he'd probably have to admit that he was in love with his best friend. So he never let himself think about it. Or, at least, he *tried* to never let himself think about it. And whenever he *did* catch himself thinking about it, he made himself knock it off.

Because Becca didn't feel the same way about him. Yeah, she loved him, but it was in the same way she loved her other—female—friends. She wasn't *in* love with him. And he wasn't about to bare his soul to her and tell her how he really felt, because he was afraid he'd lose her if he did. She'd always been the one to put a stop to things whenever the two of them had gotten physical in the past. And she'd always made such a big deal of telling him how lucky she was to have a guy friend like him, and how they were both too smart to mess it up by getting sexually involved. Because she'd seen too many good girl-guy friendships turn sexual, and after they did, everything just went to hell, and the friendship dissolved completely.

And Turner had to admit that maybe she was right about that. Sex, for being such a basic, natural act, did have a tendency to screw up relationships for some reason, sometimes beyond repair. It was probably best just to keep things the way they were. He'd rather have Becca for a friend than not have her at all. And if that meant he had to carry a torch for her for the rest of his life…

He'd just do his best not to set fire to anything. Unless it was an ancient castle full of zombies.

As he studied her more closely, he realized she was carrying a bigger bag than she usually carried. A bag big enough to hold, say…a change of clothing. And maybe something to sleep in. And girl stuff like makeup and a toothbrush. Like maybe she was planning to…

"Oh, no," he said when he realized her intention. "No, no, no, no, no. No way. No how. Nuh-uh. *Não. Nem. Ikke.*"

Hey, he'd known those cassette tapes from the "How to Talk to Any Girl in Any Language" correspondence course he'd taken in college would come in handy someday. Except he'd planned to use all the "yes" words instead of the "no" words. He'd bagged the whole Grand Tour of Europe thing, though, when he ended up spending most of the money he earned waiting tables to buy cigarettes, instead of socking it into a Grand Tour bank account, the way he'd promised himself he would.

Oh, well, he thought. Maybe he'd still meet a woman named Deolinda or Sziszi or Frøydis someday. It could happen. Hey, Indiana was a *huge* draw for European women. Everybody said so.

"You are *not* spending the night here," he finally concluded.

"What makes you think I plan to spend the night?" Becca asked innocently.

He eyed her warily. "Then why are you here?" he asked flatly.

"I'm spending the night," she told him, taking a step forward.

Immediately, Turner braced his forearms against both sides of the doorjamb. Hard. Then he leaned forward to crowd into her space, which was really his space anyway, on account of he rented it.

"Why?" he asked.

Becca halted when she realized he had no intention of letting her in. But she didn't back away, something that left her standing barely an inch from him. Turner could smell the faint soapy scent of her and knew she'd showered before she came over. Her skin was probably still warm and rosy from the hot water gushing over her naked body, and she was probably soft and silky to touch. She was standing close enough that, if he'd wanted to, he could have slipped a hand right under her sweater to find out. He could have moved it up over her torso to her breast, could have caught her nipple in his fingers and thumbed it to life while unbuttoning her jeans with his other hand and slipping it between her legs. She'd still be damp there, he thought, but not from the shower. And he could make her wetter, raking the pad of his thumb over her sweet little clit, driving his long middle finger in and out of her, again and again, until she came in the palm of his hand.

He bit back a groan. Dammit, he had to stop thinking about her like that. She wasn't interested in him as anything but a friend. Even if she had sighed with pleasure the night he had licked and sucked on her nipples, and even if she had cried out with delight the night he'd stroked her sweet little clit. Even if he could think of no greater pleasure in the world than going further still, and making love to her, just once.

Of course, once would never be enough with Becca. But, hey, it would be a hell of a start.

"I don't trust you," she said. "That's why."

Well, hell, that made two of them, Turner thought. Then he remembered she was talking about something completely different from what he was thinking about. He just wasn't sure what.

"What are you talking about?" he asked.

"Our bet," she said.

Oh, right, he thought, still dreading having to go the whole day tomorrow without lighting up.

"Of course you can trust me," he said. Lied. Whatever.

"Hah."

"Becca…"

"From the moment you wake up tomorrow morning," she reminded him. "Until the moment you go to sleep tomorrow night."

"I know. I will. I mean, I won't."

She nodded. "I'm here to make sure of that."

He expelled an incredulous sound. "You *don't* trust me."

"Didn't I just say that?"

"Becca, I'm crushed that you could think of me as being untrustworthy."

"Stow it, Turner," she said as she reached for one of his arms and shoved it down to his side. Then she breezed past him into his apartment, toward the very couch he had just vacated. "I'm going to be here the minute you wake up tomorrow," she said as she tossed her bag onto one end of it, "and I'm still going to be here the minute you go to sleep. Just to make sure you don't renege."

He gaped at her. "I have never reneged in my life," he assured her. "I do not now, nor will I ever, renege. I am not a reneger."

She didn't look anywhere near convinced. "Got any popcorn?"

In response, Turner growled something under his breath that he hoped she didn't hear and slammed his front door.

It was going to be a long Saturday.

"I JUST LOVE THIS MOVIE," Becca sighed as she thumbed the volume up on *Now, Voyager* and stuffed her hand into the popcorn bowl—the second batch she and Turner had shared so far tonight.

Before *Now, Voyager*, he recalled distastefully, she'd insisted on watching *Camille*. He hated to think what other sappy—crappy—sentimental movies she'd brought with her. He'd bet good money there wasn't a rubber monster to be had in any of them. Give him a Wasp Woman or Fresno Fiend over this stuff any day. At least the death scenes in his favorite movies had some action. And there was a hell of a lot more honor going to meet his maker by eye socket heat lasers than some disease-of-the-week. Not to mention his obituary would be a lot more interesting.

"Go easy on that popcorn," he said. "It's all that's left."

It was his way of telling Becca that 1:00 a.m. was a good time to start winding down, but she didn't take the hint. Instead she reached for the cigarettes on the end table and shook free the last one. Not that Turner was concerned. Like any good smoker—or alcoholic or drug addict, he couldn't help thinking—he had stashes all over the apartment. And at work. And his car. And the basement laundry room.

"Do you mind?" she asked.

"Be my guest," he told her.

"But it's the last one in the pack. It could be *your* last one, ever."

He shook his head. "Not really."

"If you light up tomorrow—today—after you wake up in the morning, then you have to go to a hypnotherapist with me, and that'll be the end of the smoking," she reminded him. "Are you sure you don't want this last one?"

"Number one," he said, thrusting up his index finger to punctuate what he was about to say, "that's not the last cigarette in the apartment. I mean, what kind of smoker would I be if I let myself run out of cigarettes? Number two," he continued before she had a chance to comment, bringing his middle finger into the action, "even if we go to a hypnotherapist, it ain't gonna work, so I don't have to worry about never smoking again. Number three," he concluded, flicking his ring finger up to join the other two, "you said I have to not light up from the moment I wake up Saturday until the moment I go to sleep."

She nodded, eyeing him suspiciously. "Yeah…"

He dropped his hand back into his lap. "I'm not going to sleep tonight. Which means I won't wake up tomorrow, something that rather blurs the terms of the bet. I could go so far as to say it negates the terms of the bet. So I can smoke all I want tomorrow…today…whatever."

She emitted a rude sound of disbelief. *"What?"*

"If I don't go to sleep, then I won't wake up, and then you can't hold me to the bet."

"But that's not fair!"

He thrust his hand into the popcorn bowl. "Of course it's fair. You're the one who set the terms of the wager. I'm just going to use them to my own ends. I've decided I'm not going to go to sleep tonight. Therefore, I can continue to smoke. Therefore…Four," he concluded, "you lose the bet. I don't have to go to see the Amazing Mesmiro with you."

Becca narrowed her eyes at him, but said nothing for a moment. Then, suddenly, her expression lightened. "Did I tell you what other movies I brought with me?" she asked.

Uh-oh…

"After *Now, Voyager* is *Dark Victory*. And then *Stella Dallas*. And then *Imitation of Life*. And then," she said, her eyes widening, "the coup de grâce. *An Affair to Remember*."

Oh, hell, Turner thought. No way could he stay awake through all that. And even if he could, he'd die of estrogen overload. His obituary would be so embarrassing he'd never live it down.

He looked at the cigarette Becca held delicately between her fingers. Then he looked at the TV. Then he looked at Becca's smug grin. Then he looked at the cigarette.

"Gimme that," he said as he snatched it away from her.

She chuckled as she held the lighter for him. "You won't last till noon," she predicted.

"Watch me," he warned her as he blew out a thick stream of white.

"Oh, I will," she assured him. "I'll be watching you *very* closely, Turner. You can count on it."

EVEN THOUGH TURNER WENT down for the count right about the same time Bette Davis wasn't asking for the moon, he at least managed to sleep until almost noon, thereby lasting until noon—take *that,* Becca—and, even better, thereby knocking out half the day. As he squinted blearily at the jackpot clock from where he lay sprawled on the couch, he was relieved to note that there were only twelve hours, four minutes and thirty-two seconds left to go until bedtime. Thirty-one seconds. Thirty seconds. Twenty-nine…twenty-eight…twenty-seven…

Hell, maybe he'd just spend the whole day right here on the sofa, watching the seconds tick past. That might keep his mind off of just how badly he wanted a cig—

Shit.

He battled the urge to reach up onto the end table for the pack that habitually lay there. Then he remembered it wasn't there anyway, because he had smoked the last cigarette it held hours earlier. Not long before Becca had evidently tossed a blanket over his sleeping form, he thought when he noted the cotton covering tugged up to his chest. Man, he must have slept like a rock not to have dislodged it—or himself, for that matter—from the cramped sofa.

Which meant that, at the moment, not only did he have a wicked crick in his neck, but Dishwaterblondilocks was probably still sleeping in his bed. And realizing that just made Turner crave a cigarette more. Because ever since the two of them were teenagers, he'd wanted nothing more than to find Becca in his bed. Just, you know…with him. But hey, at least he had her halfway there now, right? Because she *was* in his bed. Just, you know…with*out* him. Still, she was probably all rumpled and warm and contented, the way he'd figured she *would* be when she was in his bed. She just wasn't that way because *he* had spent the night making her all rumpled and warm and contented.

Trying not to think about the fact that the only reason Becca was in his bed in the first place was because she didn't trust him, and with a heartfelt groan of frustration, Turner jackknifed into a sitting position on the couch. He rolled his head back and forth to relieve the tension in his stiff neck—and tried to ignore his stiffness elsewhere. Then he scrubbed his hands over his face and through his hair in an effort to rouse himself.

Coffee, he thought. That was what he needed most. Well, maybe second most, he amended as he pushed himself up to standing. What he needed most was fast asleep in his bed—without him. And even if she wasn't fast asleep, she'd still be oblivious to his feelings for her.

Automatically, he moved in the general direction of his kitchen and went about making coffee. And he tried to make as much noise as he could, so Becca would be jolted awake—hey, why should *she* wake up feeling good when *he* was going to feel like hell all day? But he never heard a sound of stirring. Obviously, she slept like a rock, too.

He inhaled a deep lungful of the coffee as it was brewing, and that fortified him enough to find his way to his bedroom. The door was standing half-open, so he peeked inside. Then he immediately wished he hadn't. Because not only was Becca still sleeping soundly in his bed without him, she had kicked the covers down to the foot. And although what she chose to sleep in was in no way sexy—a shapeless, long-sleeved nightshirt imprinted with nauseatingly cute cats wearing nauseatingly cute nightshirts—it was bunched up around her waist, so that her sweet ass, encased in soft red cotton, was right there in plain sight, as were the delectable thighs Turner had spent many nights fantasizing about burying his head between.

His libido launched into the lambada just looking at those loins.

And it actively annoyed him how he was always alliterative when aroused.

He squeezed his eyes shut tight to block out Becca's bodacious butt, something that only made the image more graphic. Probably because closing his eyes enabled him to start fantasizing. And since the object of his fantasies was right smack in the middle of his reality, not to mention oblivious to the fact that she was frequently front and center—especially her front and center—in his fantasies, that wasn't necessarily a good thing. So he opened his eyes again, just in time to see the object of his fantasies—and her bodacious butt—beginning to stir.

He told himself to duck out before she caught him staring at her like a lovesick teenager. But he couldn't make himself move away from the door. Mostly because Becca chose that moment to roll over onto her back and propel herself into a full-body stretch, something that made her nightshirt ride up even higher. It also had her gripping the wooden spools of his headboard with both fists as she spread her legs toward the lower corners of the mattress.

And oh, *God,* did that make him want to do things he

knew he shouldn't want to do. Not with his best friend who didn't return his feelings. Call him crazy, but Becca might be a little alarmed if he hurtled himself onto the bed, pulled down her panties, buried his head between her legs and ate his fill of her while penetrating her with his fingers.

Of course, he pondered further, that would probably go a long way toward finally waking her up….

He must have made some sound that reflected his yearning, because she suddenly stopped stretching and looked toward the bedroom door. "Good morning," she said with a sleepy smile.

"Afternoon, you mean," he corrected her. That much, at least, he would concede. It *was* afternoon. It just wasn't necessarily good. Then, because he couldn't stop himself, he smiled back and added lightly, "I see England, I see France."

She narrowed her eyes at him in confusion. Okay, so maybe she wasn't quite as awake as she seemed.

"I see Becca's underpants," he added for clarification.

She glanced down, then hastily back up at Turner. And for one delirious second, he thought—hoped—that instead of rearranging her clothes, she was going to ask him in a silky, seductive voice why didn't he come on over there to see even more of Europe. There was just something in her eyes—okay, so obviously she *was* still half-asleep—that made him think she was as hot and bothered at the moment as he was. Then whatever had sizzled between them was gone—if it had ever been there to begin with—and she began to tug her nightshirt back down, over England, over France, over her sweet ass.

"Uh…sorry," she said as she awkwardly completed the action.

Not me, Turner wanted to reply. But he said nothing, not trusting what he might say—among other things—at the moment.

Unable to help himself—probably because he was a glutton for punishment, or maybe because he hadn't had enough sleep, or maybe because he felt edgy not being able to smoke, or maybe all of the above—he strode into the bedroom, until he was standing only a couple of feet from the bed. Then he sat right next to her and arced his arm over her body, to brace it on the mattress on her other side.

Yet she said nothing, only gazed at him with huge brown eyes that were filled with something he told himself he'd be better off not pondering. Mostly because he was afraid if he pondered it, he'd figure out what it was, and he wasn't sure he wanted to know, because as long as he didn't know, he could still harbor a hope, however crazy, that maybe someday she'd be in his bed, *with* him, not just because she trusted him implicitly, but because he made her hot as hell.

So instead of pondering, Turner leaned forward, closing what little space was left between them, until his face was scarcely inches from her own. She really was rumpled and warm from sleep, he couldn't help noticing, her face flushed and her breathing shallow from that early morning sort of breathlessness. Somehow, though, he kept himself from reaching out to her, from skimming his fingertips over her fine skin and silky hair.

He couldn't avoid the scent of her, however, because it rose up to encircle him, entice him, enchant him. She smelled like summer soap and springtime laundry, a fragrance made all the more poignant because the weather outside was cold and gray, heralding the onset of winter, and it would be a long time before he encountered such warmth and sunshine again. Better than that, though, she smelled like cigarettes, something he wanted almost as badly as he wanted Becca, which made her doubly desirable.

Her eyes, like polished onyx, had grown larger, darker, as he'd drawn nearer, and they searched his face, so close to her own now, as if she were seeking the answers to the mysteries of the universe there. Her fingers curled tightly into the fabric of the pillowcase on each side of her head, almost as if she were trying to keep herself from reaching out to touch him, too. More than anything he had ever wanted in his life, he wanted to loosen those fingers and see where she would put them.

And he wanted, too, to kiss her. For starters. So he leaned in a little closer, his mouth hovering now scant millimeters above her own. And then very, very softly, and very, very seductively...

"Would you like some coffee?" he asked.

3

IT TOOK A MOMENT for Turner's question to register with Becca, because she was way too busy being bewitched, bothered and befuddled to try and figure out what the hell he was yammering about. All she could do was wonder about the weird, wanton wistfulness winding through her, and how her body temperature had been rising ever since she'd awoken to find him gazing at her from the bedroom door.

God, he was sexy in the morning. In all their years as friends, she'd never spent the night with him, so she'd never seen him like this, all tousled and sleepy-eyed and unshaven. His jaw was dark and rough and uncivil looking, and his black hair hung over his forehead in a way that made her want to lift a hand to brush it back. In fact, she wanted to thread her fingers repeatedly through those silky locks, then skim her palm back over the crown of his head, until she could curl her fingers around his warm nape and pull his head down to hers, and take his mouth in a hungry kiss that just went on and on and on. Then push his head lower, down over her breasts and belly, then lower still, between her legs and—

And what the *hell* was she thinking? she wondered when she realized where her thoughts—and Turner's mouth—were going. Obviously, she hadn't gotten enough sleep last night. But that was what happened when you stayed up late watching old movies and then stayed up even later watching your best friend sleep because you'd never realized before how sexy he was when he did that. And now here Turner was, crowding her space, looking all hot and smelling all earthy and sounding all seductive, and gosh, would he think her untoward if she just sucked on his lower lip a little bit, just for a minute, and then maybe moved her own head lower, over his chest and torso, and then lower still, between his legs to suck some more, this time on his—

And what the *hell* was she thinking? Turner was her *friend,* she reminded herself ruthlessly. He was her bestest buddy in the whole wide world. You weren't supposed to suck the, um, lower lip of your best friend, not even for a minute. Everybody knew that. It was like rule number two of friendship, right after "You should never fool around with your best friend's boyfriend." Which actually didn't even apply with Turner, so the, um, lower-lip-sucking rule would be numero uno for them. She'd told Turner things she'd *never* tell someone whose, um, lower lip she wanted to suck. So why would she even be thinking about sucking his, um, lower lip? And why would thinking about that make her feel so freaking hot?

Man, she needed a cigarette. Bad. But how unfair would that be, to smoke in front of Turner, when he had to go the whole day without? Then again, why did she care? He wasn't exactly being fair, either, looming over her looking all sexy and sounding all sexy and smelling all sexy and being all sexy and making her want to suck his, um, lower lip.

She expelled a long, unsteady breath she hadn't even been aware of holding, and took a minute to let her heart stop racing. But when she realized it was going to be awhile before her heart stopped doing that, she gave up. Trying not to sound as breathless as she felt, she replied, "Sure, I'd love some coffee."

He smiled in a way that made her think he knew what she really wanted—and it *wasn't* coffee—and she couldn't help wondering if he suspected her of that, um, lower-lip-sucking business. Nah, she immediately reassured herself. Turner only thought of her as a friend. As his bestest buddy in the whole wide world. Dammit. He couldn't possibly suspect her of wanting to suck his, um, lower lip.

And she didn't want to suck his, um, lower lip, anyway, she reminded herself. She *didn't*. She'd just woken up feeling horny, like ninety percent of women in her demographic—that demographic being single, twentysome-thing, professional females who had gone date-free for *way* too long. And since Turner was the only human being in the vicinity with a Y chromosome, it was only natural she'd want his, um, lower lip. Simple chemistry. No, she quickly corrected herself. Simple biology. She and Turner didn't have any chemistry together. Well, not since their ju-nior year in high school. And the kind of chemistry she was talking about now didn't involve beakers and Bunsen burn-ers. Well, not in the way they were supposed to be used, anyway.

Oh, stop it, she told herself. Thinking that way was only going to make this day longer than it already promised to be. Turner was her friend. Period. And she wasn't about to let *anything* change that. Friends, good friends, the kind you could trust no matter what happened, were too hard to come by in this life. What she and Turner had was too spe-cial to mess with. She needed to wake up a little more, that was all. The day was going to be just fine.

But when she inhaled another breath to steady herself, Becca pulled the musky, masculine scent of Turner—mixed with the aroma of forbidden tar and nicotine—deep into her body with it. And even as he leaned away from her and rose from the bed, she noted again how his T-shirt stretched taut across his brawny chest and muscular arms, and how his rough, dark jaw gave him a feral look, and how his blue eyes seemed to be sizing her up for…something.

And she started thinking that maybe, just maybe, the temptation offered by cigarettes wasn't going to be the biggest obstacle she faced today. Maybe, just maybe, the toughest thing she was going to have to battle would be her own wayward thoughts.

BECCA HAD JUST FINISHED making Turner's bed when she heard the water shut off in the bathroom. He'd magnanimously offered to let her shower and dress first, so she'd figured the least she could do was change his sheets for him—especially since she'd probably drooled all over them during that odd little morning interlude that had so confused her at the time.

Of course, now that she was dressed in a fresh pair of jeans and a cropped red sweater, and now that she was fortified by coffee and Cap'n Crunch—honestly, did men ever eat *anything* healthy for breakfast?—she was confident she knew *exactly* what had been behind that odd little… That unusual little… That strange little… That weird little… That mysterious little… That bizarre little…*thing*. Now she was confident that what had passed between the two of them earlier had simply resulted from a lack of sleep and nothing more.

There was a reason why some governments used sleep

deprivation as a form of torture. It made a person crazy. Crazy enough to do and say things they would normally never say or do. Like drool on their best friend's pillow because their best friend suddenly seemed kind of sexy, where he would never seem sexy if one had gotten enough sleep and was in one's right mind.

That was her story, and she was sticking to it.

Unfortunately, her adhesive must have collected some lint or something while she was changing the bed, because Becca became decidedly less stuck to that story when the door to the bathroom just outside the bedroom flew open, and Turner emerged in a puff of steam, completely naked, and she found herself wanting to be stuck to him in the most basic, most wanton way two people could be stuck together.

Oh, no, wait, he wasn't quite naked, Becca was relieved—sort of—to realize. He had a towel slung around his midsection—sort of. So he was decent—sort of. Of course, the thoughts that popped into her head just then, not to mention the feelings that went zinging through her bloodstream, were anything *but* decent. Because as sexy as Turner had been that morning all rough-jawed and sleep-rumpled, he was ten times more so all wet-skinned and steamy.

Lack of sleep, she reminded herself, closing her eyes against the sight. *Note to self: Must be in bed at a decent hour tonight so Turner will get laid. Ah, that is to say, so that all errant* thoughts *of Turner will be* laid *to rest.*

Right.

"Oh, sorry," he muttered as he backed into the bathroom and pushed the door half-closed in front of himself. "I didn't realize you were in here."

"No, I'm sorry," she hastily told him, heading for the

bedroom door. Which meant she also was headed toward the bathroom door. And Turner. And Turner's towel. Among Turner's other things.

"I thought you'd be longer in the shower," she added as she made herself race through the bedroom door and into the living room.

"Longer?" he echoed as he poked his head back out to look at her. "All I had to do was get clean. What else would I be doing in here?"

Don't answer, she told herself. *Don't even* think *about an answer.*

Oh, damn. Too late…

"Uh…" she began as she turned her back on Turner to give him some privacy and herself some sanity. "I'll just be out here in the living room, 'kay?"

Out in the living room trying not to think about you all naked and steamy, with water streaming down over your skin, and you pushing the soap across your chest and over your abs and stomach, the frothy foam oozing between your fingers and over taut muscle, and then your hand moving lower, over your lean thighs and toward your, um, uh…lower lip?

She cleared her throat indelicately. "I'll be out here in the living room," she repeated, striving for lightness in her tone, but thinking she probably only succeeded with lewdness instead.

She wasn't sure, but she thought Turner mumbled something in response. She was too busy not thinking about him to ask him to repeat himself. Though she was pretty sure she heard the words *crazy lunatic female* somewhere in the mix. She also thought she heard the sound of a towel being whipped from a wet, steamy, hard body, but that could have just been her imagination. Wishful think-ing. Whatever.

Oh, where *had* she put her cigarettes?

Recalling that she had smoked the last of them before going to bed, she gave herself a good mental shake and told herself to calm down. It wouldn't be fair, anyway, to smoke in front of Turner when she'd bet him he couldn't go all day without. She could go without, too. She'd just have to keep her thoughts focused, that was all.

Yeah, focus, she reiterated to herself. *That's the ticket.*

Unfortunately, when Turner emerged a few minutes later from his bedroom, wearing snug, faded jeans and an even more faded denim work shirt that he hadn't bothered yet to button up, Becca's focus flew immediately to his per-son. To be more specific, her focus flew to that part of his person that was currently uncovered. And then her focus focused way too well. The rich scattering of dark hair that peeked out from his open shirt spanned his chest from shoulder to shoulder, she knew, because she'd seen him shirtless on more than one occasion.

But somehow, seeing him this way now felt different from the way it had on those other occasions. Before, when Turner had been shirtless around her, it had been in some public venue. Because they were swimming or he was working out in his parents' yard or playing basketball or something else equally harmless. Now his state of disha-bille seemed anything but harmless. Here, in the privacy of his apartment, when it was just the two of them, alone, it seemed more intimate somehow.

Lack of sleep, she reminded herself again. Yeah. That was for sure why she suddenly felt so restless around him.

"So what do you want to do today while you're not

trusting me to light up in secret?" he asked as he began to button his shirt. "Besides pretend we *both* don't want a cigarette, I mean."

Becca shrugged. "I don't know. We could see a movie."

He gazed at her through narrowed eyes. "Oh, I don't *think* so."

"Had enough, have you?"

"Let's just say that when it's my time to go to that big disease-of-the-week in the sky, I'll know all the right things to say about moons and stars and no regrets."

"Mmm."

She watched as he finished buttoning himself up, and continued to watch as he rolled back his sleeves over strong forearms, and continued to watch as he dragged both hands through his still-damp hair, slicking it straight back from his face. And then she continued to watch some more as he gazed back at her.

"What?" he asked.

"What, what?" she replied.

"Why are you looking at me? Do I have toothpaste on my lip or something?"

Oh, she really didn't want to talk about his lip right now. "It's nothing," she said quickly.

Probably a little too quickly, because he narrowed his eyes even more. "What's wrong?" he asked.

"Why do you think something is wrong?"

"I don't know. You're looking at me kind of funny."

"Well, I don't know why. I don't feel funny."

"How *do* you feel?"

Oooh, not a question she wanted to answer right now. She needed a diversion. Quick. So she strode across the room to where she had slung her purse over the back of a chair, rummaged through it until she found what she was looking for, then shamelessly withdrew a limp, bent, God-only-knows-how-long-it's-been-in-there cigarette, plus her lighter, and strode back over to Turner.

"Hey," he objected. "You can't smoke today."

"Why not?"

"Because we have a bet, that's why."

"*I* didn't make any bet," she pointed out as she tucked the cigarette between her lips. "You did. I can smoke if I want to."

He gaped at her. "But that's not fair!"

She smiled. "Yeah, I know."

"But…but…but…"

She withdrew the cigarette from her mouth and extended it toward him. "Would you rather have it yourself?" she asked sweetly.

For some reason, it suddenly seemed imperative that she get him to smoke. Not just because she needed him to lose the bet in order to accompany her to the hypnotherapist, but because the sooner he lit up, the sooner she could win the bet and vacate the premises. Then, in the privacy and safety of her own home, she could wonder just why the hell she suddenly felt so weird around Turner. So she moved the cigarette closer, rolling it between her fingers in an effort to free the sweet aroma of unsmoked tobacco, a fragrance she knew he wouldn't be able to resist.

"C'mon," she taunted him. "You know you want to. Can't you smell it?" she cooed in the sexiest siren voice she could muster. She took another step closer, until her body was almost flush with his, then pushed the cigarette even closer to his face. "Smell how *good* it smells," she entreated him seductively.

But Turner glanced away, silently declining her offer. She frowned at the rebuff, feeling strangely rejected. So she lifted her free hand to his face, cupping his jaw in her palm until she could turn his head toward the cigarette again.

"Look at it, Turner," she said softly.

"I don't want to look at it," he replied, turning his head away again.

So Becca cupped his jaw more firmly and urged his face to where she'd held it before. "Look at it," she instructed him more forcefully, her voice sounding throatier now, though she couldn't recall making a conscious effort to have it do that. "Look how smooth and round it is."

He did as she told him to, glancing down at the cigarette, then hastily back up at her face. "Yeah. So?"

"Don't you want to touch it?" she whispered, arching one brow.

He shook his head slowly, but his gaze flittered back down to the cigarette she held out to him. "No," he told her roughly. "I don't want to touch it."

"Of course you want to touch it," she said sweetly. She threaded her fingers intimately into his hair. "You want to touch it sooooo bad."

"No, I don't," he declared.

"Yes, you do," she insisted. "You want to caress it, and stroke it and hold it in your hand. You want to run your fingers over it, up and down and around and around. Then you want to put it between your thumb and forefinger and roll it back and forth. It feels so good to do that, doesn't it? I love how that feels."

Becca lifted the cigarette to her mouth, and Turner's gaze followed. Instead of tucking it between her lips, however, she raked the cigarette slowly across her mouth. "But as good as it feels to touch it, there's nothing like putting it in your mouth, is there?"

"Becca…" he said, the warning in his voice unequivocal.

"You want to feel it against your lips," she murmured. "Taste it on your tongue. You want it in your mouth, don't you, Turner?"

"No. I don't." But his words were quiet, uncertain.

"Yes. You do," she said. "You want your mouth on it, sucking hard. Don't fight it, Turner. Take what you want. Take it *now*."

For a moment, she thought he would succumb, because he actually lifted his hand toward her—or, rather, toward the cigarette. His fingers hovered there for a moment, lingering…lingering…. Then he drew his hand away again and crossed his arms over his broad chest.

"No," he told her, his voice still a little shaky. "I'm just saying no. I will not submit to peer pressure." And then, as if he wanted to physically illustrate that, he took a solid step backward, away from the cigarette, away from Becca.

Dammit. They had been so close. Though, somehow, what they had actually been close to doing wasn't the thing she had *wanted* them to be doing. Or worse, maybe they *had* been close to doing that.

She made herself roll her eyes, as if she were as unconcerned as he. "Fine," she conceded petulantly. Then, smiling playfully again, she placed the cigarette between her own lips and said, "Then you won't mind if *I* smoke."

He opened his mouth to object again, then closed it. "Feel free," he said. "This is by no means a smoke-free environment."

"Thanks," she replied, her tone just as clipped as his. "Don't mind if I do."

But the reason Becca lit the cigarette wasn't so much to tempt Turner by smoking in his presence as it was an effort to calm her own nerves. Because their little exchange just now had left her feeling edgy and irritable and very close to blowing her top. Or something.

It made no sense. There was no reason for her to feel edgy or irritable around Turner. Just because he wasn't folding as quickly as she'd thought he would, and just because he obviously had more willpower than she did, and just because it looked as if she might lose this bet instead of him, that was no reason for her to get edgy and irritable.

Funny thing was, she suspected her bet with Turner had nothing to do with her current state of unrest.

Deciding not to think about any of that, she palmed her lighter and thumbed the flame to life, moving it to the tip of her cigarette. Inhaling deeply, she savored the warmth of the smoke filling her mouth and lungs, and relished the false heat that wound through her body. Nothing felt as good as smoking, she thought. She couldn't imagine a greater physical pleasure than that soothing, pleasant sensation curling through her body.

Until she glanced up to find Turner gazing at her—or, rather, the cigarette—with unmistakable desire and unmitigated hunger. And then she began to imagine, too well, a physical pleasure that might rival, or even surpass, the one she was enjoying now.

"You're playing dirty, Becca," he said as he watched her enjoy herself. And without awaiting a reply—not that his comment really needed one—he spun on his heel and went back into his bedroom, slamming the door behind him.

It was all Becca could do not to follow him. And not because she feared he might light up in secret, either. But because she felt hungry and wanton herself. So she inhaled deeply on the cigarette again, waiting for the familiar sensation to calm her down.

But for the first time she could ever remember, smoking did nothing to soothe her nerves.

IT WAS AFTER ELEVEN that night when Turner finally gave up all pretense of being unaffected by the day's events, and surrendered to the urge to smoke. Because even at that late hour, he knew sleep was a long way off, and he'd spent most of the day feeling half-crazy as it was. The craziness had resulted less from going smoke-free, however, than it had from watching Becca move about his life as if she belonged there.

It wasn't that they did anything unusual together, but that was just the point. They spent the day doing the most mundane things two people—two *friends*—could do. They ate lunch together at a nearby fast-food restaurant, and they had dinner at a favorite pub near Englund Advertising where they had had dinner together a million times before. In between, they went to a home improvement store so Becca could look at paint chips and other items because she was thinking about redecorating her condo.

Normally, Turner loved home improvement stores. Normally, he could pass an entire day in one without ever marking the passage of time. Normally, he experienced an almost erotic gratification at handling power tools and light fixtures and PVC tubing. But normally, he wasn't with Becca when he was visiting one. Throw her into the mix, and suddenly one of his favorite activities felt totally *ab*-normal. Well, except for the part about experiencing erotic gratification. Because having her hovering over his shoulder while he handled power tools and light fixtures and PVC tubing just made all of those items seem overtly sexual somehow. So by the end of the day, his nerves were frazzled to bits.

Even so, he managed to make it through the day without lighting up. Without lighting up a *cigarette,* anyway. His libido was another matter. It raged completely out of control. Especially when Becca had been bent over to inspect the color on a can of paint, and her round, firm ass brushed against his hip, and he'd wanted nothing more than to bury himself in her from behind. Still, he had survived. Even more difficult, he had kept his hands to himself.

The clincher came after they arrived back at his apartment and were settling in for another movie marathon—this time with *his* choice of cinema. Because just as he was popping a copy of *Mothra* into his DVD player, Becca exited his bedroom dressed for spending the night again, because she didn't want to leave until morning, to witness him falling asleep, thereby proving he hadn't lit up from the moment he awoke until the moment he fell asleep.

The problem for Turner, however, wasn't that he had to watch Becca exiting his bedroom alone when he'd rather see her entering it with him. Still, seeing her anywhere in the vicinity of his bedroom certainly wreaked havoc with his carnal appetite. Of course, seeing her breathe today had wreaked havoc with his carnal appetite. No, the problem was, and the thing that *really* sent his carnal appetite into overdrive, demanding some kind of, ah, nutrition—and if it couldn't be sex, then it had damn well better be nicotine—was the fact that when she emerged from his bedroom, she was wearing nothing but his old college football jersey and a pair of knee socks.

Turner had to do a double take to be sure he wasn't see-ing things. And when he realized he had actually seen what he thought he saw, he could only sit on the sofa staring openmouthed at the vision. Never mind that the jersey fell to midthigh on Becca and covered everything that needed to be covered. That was beside the point. The point was that the outfit she had on was the one she always wore in his second favorite sexual fantasy about her, the one where she got stranded at his apartment in a snowstorm, and all she had to wear was the very thing she had on now. And the realization that sexual fantasy number two was about to be played out in his very *non*sexual reality was just a little more than Turner could stand.

Sexual fantasy number one was the one where she came on to him at the office when they were working alone to-gether late one night. In that fantasy, Becca suddenly re-alized she had a powerful sexual attraction to him and had for years, one that was so ferocious and demanding that, although she managed to get all of her own clothes off, most of his stayed on, and he ended up bending her for-ward over the big table in the Englund Advertising board-room to take her from behind. Then, it went without saying, he took her again in her cubicle, spilling pencils off her desk and knocking over that stupid coffee mug Doug in ac-counting had given her as her secret Santa last Christmas, the one that said "Let's get naughty for Christmas...it'll be SO nice" in big red letters, and breaking it into a million pieces. Doug in accounting was such an asshole.

There were other sexual fantasies starring Becca on Turner's list, too, of course. The one with the roller coaster at King's Island was a favorite, as was the one where Becca bought him at a bachelor auction and then handcuffed him to her bed for days. And then there was the one where they got jiggy in the back seat of a Rolls Royce, but fat chance that was ever going to happen since the only person Turner knew with a Rolls Royce was his employer's father. But the football jersey/knee-socks fantasy held firm at number two, and there was Becca in his reality now, all decked out to play.

Next thing you know, he thought, *she'll be doing just like in the fantasy and telling me how sorry she is that she has to wear my clothes, but she spilled something all over herself, and this was the only thing she could find to wear.*

"I'm sorry to have to borrow your stuff," she said as she took a few steps into the room, tugging on the hem of the jersey and looking way more nervous than she should, seeing as how they were just friends and shouldn't have any reason to feel nervous around each other. "But when I went to pour milk on my cereal this morning," she continued, "I dropped the carton, and it spilled all over my nightshirt. This was all I could find to sleep in."

Uh-oh…

"I hope you don't mind," she added, sounding nervous, too. "This is the only thing you have that's big enough to cover my, um…my assets," she added with a sheepish grin.

The minute she said it, Turner was helpless to do anything but look at her…assets. And as his gaze roved over her from the top of the silky hair he longed to run his fingers through to the tips of the knee-sock-clad toes he wanted to suck, he was damn near overcome with a sexual urge unlike any he had ever experienced before.

And then all he could do was reach for the pack of cigarettes she'd tossed onto the end table earlier, shake one free and say, "So. What time is this appointment with the Amazing Mesmiro? And do you want to drive, or shall I?"

4

THE NAME ON THE OUTER office door, Becca noted when she and Turner arrived for their Tuesday morning appointment, said not the Amazing Mesmiro, but rather Dorcas Upton, RN, BSN, LHT. And then, below that, to make matters clearer, Licensed Hypnotherapist.

"Registered Nurse," Becca said brightly to Turner, pointing to the first two letters that followed Dorcas Upton's name. "That's good. That shows she's not a flake."

"Doesn't prove she never played Vegas," he replied grudgingly. "What's BSN stand for?" he asked. "And LHT?"

"Licensed hypnotherapist," Becca guessed for the latter. Especially since it was spelled out right there. Duh. For the former, however, she hadn't a clue. "I'm not sure about the other letters, though," she said.

Turner considered the sign for a moment himself before declaring, "I'm guessing BSN stands for Blatant Staggering Nutcase."

"I doubt it," Becca replied through gritted teeth.

"Big Simpering Neurotic?" he suggested further.

"Um, no," she replied as patiently as she could. "Just a shot in the dark, but…I'm thinking not."

"Blithering Schizoid Nitwit?"

"Turner…"

"Brilliant Scholar Not?"

"*Turner.*"

"I know. Bunch of Stupid Nonsense."

"Turner, stop it," she finally hissed under her breath. And then it hit her. The RN designation ultimately gave it away. "Bachelor of Sciences, Nursing!" she said triumphantly. "That *really* shows she's not a flake if she has a bachelor's degree."

Turner said nothing in response to that. And just to show what a good sport Becca was about such things, she didn't even grin smugly and lean in close and tell him—

Oh, who was she kidding?

"Told you so," she said with a smug grin, leaning in close.

He growled something under his breath and made a big show of checking his wristwatch. "We're more than half an hour early," he said.

Becca glanced at her own wristwatch. He was being generous. They were closer to forty-five minutes early. She'd made the appointment for ten o'clock, and it was just past nine-fifteen now. "I thought traffic would be a lot worse," she said lamely. "I wanted to get an early start."

The real reason she'd wanted to get an early start was because she'd figured Turner would put up more of a fight about coming, so she'd shown up at his place extra early to allow time for the argument. But he'd been surprisingly cooperative about everything. He'd also been pretty yummy-looking in his faded blue jeans and a navy-blue sweater that made his blue eyes seem even bluer somehow, especially when he pulled a disreputable-looking denim jacket on over it. Becca, too, had opted for blue jeans today, pairing hers with a white, scooped-neck T-shirt and black blazer.

The day outside the downtown office building where Dorcas Upton and all the letters following her name had sited their office was coolish but sunny, the perfect weather, Becca couldn't help thinking, for a good hypnotizing. She and Turner had both taken a personal day off from work, feeling not one bit guilty about it since they had to be present for a big meeting at the office on Saturday morning. Robert Englund hadn't complained, and besides, they were doing this as much for him as they were for themselves.

Well, okay, maybe that was pushing it. But tomorrow, Becca and Turner would put the finishing touches on their pitch for a big new account Englund Advertising was trying to land—an account that could bring in loads of money, not to mention a nice, fat promotion for Becca and Turner both—and the meeting Saturday would herald the big reveal. It made sense that the two of them would want to be at their best for the rest of the week.

And their best, Becca had decided, would be smoke-free. That way, they could work on the campaign with one hundred percent of their focus, instead of always being distracted by when they might be able to sneak away for a cigarette.

"Maybe Ms. Upton can take us early," she said now as she reached for the knob and opened the door. "I didn't have any problem making the appointment yesterday. That makes me think she can't be booked solid all the time."

"It makes me think she's a quack," Turner muttered.

Becca shushed him, but had to admit he had a point. And that point was made even finer when they entered the hypnotherapist's office to find it completely empty. Although there was a little frosted window pushed open over a counter where a receptionist might normally be seated, there wasn't a receptionist sitting there now.

Still, it was a very nicely appointed office, with wallpaper in a pale yellow stripe, plush, plum-colored seating, soft lighting and lots of ferns. And someone must be around, because there was soft classical music playing, and somewhere on the other side of that frosted window, down a hall or in another room, someone was talking on the phone.

"Place doesn't seem to be hopping," Turner said. "I bet she could take us early."

Becca nodded. "If she's here…"

No sooner were the words out of her mouth than a door on the other side of the room opened and a slight, wiry woman came striding through. When she saw Becca and Turner, she seemed to be as surprised as they were, but she quickly recovered and smiled. "Well, hello there," she said. "I'm Dorcas Upton. Can I help you?"

Becca wasn't sure what she'd been expecting when it came to hypnotherapists, but she was pretty sure it wasn't this. Dorcas Upton had more in common with Mother Goose than she did with the Amazing Mesmiro. Probably around sixty years old, she had her gray hair fixed atop her head in a tidy bun, and beaded black half-glasses were perched on the end of her nose. Slender to the point of being almost angular, she stood a good three or four inches shy of Becca's own five-six, even though she was wearing sensible black pumps with a one-inch heel. Her outfit, too, was mostly black; a plain, straight skirt that fell to midcalf and a black, pearl buttoned sweater open over an ivory blouse.

No white coat after all, Becca mused. For some reason, that made her feel better, though. Dorcas Upton looked like a school librarian, her dark eyes reflecting intelligence, proficiency and good humor. Becca liked that in a hypnotherapist.

"I know we're not on time for our appointment," Becca said by way of a greeting, not quite able to quell the anxiety she could hear lacing her voice. Probably because she couldn't quite quell the anxiety coursing through her brain and body, too. "But is there any chance we could still see you?"

"Certainly," Ms. Upton said. She smiled as she tilted her head toward the empty waiting room. "As you can see, I've no one else waiting at the moment. If you'll just follow me?"

She swept her hand toward the open door behind her, and Becca turned to look at Turner. He was studying the hypnotherapist through slitted eyes, but he seemed resigned to going through with it. Becca tried to smile at him reassuringly, then reached out and took his hand. Though she honestly couldn't have said whether she did that for his benefit or for her own. It just felt better holding his hand.

"Come on," she said softly, tugging gently. "In a little while, it'll all be over. And then we'll have the rest of the day off from work to celebrate our new commitment."

Turner smiled back, a little halfheartedly, but he nodded. "This better work," he told her. "That's all I can say. Because we're both going to be frustrated in the extreme if it doesn't."

DORCAS UPTON SMILED at the couple, deciding immediately that she would forgive them for being twenty minutes late for their appointment. And not just because they were the cutest couple she'd ever seen, either, single *or* married, and obviously perfect for each other. But also because she had just hung out her shingle two months ago, and she wasn't exactly overrun with clients yet.

Starting a new business wasn't easy. And she hadn't been a hypnotherapist for very long. Dorcas was still working the bugs out both her method *and* her office. So even if Mr. and Mrs. Feder were late for their nine o'clock appointment, she'd see them. And she'd take care of their problem for them. And then, as Mrs. Feder had just said, they could go home and celebrate their new commitment. To each other, and to a happily wedded way of life. Once Dorcas was finished with them, they wouldn't be frustrated anymore.

Because she was confident she could help the shy newlyweds iron out their little problem. And a delicate little problem it was, too. She wasn't surprised they'd arrived late for their appointment. If their extreme shyness and inhibitions were keeping the two of them from making love, then certainly it might result in the sort of nervousness and hesitation that would make them late for an appointment to remedy the problem.

"Won't you come into my office?" she asked the Feders, smiling with as much encouragement as she could. Didn't want the precious—though nervous—lovebirds to bolt, after all.

The couple exchanged one final, reassuring glance, then Mrs. Feder nodded. "We're ready," she said.

They followed Dorcas into her office, which did have the bugs worked out of it, at least where the decor was concerned. In an effort to make her clients feel as comfortable as possible, she'd opted for muted earth tones with splashes of pastel blue, hoping to evoke an earth-and-water feel that might appeal to more elemental aspects of the human psyche. An electric desk fountain bubbled pleasantly atop a bookcase on the other side of the room, and the classical music of the waiting room was replaced here by a recording of a windswept canyon in New Mexico. The atmosphere certainly made Dorcas feel relaxed and contented. Hopefully, her clients felt that way, too.

As she rounded her desk and took a seat behind it, she glanced down at her appointment book in an effort to discern the Feders' first names. But she frowned when she realized her receptionist hadn't written them down when she recorded the appointment, only "Feders."

Ah, well, Dorcas thought. There was time enough to get acquainted. Although her next appointment was at ten, that would be a fairly mundane quit-smoking session. Dorcas could do those in her sleep. They didn't take long. This one with the Feders, though…

It wasn't every day you ran across two people who wanted to make mad, passionate love and couldn't get over their combined inhibitions to do it. And newlyweds to boot! But that was all right. They'd be at it like rabbits when she was finished with them.

"I'm sorry about the timing," Mrs. Feder stated as she took a seat in one of the chairs opposite Dorças's desk. "This was just one of those mornings when—"

"Say no more," Dorcas interrupted gently in as soothing a voice as she could manage. "And don't think anything of it. It isn't a problem, honestly."

In spite of her reassurances, Mrs. Feder seemed a little nervous about the session ahead. And Mr. Feder, who still stood at the door, looked too wary to even enter the room.

"I'm sorry," Dorcas said, "but you'll have to tell me your first names again. My receptionist didn't write them down in my appointment book."

Mrs. Feder smiled. "I'm Becca, and this is Turner."

Dorcas smiled in return. "And you must both call me Dorcas. Well, since time is of the essence, let's get started right away, shall we?"

Becca turned to look at her husband, who still seemed reluctant to enter. Funny, Dorcas thought, but he didn't look like the sort of man who would have trouble consummating his marriage. On the contrary, he looked like the sort of man who would pounce on whatever female held his interest. He also seemed extremely interested in his wife, if the expression on his face when he looked at her was any indication.

He turned to Dorcas. "You're not going to make us bark like dogs for your own amusement while we're under, are you?" he asked.

She smiled. "Of course not." She waited until he looked relieved before adding, "I'm going to make you flap your arms like a chicken. I find that much more entertaining." Then she chuckled good-naturedly at his panicked expression. "I'm sorry. Couldn't resist. Just a little hypnotherapist humor there."

He said nothing, looking as if he wasn't sure whether to believe her or not.

"It will be fine, Turner," she said. "I run a professional, legitimate business. Hypnotherapy may not be understood by most people, but it is, without question, a viable treatment for many." She offered him her most reassuring smile. "It may interest you to know that not all people are able to be hypnotized."

"Really?" Becca asked, her voice tinged with a mixture of both curiosity and concern.

Dorcas nodded. "And of those who *are* able to be hypnotized, not all respond to hypnotherapy. Should that be the case with one or both of you, I can recommend another therapist who might be able to help you with your problem through more conventional methods."

"We've already tried those," Becca said. "This is kind of a last resort for us. If you can't help us…"

She didn't finish the statement, only looked forlorn at the prospect of what might lie ahead, should this session fail.

"Well, don't you worry," Dorcas said. "Just relax, and we'll give it our best. Truly, I think you'll be pleased by the results. Now, then, Turner, if you'll take your seat next to Becca, we can get started."

As Dorcas extended her hand toward the vacant chair, Turner pushed himself away from the door and strode with obvious reluctance toward it. After a moment's hesitation, he took a seat.

"That's fine," Dorcas said, still smiling. "Now let's get you two hypnotized."

She began the session the way she always did, with some relaxation techniques that included deep breathing and mental visualization. Little by little, Dorcas took the Feders through the steps, until she was confident that both were in a state of deep hypnosis. Only then did she give them the posthypnotic suggestions that they wouldn't be able to remember consciously once they were brought back, but which they would hopefully act upon when confronted by the proper stimulus.

She'd given much thought to the stimulus in this case, thinking it would be best if she gave the Feders a word to respond to. But it had to be a word they would be most likely to use or hear only in the privacy of their own home. She didn't want the two of them to be overcome with passionate desire for each other in a public place. Ultimately, she had decided on the word *underwear,* thinking it was one that wasn't used too often, and one they would most likely only say when they were at home together. Nevertheless, it *was* common enough that it would come up eventually.

If one could pardon the pun.

And Dorcas was confident it would only need to be spoken or heard once, because after the Feders made love that first time, their inhibitions and shyness would most likely disappear, regardless of whether they had been hypnotized or not. Once they experienced sex with each other, they wouldn't need a stimulus like the word *underwear* for it to happen again. Because after that first time, they would realize there was no need for shyness or inhibition, and they would respond to each other naturally. Until that happened, however, the trigger word would do the trick.

So Dorcas told the Feders that any time either of them heard the word *underwear,* he or she would be completely overcome with desire for the other, and would initiate lovemaking with complete and uninhibited abandon.

"Upon hearing the word *underwear,*" she said softly as the couple sat still and silent, "each of you will think of or look at the other and will immediately want to make mad, passionate love. You will feel no inhibition about sex whatsoever. You will feel no shyness, no guilt, no shame, no worry. You will be eager to explore any sexual impulse, fantasy, act or position either of you wishes to try. You will each respond to your partner without fear or reserve or modesty. Whenever you hear 'underwear,' that's your signal to forget your inhibitions and turn to each other with all the desire and passion you feel for each other. Whenever you hear that word you will stop whatever you're doing and be as sexual together as you want to be."

Dorcas paused for a moment, thinking she should also give them a turn-*off* switch for their passion, too, just in case they found themselves in a situation where they heard the word but weren't together, or where having sex wouldn't be possible. No reason to make the two of them wander around in a state of constant arousal, after all.

So she said, "The only thing that will assuage your desire will be to engage in sex, or to sleep."

Now if one of them had to travel without the other, they could at least feel better in the morning about not having been able to have sex when they wanted it.

That should do it, Dorcas thought. Now the Feders could go home and do it, too. Over and over again. To their hearts' content. And with that escape valve of sleep, they shouldn't have to go around in a perpetual state of wanting without being able to have. Her work here was finished.

Gradually, she brought Becca and Turner back to consciousness, reminding them before total awareness recurred that they would consciously remember nothing of what they heard while under hypnosis, and that they would feel rested and relaxed upon waking. And then, with a slow, steady count to five, Dorcas woke them.

Their eyes fluttered open in unison, almost as if they were of one body. Becca smiled a dreamy little smile as she brought her hands out in front of her, threaded her fingers together and stretched. But Turner immediately jumped out of his chair and stood, frowning as he looked around at the office.

"I don't think it worked," he said. "You never even got me under."

"Yes, I did," Dorcas replied easily. This wasn't an unusual response for people, especially men, to have. "You won't remember it, because I told you not to. But you were most assuredly under hypnosis, Turner."

"Did I bark like a dog?"

Dorcas grinned. "No. And I didn't make you flap your arms like a chicken, either."

"I don't feel any different," he told her.

"That's not unusual," she said. "You're not supposed to feel any different." Well, not yet, he wasn't, she added to herself. Just wait till he heard the word *underwear.* "Unless perhaps it's to feel rested and relaxed, since I told you to feel that, too."

"I don't feel rested or relaxed," he said.

"I do," Becca said. "I feel very rested and relaxed. Like I just had a nice, long nap."

She was going to feel even better after she heard the word *underwear,* Dorcas thought, still grinning.

"Well, regardless of how you feel at the moment," she told the Feders, "I gave you both a posthypnotic suggestion that should help you with your problem. If you're still having trouble this time next week, call me, and we can try again. But you were both well under, I assure you. Do you remember anything that I said to you?"

The Feders exchanged a glance, then shook their heads and turned back to look at Dorcas.

"Then I think you'll see some results," she told them. "As I said, if not, do let me know, and we'll see if another session will take care of it. But I think the two of you will be pleased."

Oh, Dorcas did so love being able to help people. And the Feders seemed like such a nice couple.

"Now go home and relax," she told them. "Take the rest of the day to yourselves and see what develops. Maybe you could do a little laundry," she suggested helpfully. "A load of lights. See what happens when you go to put it away. You can settle up with my receptionist on the way out. She should be off the phone by now."

The Feders gazed at her with obvious confusion about the laundry recommendation, but Dorcas only smiled and showed them out. She needed to get them close to some underwear as soon as possible. Whatever it took to get these two lovebirds in the sack going at it. As often and as long as possible.

Becca and Turner Feder were in for a pleasant surprise, she thought as she watched her office door close behind them. And with any luck at all, it would be soon.

TURNER KNEW THE HYPNOSIS hadn't worked on him as soon as they hit the street. Because not only did he not feel in any way rested or relaxed—though he had to admit Becca seemed more mellow at the moment than he'd seen her for a while—he was craving a cigarette more than he'd ever craved anything in his life.

Well, except for Becca, natch.

But he *was* craving a cigarette. Something fierce.

"It didn't work up there with the Amazing Dorcaso," he said after they exited the building and began the walk toward where they'd parked her car.

"What do you mean it didn't work?" Becca echoed, halting in her tracks, forcing Turner to stop walking, too. He turned to face her as she added, "How do you know it didn't work? It's too soon to know that."

"I know because right now, I want a cigarette real bad," he told her. "Don't you?"

She thought about that for a moment, then frowned. Dejectedly, she confessed, "Yeah. I do."

"I told you hypnotherapy was a load of crap," he said.

They started walking again, more slowly this time. "Well, Dorcas said we could try again," Becca reminded him. "Maybe we could go back up right now. It's ten o'clock, when our original appointment was scheduled. She'd have time to see us again for another session."

"No way," Turner said decisively. "I'm not going through that hoodoo again. If it didn't work once, doing it again won't make any difference."

She eyed him thoughtfully for a moment before asking, "What do you think she meant by all that 'go home and do laundry' stuff?"

"Got me," he replied.

Becca's disappointment was obvious. "I was so sure it would work," she said. "Now what are we going to do?"

Turner glanced up the street, at a drugstore on the corner. "I don't know about you, but I'm going for a pack of smokes." He started off, but Becca's hand on his arm halted him.

"Wait," she said.

"What?" he asked, turning around to face her.

"Maybe we could still try to quit on our own. Cold turkey."

He expelled an irritated sigh. "We tried that already, remember? Back in college. It was pointless."

"But we were kids then," she reminded him. "We'd do better now. We're grown-ups. We have more stamina."

Oh, she had to use a word like *stamina,* Turner thought. Yeah, he'd love to show her some stamina now. Except not where it came to quitting smoking. On the contrary, he wanted to *start* smoking with her. And there wouldn't be a cigarette in sight when he did. Screw the statistics that said college boys had more stamina than guys his age.

Turner could prove it all night to Becca if she gave him half a chance.

Oh, yeah, baby. I got your stamina right here.

"Turner?" she said, bringing him out of his reverie. His daydream. Fantasy. Lurid desire. Whatever.

"What?" he asked, unable to curb his irritability.

"You look kind of…"

"What?" he demanded again, even more grouchily this time.

But instead of answering him, Becca began to nibble her bottom lip worriedly. Oh, hell. He hated it when she did that. Because it made him want to nibble her bottom lip, too. And still she had her fingers curled so tentatively— and so temptingly—into his forearm, making him want to curl his fingers less tentatively—and more temptingly— into parts of her.

Dammit, why did she have to value their friendship so much? Why couldn't she dislike him enough to become sexually involved with him? Life was so freakin' unfair.

"I'm sorry," he murmured, gentling both his voice and his attitude. "I just get a little irritable when I go too long without smoking." And he wasn't just talking about cigarettes there, either. It had been too long since he'd smoked up the sheets with a woman, too. Which, now that he thought about it, could also be contributing to his need for cigarettes lately. Not to mention compounding his need for Becca.

"Well, since you're already irritable," she said, "what's the harm of trying to go longer between cigarettes? We don't have to go cold turkey yet. Just cut back. How about that?"

God, she was so beautiful, he thought, scarcely hearing her question. Behind her, a streetwise maple tree was still clinging to what was left of its reds and golds and oranges, and the sun overhead lit reddish-gold fires in Becca's tawny hair. The cool autumn breeze danced with the silky locks, nudging a few errant strands over her shoulder and into her eyes. His fingers itched to reach up and tuck the wayward tresses behind her ear, but she beat him to it, carelessly flipping her hair back on her own.

He'd touched that hair himself, he recalled, had sifted it through his fingers and buried his hands in it. And he'd touched other parts of Becca, too. Parts he wouldn't mind exploring again, though years had passed since the last time it happened. He'd touched his lips to hers, had tasted her deeply. He'd held her breast in the palm of his hand, and his fingers had been slick with the damp heat of her. Maybe it had only happened a few times, and maybe only because they'd both been under the influence of either raging hormones or holiday spirits of the alcoholic variety. But he had tasted and touched Becca once upon a time. And he remembered every single moment of every single time.

Someday, he hoped, he would touch and taste her again. Only the next time it happened, the sole influence they'd be under would be their feelings for each other. And their need for each other. Someday, he told himself again. He just had to be patient, that was all. But it would happen again.

Someday.

"Look, we have the whole day off from work," she reminded him. "Let's do something fun. Something that will distract us from smoking. Let's go to a movie. I'll even let you pick which one. And then I'll cook dinner for you at my place."

"We should probably talk about the new account at some point," Turner told her, deliberately replacing thoughts of their personal relationship with thoughts of their professional one, since that was so much easier to think about. "We may have taken the day off from work, but we still have a lot to do on our presentation before Saturday."

"We'll do it tomorrow," she told him. "We have the rest of the week before we have to present it, and we don't have that much more to do. And, all modesty aside, I think we both realize how brilliant our pitch is. If we don't land that account for Englund Advertising, nobody can." She smiled with much satisfaction as she looped her arm through his and began to walk leisurely up the street. "By Monday morning, Turner, you and I will be working on the ad campaign for real. I just know it. By Monday morning, the account for Bluestocking Lingerie is going to be *all* ours."

5

HIS AND BECCA'S PITCH might be brilliant, Turner thought the following evening when everyone *else* at Englund Advertising was packing up to go home, but it wasn't finished yet. Which was why everyone *else* at Englund Advertising was packing up to go home, and he and Becca were still seated in her cubicle working on their pitch. Yeah, they still had two more days to perfect it, but he knew they'd both feel a lot better if it was perfect *now*. And since neither of them had any plans for the evening, neither had seen any problem with hanging around a little longer to do some more work on it.

Except for the fact that he, for one, was craving a cigarette something awful.

Damn hypnotherapy anyway, he thought. What a racket. By day's end yesterday, he and Becca had both succumbed to their need to smoke, a half-dozen times at least. Whatever the Amazing Dorcaso had said to them while they were under, it hadn't worked worth a damn. Not that he was surprised. Yeah, looked like it was going to be an early, stinky grave for the two of them, after all.

"We just need a catchier slogan," she was saying now from her seat behind her desk.

Her cubicle, like his, was a perfect square, eight feet by

eight feet, which was by no means large, but was larger than most of the Englund Advertising employees had. That was because Turner and Becca were next in line for promotion to account managers, something that would net them an honest-to-God office. Interior, without windows, at first, but eventually, if enough of their colleagues quit or retired—or, you know, died—they'd have the breathtaking view of the Indianapolis skyline visible from the best offices and the boardroom.

In the meantime, Becca, at least, had created her own view for her cubicle. Among the requisite calendar and phone list attached to the beige fabric walls, she'd tacked up pages pulled from magazines of print ads that the two of them had worked on together. There were glossy shots of everything from a local microbrewery and its assorted ales, to a local vineyard and its assorted wines, to a local five-star restaurant, to an exclusive condominium highrise recently added to that breathtaking view of the Indianapolis skyline. Only in the past couple of years had Englund Advertising expanded into markets beyond Indianapolis, but in that short time, they'd won a number of high-visibility national accounts. Turner and Becca, however, had continued to work with local clients.

Until now.

Bluestocking Lingerie would be Englund Advertising's biggest client yet, if—no, *when,* Turner immediately corrected himself—they landed it, since the underwear company was fast becoming synonymous with expensive, expertly fashioned, very sexy female underthings. It was Turner and Becca's job to create a campaign that would turn that *fast becoming* into a fait accompli. If they had their way, any woman worth her weight in Belgian lace would want to own Bluestocking products, and every woman would know to head to a Bluestocking boutique when it came to shopping for her wedding night. Or any other night when an enormous amount of gratuitous, unbridled sex was on the agenda.

Because most of the pieces Bluestocking had sent over to Englund Advertising for Turner and Becca to inspect weren't exactly the sort of thing a woman would wear for comfort and-or function. Even Turner could see that. When Becca had dumped the box of lingerie onto her desk, there had been things in the lacy, silky—and in a few instances, leather-studded—mélange that Turner had never seen before. And he'd always considered himself a connoisseur of what women wore under their clothes, so that was saying something.

Inescapably, though, as he'd picked through the assortment of barely there attire, he had found himself wondering if Becca owned any of Bluestocking's products herself, and if so, which ones? At the moment, however, he was trying very hard *not* to wonder about that. Unfortunately, it was with dubious success.

He had wheeled his own chair into her cubicle for the after-hours conference, and now sat wedged between the cubicle's wall and the side of her desk, his khaki-covered legs propped negligently on its surface as he leaned back. He loosened his psychedelically colored Jerry Garcia necktie and rolled the sleeves of his white oxford shirt up to his elbows, not so much because he wanted to get down to work, but because it was a little stuffy in the tiny space.

Becca seemed restless, too, because she leaned impatiently back in her chair, then reached up to undo her tortoiseshell barrette. She scrubbed her hands absently through her hair, then gathered it together again in a tidier ponytail than before and clipped it back into place.

Turner watched her with veiled interest, noting the way her breasts surged against the creamy fabric of her blouse as she completed the task, and how that blouse gaped open just enough for him to glimpse the champagne-colored lace of her bra beneath. He bit back a groan and forced himself to glance away. But that left him looking at the slender length of leg encased in smoky black silk that extended from the hem of a brief black skirt.

At least she'd kicked off her spiky high heels, he tried to reassure himself, telling himself stocking feet couldn't possibly be as erotic as he suddenly found Becca's to be. Nevertheless, the images of hair and breast and leg and foot had all lodged firmly in his brain, and together they generated a PowerPoint presentation of other images that grew steadily more graphic.

Oh, yeah. Turner could definitely use a smoke right now. But it wasn't the cigarette kind of smoking that overwhelmed him just then.

"We need something short, but memorable, for a catch phrase," Becca continued efficiently, oblivious to Turner's state of agitation. "Something that will strike a chord with the upwardly mobile, professional woman that Bluestocking Lingerie wants to target for their line of products."

"I still like my suggestion," he said, not quite able to keep the petulance out of his voice in light of her having so resoundingly denounced what he thought was an extremely catchy slogan.

She rolled her eyes at him. "Gee, color me skeptical, but I'm not convinced that the women of America would respond in a positive manner to Bluestocking Lingerie—Put it on, and put out."

"No, not that one, the other one," he told her.

"Bluestocking Lingerie—When your fling is the thing?" she asked.

"No, no, the one after that."

"Bluestocking Lingerie—He'll get a big shock and you'll get a big cock?"

"No, the other one after that."

"Bluestocking Lingerie—You're in luck, you, when he wants to—"

"No, the *other* other one after that."

She thought for a minute. "Oh, right," she said, remembering. "Bluestocking Lingerie—When there's boffing in the offing."

"That's the one," Turner exclaimed.

"Actually, I think that's not the one," she stated.

"Well, it *is* short and memorable," he pointed out.

"I don't think it's what the client is looking for," Becca replied evenly. "Come on. There's got to be something. This is usually the easiest part of the campaign for us. Maybe we should focus on a handful of the designs instead of the collection as a whole," she suggested.

She sorted through the scanty garments littering her desk, the items Bluestocking seemed to be most interested in promoting. To Turner, it just looked like a bunch of bras and panties that had little to distinguish themselves from each other.

"They all look alike to me," he said. "I think we should stick with the collection as a whole."

"Alike?" she repeated, clearly aghast. She laid out a few pairs of panties and a few assorted bras. "They're not all alike. It says so in the Bluestocking portfolio they sent along. Look at the panties, for instance."

Turner did. But he still didn't see any notable differences aside from color and fabric. "Yeah? So?"

"So," she said. She directed her attention to the first pair, and reading the tag attached to it, added, "Here, you have your briefs." She moved on to the last pair and flipped up that tag, too. "And here, you have your string bikinis. In between," she continued, moving back to the other garments and reading their tags, "you have your hemi-brief… and then your semi-brief…and then your, ah, your demi-brief. And then your bikini, and your mini-bikini, and your micro-bikini, and your mini-micro-bikini."

He narrowed his eyes as he followed the movements of her hand. "What's the diff?"

She opened her mouth to tell him, then shrugged. "I don't know. Those in the middle all look pretty much the same to me. But the briefs and the string bikinis are totally different. And the thong…" She pulled another garment—though it looked like it was little more than a remnant of black lace to Turner—from the others.

"Oh, now with *that* one I can certainly see the difference," he said enthusiastically. And he would have loved to see more of it, too. Especially on Becca.

"Mmm," she said noncommittally.

"What about the bras?" he asked, warming to the subject matter now, and wondering how he might broach the subject of having Becca model each and every article of clothing there. Because, ya know, that could be really helpful. It would totally inspire him to do his best work. On the campaign, he meant.

Becca seemed not to notice his preoccupation, because

she was straightening the assortment of bras, flipping up and reading their tags, too. "Full cup," she said, pointing to the first one. "Hemi-cup." She continued on to the second. "Then…semi-cup. And, um, demi-cup." She moved to the next row and continued, "Mini-cup. Micro-cup. And then mini-micro-cup."

"This sounds vaguely familiar," Turner said. "But I want to know where the thong cup is."

He looked up to find her rolling her eyes at him again. "There's no such thing as a thong cup."

"Well, why the hell not?" he demanded.

She bit the inside of her cheek. "Just a shot in the dark, but probably, it would be kind of uncomfortable to the wearer. Not to mention offer no support whatsoever."

"Oh, and a scrap of lace lodged between your butt cheeks isn't uncomfortable?" he countered. "Never mind supporting. Here's a news flash for you, Becca. Women don't wear stuff like this for comfort and support. They wear it because they want to turn on their guy."

"Not always," she said. "Some women like to wear frilly, girlie stuff under their clothes because it makes them feel sexier and more feminine."

He eyed her thoughtfully. "You talk like you're speaking from experience."

Which, of course, he knew she was, having just glimpsed what she was wearing under her own business attire. He was just trying to bait her. Though why exactly he was trying to bait her, he wasn't sure he wanted to think about.

She gritted her teeth, but said nothing more, only scooped up all the pieces of underwear and piled them into an untidy heap that she pushed to the side of her desk.

"Okay, so then maybe we should look at the collection as a whole," she conceded.

Turner did his best to stay focused on the matter at hand after that, but his gaze kept straying to the buttons on Becca's blouse, and his mind kept straying to how much he wanted to reach across the desk and undo every last one of them, to get a better view—among other things—of what lay beneath.

Okay, so maybe that was why he had been baiting her....

Man, he had to do something about his preoccupation with Becca. Ever since the two of them had started working on this pitch for Bluestocking Lingerie, he'd been way too in tune to his feelings for her. Normally, he could ignore his attraction to her and be around her with fairly little discomfort. He'd gotten so used to his feelings for her over the years that he no longer had trouble dealing with them. He'd decided a long time ago that he'd rather pine incessantly for her than lose her completely. Eventually, it had just become second nature to him to want Becca and know he couldn't have her.

But for the past few weeks, being faced every day with such incredibly sexy lingerie, and watching her fondle it, and fondling it himself, and thinking about how it would look on her, and how unbelievably erotic it would be to take it off of her... Being confronted on a daily basis with the intimate tools of a woman's trade when it came to seducing a man... Turner had just been in a perpetual state of arousal, that was all. And Becca's constant nearness had been almost too much for him to bear. There hadn't been a single day in the past couple of weeks when he hadn't succumbed at some point to fantasizing about being naked with her, cupping his hands over her bare ass, sucking on her ripe breasts, burying his head between her legs to run his tongue over and into the melting center of her....

Oh, God, not again....

He should just go out, find a willing woman and get laid, he told himself, not for the first time. That new redhead Englund had hired last month had made clear her interest in doing the horizontal boogaloo with him. What was her name again? he wondered. Linda? Laura? Louise? Lucy! That was it. Maybe Turner ought to try thinking about her instead of Becca when he started feeling randy. Hell, who knew? Maybe Lucy could make him forget all about Becca. And how those skimpy bras and panties would look on Becca. And how it would feel to have Becca's smoky-stockinged legs braced on his shoulders while he rammed himself into her....

Oh, dammit. Here came the PowerPoint presentation of all of Becca's parts again....

He rubbed his eyes wearily as he leaned back in his chair, trying to put thoughts of her out of his mind. "Man," he muttered irascibly, "I can't believe all the trouble we're going to just to sell some stupid underwear."

He dropped his hands back into his lap and surrendered to his urge to look at Becca. To his surprise, he found her gazing back at him with much interest, as if she were studying him in an effort to discover what made him tick.

"What?" he said, still sounding irascible. Still feeling irascible.

"What did you just say?" she asked, her voice soft and low and sounding strangely...aroused? Oh, surely not. That was just wishful thinking on his part. He was aroused, so naturally he'd think everyone else was, too.

He narrowed his eyes at her. "I said I can't believe all the trouble we're going to just to sell some stupid underwear."

She nodded slowly, her gaze still fixed on his face. "That's what I thought you said."

And there was still something really weird about her voice, he noted. He'd seen enough of her chick flicks to recognize a little Greta Garbo when he heard it. Next she'd be telling him she vahnted to be alooone.

But it became obvious pretty quickly that she *didn't* want to be alone, because she smiled at Turner in a way he'd never seen her smile at him before. But it was a smile he did recognize, because he'd seen it from other women in the past. It was the kind of smile to which a woman treated a man when she was in the mood for an enormous amount of gratuitous, unbridled—

Oh, no, he immediately told himself. No, no, no, no, no. No way. No how. Nuh-uh. *Nej. Neen. Ie.* He was just imagining things again.

"Do you know," she said, propping her elbow on her desk now and settling her chin into her palm, "that you have the most beautiful eyes? I never really noticed before. But they're incredibly blue."

Turner again narrowed his eyes at her. "You never noticed that my eyes are blue?" he asked skeptically, wondering what kind of game she was playing here.

"Oh, I noticed they were blue," she said, wheeling her chair closer to the edge of the desk—and closer to Turner, too. "But they're just really, *really* blue, aren't they?"

What the hell was she up to? he wondered. She was acting like she was…flirting with him or something. No, she was going beyond flirting, with that smile and those smoldering looks. She was acting as if she wanted an enormous amount of gratuitous, unbridled—

No. No way. *Ne. Nei. Lo.* He was just misunderstanding whatever the hell it was she was doing.

"My eyes aren't any bluer than they were this morning,"

he said. At least, he didn't think they were. Were they? What the hell was she talking about?

She said nothing in response to that, only continued to gaze at him in a way that was extremely... The word *steamy* came to mind. Along with a few others he'd be better off not thinking about. And that smile, he thought, studying her mouth again. If that wasn't a smile meant to tempt men to commit sexual mayhem, he didn't know what was.

She scooted her chair to the very edge of her desk, bringing her within inches of where Turner sat, then propped her elbow on her desktop and cradled her chin in her palm again, the way she had before. Not once did she take her eyes off of his face, and she continued to smile that smoldering— and other words he'd better not think about—smile.

"You smell really good today," she said out of nowhere. "Is that a new fragrance you're wearing?"

"I don't wear fragrances," he told her. "You know that. It isn't manly. Real men don't smell like pine trees or ocean breezes."

She inhaled deeply and released the breath slowly. "Well, you smell good, anyway," she said. "Very, *very* manly. Much better than pine trees and ocean breezes. Maybe it's the fabric softener you use."

He narrowed his eyes even more. "I don't use fabric softener. It *really* isn't manly to smell springtime fresh."

"Mmm," she replied, scooting her chair closer still. "Do you remember..." she began, and he was grateful she was changing the subject. Until she finished, "...the office Christmas party a couple of years ago, when you and I drank too much of the eggnog Dennis poured all that spiced rum into?"

Oh, as if Turner would ever forget *that*. The night the two of them had escaped to their smoking closet to do some *real* smoking was easily one of his top five most re-played memories of his entire life. When he was at death's door, that was a scene he hoped would go in slow motion while the rest of his life was flashing before his eyes. But why was Becca bringing it up? She'd made clear after it happened that it had been a mistake and that she never wanted to talk about it again.

"Yeah, I remember…." he said tentatively. "What about it?"

The hand that wasn't cupping her chin inched across the desk toward his legs, still propped up on her desk. Turner watched, fascinated, waiting to see where she would stop it. But she didn't stop until her fingers were wrapped lightly around his ankle. And when her thumb began to trace an idle circle over the lower part of his shin, he nearly jumped out of his skin. Instead of dropping his leg from the desk, he only watched the laconic motion of her thumb and did his best to ignore the stream of heat that rushed through his belly.

"I've been thinking about that night a lot lately," she said as she stopped drawing those lazy circles, and moved her hand up over the cuff of his pants. "Remembering what happened in our smoking closet that night. It was pretty memorable, after all."

What the hell…? Turner thought as she dragged her hand higher, up over his knee. She pushed her chair forward again so that she could curl her fingers over his thigh. Heat shot through him again at the contact, and his cock stirred between his legs.

"Becca…" he began. But for the life of him, he couldn't make himself say another word.

"What?" she asked.

"What do you think you're doing?"

She smiled that smile again, and his blood went zinging through his veins. "Nothing," she said with mock innocence.

"Then could you take your hand off my leg?"

She curved her lips into an almost convincing pout, but dropped her hand as he'd requested. "If I have to take my hand off your leg, then you have to take your legs off my desk," she told him petulantly.

Oh, so that was what it was all about. Well, hell, if she'd wanted him to move his legs, why hadn't she just said so? Immediately, and with much relief purling through him— kind of—he shifted his feet to the floor. His body was fast reaching a state she didn't need to see up close, anyway.

And no, it wasn't the state of Rhode Island.

"There," he said. "Satisfied?"

Her smile went nearly incandescent. "Well, actually, if you must know…"

But she never finished whatever she'd intended to say. Not verbally, at any rate. Instead she rose from her chair and, without even having to take a step, swung one leg over both of Turner's and dropped down into his lap, facing him, her fingers curled now over both of his shoulders. But as startling as her action was, it wasn't what caught Turner's attention the most. That would have been how the action made her brief skirt ride high on her thighs, offering him a glimpse of naked flesh where her black silk stockings ended and black satin garters began.

Holy cow, he thought. He'd had no idea Becca wore stuff like *that* under her clothes…

It took a moment for the realization of what she had done to set in, a moment Turner used to try and think of something to say. But try as he might, he couldn't pull his gaze away from that tempting bit of black satin, and the only words that came into his head ran along the lines of *I want to sink my teeth into your sweet honeypot, baby,* which, call him crazy, probably wouldn't have helped matters much.

Not in the way they needed to be helped at the moment, anyway. Because as often as he had fantasized about Becca straddling his lap exactly as she was now—except, um, without her shirt on—for some reason, Turner was hesitant to accept this at face value. Mostly because he wasn't looking at her face. Oh, no, wait, that wasn't it. Mostly because he was certain she was up to something and couldn't be serious about…whatever the hell she seemed to be doing.

Maybe she was just trying to inspire him to come up with a new slogan? he wondered lamely. Though she'd never been quite this, ah, persuasive before when it came to giving him a nudge…. And if that were the case, then her plan was going to backfire. Because everything whizzing through his muddled brain at the moment included the same ol', same ol' words like *putting out* and *fling* and *boffing* and *cock* and—

"Uh, Becca?"

"Hmm?" she purred. Really. Purred. Turner could honestly say he had never heard a woman purr until that moment. And hearing Becca do it now…

Oh, man…

He told himself to say something—anything—that would make light of the situation. Because he did need to make light of the situation. If he didn't, the boner that was growing in his pants was going to come to light instead. Or maybe it would just plain come.

But anything he might have said dried up in his throat when Becca removed her hands from his shoulders and lifted them to her blouse. She immediately began to unbutton it, hesitating not a second as she pushed each pearly little button through its hole.

"Becca?" he said again when he realized she had no intention of stopping until the garment was completely undone. "What are you doing?"

"It's hot in here," she said, jerking her shirttail from the waistband of her skirt. "The thermostat must be set up too high. Don't you feel hot?"

Hell, yes, he felt hot. But it wasn't because of the room's thermostat. That was for damn sure.

"Becca?" he said once more. "What are you doing?"

"I need to cool off," she told him.

Oh, and like he didn't?

She shrugged completely out of her shirt and tossed it to the side without even looking to see where it landed. "You don't mind, do you?" she asked belatedly. "I mean, we know each other well enough that we can take off our shirts in front of each other, right? It's no big deal."

Actually, it wasn't a deal Turner was worried about getting big. "Uh…" he began eloquently.

Words deserted him after that, though, because he was way too busy appreciating the view. The bra he'd glimpsed beneath Becca's blouse was indeed fashioned of filmy lace, nearly the same color as her soft skin, but that was about all it was fashioned of. Meaning it was translucent, and he could easily distinguish the dark circles of her nipples and aureolas beneath it. Her breasts surged against the taut fabric, spilling from the top in a way that made him want to fill his hands with them, then lean forward and run the tip of his tongue along the smooth flesh where it joined with lace. It was only through some incredible miracle of restraint that he kept himself from doing just that.

"In fact," he heard Becca say from a million miles away, "if you want to take off your shirt, too, I wouldn't mind. You must be feeling as hot as I am."

Oh, that was the understatement of the millennium. Although he had no idea why he answered the way he did, he told her, "No, uh, that's—that's okay. I'm, um, I'm comfortable." He was also lying through his teeth, since the bulge in his pants was making him just the opposite. But she didn't need to know that.

She scooted forward on his lap and wiggled her ass against that part of him. Oh. Okay. So evidently she already knew it.

"You don't feel like you're comfortable," she said as pushed herself forward more, an action that sent her skirt riding even higher on her thighs. "And I'm not comfortable, either," she added as she looped her arms around his neck. "But I know how we can fix that for both of us."

And then, before he could object, she slanted her mouth over his, treating him to the sort of kiss he'd only fantasized about before, wet and deep and long. She thrust her tongue into his mouth and rocked her entire body against his. And instinctively, enthusiastically, Turner wrapped his arms around her waist and returned fire.

Heat. That was all he registered after that. Heat in his mouth, in his belly, in his hands, in his pants. Becca was hot all over, and so was he, and if he didn't do something to cool them off fast, they were going to spontaneously combust. And as often as he'd thought about combusting with Becca right in this very cubicle, he really didn't think

the office was the best place for that. Englund did have a
no-smoking policy, after all.

And Turner would remind her of that, too. He would.
In just a minute. Maybe two. Okay, five, but no more than
that. But she chose that moment to push herself up on tiptoe and surge forward again, lowering herself onto his now
rock-hard dick. And she punctuated the action with an
erotic little whimper of surrender that made Turner come
completely undone.

Unable to help himself, he jerked his mouth from hers
and dragged a long line of openmouthed kisses down the
column of her neck, tasting the little hollow at the base of
her throat. Then he dipped his head lower, rubbing his lips
over the soft mound of one breast, before flattening his
tongue against her nipple, over the scant covering of lace.
Again and again he licked her swollen flesh through the
fabric, drawing indolent circles with the tip of his tongue
before closing his mouth over her more completely. But he
couldn't suck her fully into his mouth the way he wanted
to, so, reaching behind her, he unhooked her bra, helped
her shrug out of it, and cast it aside.

Her breasts were glorious as they spilled free, full and
round and ripe. Never in his life had he seen a more perfectly formed woman than Becca. He pressed his face to
her again, palming one breast firmly under his hand as he
guided the other to his mouth and began licking it again,
this time flesh to flesh. She tasted…so sweet. Her skin was
hot, silky and luscious, and he knew there would never
come a time when he didn't want to fill his hands and
mouth with her. All of her.

She tangled her fingers in his hair and drew his head
closer, scooting her hips forward, toward his waist. The

friction created by the movement made his cock lurch higher, and she gasped as his hard rod rubbed against her.

He moved his mouth to her other breast. Her fingers circled his wrist, and when she shifted her hips backward again, she tugged his hand between her legs. Turner felt her heat before his fingers even made contact with her wet panties, but Becca kept her hand cupped over his, shoving his fingers against her. As he caressed her through the silk, he felt the fabric grow wetter and hotter still, and he knew she was hotter and wetter beneath it, ready for him.

He wanted so badly to free his dick from his trousers and ram it inside her to the hilt, right here, right now. Her breath against his temple was as fiery and steamy as the rest of her, coming in ragged, irregular gulps every time he stroked her.

"Again, Turner," she gasped against his ear. "Finger me again. Harder. Faster. And then I want your cock inside me."

"Oh, Becca," he said. But even as he ground out her name, he knew there was no way he could take her here like this. They were at work, for God's sake. And it wasn't long after office hours. There could still be a couple of people around. He didn't know why she suddenly wanted to have sex with him, and he figured he probably shouldn't question it. But he wanted their first time together to be someplace where they could spend more time exploring and satisfying each other. He didn't want it to be a quickie on her desk, when they weren't even completely undressed.

Although he had no idea where he found the strength to do it, he moved his head back from her breast and jerked his hand from between her legs, fighting her efforts to pull him back to both places.

"No, Becca," he said, amazed to hear himself say it. "We can't. Not here. Not now. Not like this."

Her disappointment was almost palpable. "Yes, we can," she insisted breathlessly, crowding against him again. "Please, Turner. I need you. I want you. I want your cock inside me. *Now*."

She moved her hand between his legs this time, finding his dick and rubbing it hard. He cried out at the fire that shot through him, but somehow managed to grasp her wrist and pull her hand away.

Her eyes, still dark with her passion, clouded over. "Please," she whispered again.

He shook his head. And told her again, "No, Becca. Not like this."

"But—"

"McCloud! Mercer!"

"Oh, shit," Turner said when he heard the booming voice of their employer.

Without thinking, he jumped up from his chair, taking Becca with him. She nearly fell to the floor, but he caught her and set her upright, his fingers curled around her bare arms, her naked breasts shuddering. Before he had a chance to say another word, she pushed herself up on tiptoe and covered his mouth with hers, wrapping her arms around his waist to pull him close.

She still wanted to do it, even with their boss within shouting distance. What the hell had gotten into her?

Through no small effort, Turner disentangled himself from her half-naked body and set her at arm's length, holding her there firmly when she obviously wanted to lunge forward again.

"It's Englund, Becca," he hissed, as loudly as he dared. "Our boss, remember? Get dressed. I'll stall him."

She didn't seem to have heard a word he said, because

she reached for him again. "I don't care who it is, Turner, I want you. Now."

"Get dressed," he told her again, more forcefully this time. "We'll talk about this later."

"McCloud! Mercer!"

Englund's voice was closer now, and still Becca made no move to do as Turner had instructed.

"Do you promise we'll talk later?" she asked.

"Yes," he told her.

"And then we can make love?"

Good God, what was going on? "If you still want to, yes," he told her. Though at that point, he would have said anything to get Becca to cooperate.

"It better not be too much later," she muttered.

"Get dressed," he said for the last time. And without even waiting to see if she followed his instructions, he turned and headed out of her cubicle, calling, "Right here, Mr. Englund! Sorry! We were working so hard on the Bluestocking pitch, we didn't even know you were here...."

TURNER WAS A TEASE.

A tempter.

A breaker of promises.

A liar.

Yet, still, she wanted him.

Needed him.

Hungered for him.

Burned for him.

As Becca lay awake in her bed—alone—tossing and turning and practically on fire with her unsatisfied desires and her unfulfilled needs... Or would they be unfulfilled desires and unsatisfied needs? she wondered vaguely. Oh, well. No matter. 'Cause she had *all* of 'em, honey, and it was no picnic, that was for sure, and if she didn't get some relief soon, she was going to…to…to…

Where was she?

Oh, yeah. As she lay awake in bed—and had she mentioned she was alone?—tossing and turning and practically on fire with her unfulfilled and unsatisfied…stuff, all she could think about was Turner. About how incredibly sexy Turner had been this evening. About how much she'd wanted Turner. About how much she'd *needed* Turner. About how incredible it had felt to be in Turner's arms. About how exquisitely Turner had touched her and tasted her. About how awful and horrible and despicable and nasty and evil it had been that she'd been prevented from having Turner right there in her cubicle because Englund had decided to work late, too, to supervise their progress on their pitch. About how Englund had walked down to the parking garage with both of them so that they'd had to leave in their separate cars without making any plans to meet later.

About how, when Becca had called Turner to invite him over as soon as she'd arrived home, he'd told her he was too tired to come over, and that they could talk in the morning.

And *still* she wanted him.

Acutely.

Completely.

Desperately.

She punched her pillow with much frustration and flopped over to her other side. Although a light snow had been falling when she arrived home, she'd worn only her panties and a cropped undershirt to bed because she'd been so hot. Now, the covers were kicked into a heap at the foot, and the ceiling fan rotated laconically above her, its chilly breeze washing over her heated skin, cooling her not at all.

Around her, her bedroom was silent and semidark, the night-light in the bathroom providing just enough illumination for her to see the white French provincial furnishings and floral wallpaper and accessories. Suddenly, it all looked so sickeningly sweet and girlie-girl, and she couldn't imagine what had possessed her to go with such a decorating scheme.

No wonder she'd never been able to lure Turner into her bed, she thought. What man in his right mind would feel aroused in an environment like this? Maybe, in addition to all the other redecorating she planned to do on the condo, she'd redo this room, too. Maybe in red. Deep, dark, intense red. The color of passion. Yeah. With dark, heavy Mediterranean furnishings. That would make it more masculine. And wrought-iron accessories. Like torches. And chains. And maybe some manacles affixed to one wall, to give it that certain je ne sais quoi.

Yeah, that could work….

Unbidden, she enjoyed a very graphic mental image of what, exactly, that je ne sais quoi would involve. Notably, Turner manacled to her wall, naked, with firelight bathing his muscular form while she knelt before him, her hands curved over his taut, firm ass, his cock rigid and full as she sucked it, hard and deep. Only when he was on the verge of coming would she stop, and then she would stand and push her body against his, curl one leg around his waist and rub her wet clit against his hard shaft, driving them both to orgasm.

Oh, Turner…

Grabbing the pillow from the opposite side of the bed, Becca thrust it between her legs, bucking her hips against it. But it was a lousy substitute for the man.

6

BY SATURDAY MORNING, when Becca and Turner were supposed to present their pitch to the Bluestocking Lingerie people, Becca was still reeling from what had happened Wednesday night. She couldn't begin to explain why she'd behaved the way she had with Turner, though God knew she'd tried. What was weird—well, one thing that was weird among the many weird things that night—was that she hadn't even remembered what happened until she'd arrived at work Thursday morning and saw Turner sitting in his cubicle, staring at her cubicle, waiting for her to show up. One look at him, though, and she'd been flooded by the memory of what had happened the night before.

And that wasn't all she'd been flooded with.

As insane and inexplicable as her behavior had been, she also remembered how she'd enjoyed herself *so much*. That didn't, however, excuse what had happened.

All she knew was that one minute she'd been sorting through a collection of racy lingerie, and the next, she'd been unbelievably aroused. It was the strangest thing. She'd never been the sort of woman to heat up quickly, had always liked a little playful, naughty flirting with her partner first, then lots and lots of physical foreplay—preferably oral— before the main event. Wednesday evening, however…

All she'd wanted was to feel Turner's hands all over her naked body—*now*. And she'd wanted him buried deep inside her—*now*. Forget flirting. Forget foreplay. She'd wanted out-and-out sex, as raw and as forceful and as fast as it could be. Thank God they'd been interrupted by Englund or who knew how far they would have gone? And even more important, thank God Turner had had the good sense to try and dissuade her from what she'd wanted to do, or they may have been too far-gone by the time they *were* interrupted even to notice the fact. And if Englund didn't want them smoking in the workplace, she could only imagine how he'd feel about them *smoking* in the workplace.

But even after going home that night, she'd still been thinking about Turner. About Turner naked. About Turner naked in manacles while she gave him a blow job, for God's sake. And then about Turner naked in bed with her. Beside her. And on top of her. And underneath her. And behind her. And in just about every other position the two of them could manage. And some they probably *couldn't* manage, at least not outside her delirious fantasies. After a good night's sleep, though, she'd felt like her old self again. To the point that she'd even forgotten about what had happened until the sight of Turner had reminded her. Graphically. But even then, overpowering her arousal was the fact that she'd been horrified to remember what had happened the evening before.

She'd tried to tell herself—and Turner, too—that it must have happened because of the nature of the campaign they were working on, that all the racy lingerie had just put ideas into her head.

But that didn't make any sense. If anyone was turned

on by the Bluestocking products, it should have been Turner. The items the company had sent as samples weren't that much different from what Becca wore under her clothing every day of the week. Why would *she* suddenly be turned on by *women's* underwear? That was silly.

So then she'd tried to tell herself—and Turner, too—that she'd been working too hard lately, that she and Turner were both under a lot of stress right now, feeling the pressure of coming up with a campaign for an account that could potentially result in a big promotion for each of them, not to mention a fat financial bonus they could both use.

But they'd been under stress and felt the pressure lots of other times, she'd been forced to remind herself, and neither of them had ever resorted to being physically aroused by the other. So that hadn't really explained her behavior, either.

So *then* she'd tried to tell herself—and Turner, too—that it had just been too long since she'd had sex, and that any human being with a Y chromosome would look good to her—though she hadn't put it *that* way to Turner. And although that explanation did sort of make sense—she *had* gone way too long without sex, and she'd definitely been feeling more than a little randy lately—it didn't account for why her reaction to Turner had come about so suddenly and with such intensity.

Ultimately, Becca had told herself—and Turner, too—that it must have been a combination of all three factors that resulted in her behavior Wednesday night. What else could it have been? Although certainly Turner was a very attractive man, and yes, they did have a history together, however limited, of succumbing occasionally to a physical response, it hadn't happened for years, and had only occurred then when they were both between partners and feeling natural, understandable, utterly human urges for physical closeness with the opposite sex.

That must have been what happened Wednesday, she told herself—and Turner, too. The combination of factors had just overwhelmed her, and she'd looked to him—her best friend in the whole wide world—to help her through a rough patch.

That was her story and she was sticking to it.

And Turner, though wary, had ultimately conceded that maybe she was right. Especially after she told him she had no desire to repeat the episode.

Since Wednesday, there had been no recurrence whatsoever of her aberrant behavior or wayward desires, so her theory—sorta—made sense. Ultimately, Turner thought so, too. Or at least he told her he thought so. At any rate, after talking Thursday morning about what had happened Wednesday evening, both of them had decided it had just been a weird, singular, out-of-character event, and had agreed it wouldn't happen again.

And it wouldn't, Becca knew. Because she planned to go out and find herself a man as soon as possible, to scratch whatever itch she was feeling. Donnie, she'd decided. An old boyfriend from a few years ago, from whom she had parted on good terms. She still ran into him from time to time because they both traveled in the same professional circles. She knew he was currently unattached, too. So she would contrive some way to run into him "accidentally," and then one thing could lead to another, and then the two of them could relieve a little pressure together and go their separate ways in the morning.

First, however, Becca and Turner had to get through

their pitch for the Bluestocking Lingerie people. Which, she noted as she glanced down at her watch, was only about fifteen minutes away.

For this meeting, Becca had succumbed to Robert Englund's dress code, and had opted for a berry-colored wool suit with a crisp white blouse beneath. The jacket was cropped, however, ending at her waist, and black velvet piping and buttons prevented the suit from being *too* straitlaced. At her throat, she'd fastened a flashy Art Deco, faux-ruby brooch, with dangly earrings to match it.

She didn't want the Bluestocking people to think she was a dull, joyless stick-in-the-mud who had no appreciation for more sensual pleasures. Frankly, she was still surprised they'd even contacted Englund Advertising, since the company wasn't known for being hip. Still, the pitch she and Turner had put together definitely was. If Bluestocking didn't like the campaign, then they weren't the chic, farsighted, with-it company they were striving hard to be.

So there.

Turner was already seated in the boardroom with their employer when Becca joined the group. Bluestocking had sent three representatives to hear the pitch, the highest-ranking being a raven-haired, red-lipsticked, fortysomething woman in a chic black suit who introduced herself as Donetta Prizzi, VP in charge of marketing. Becca thought she looked bored and difficult to please. And the two guys with her—both much younger and decidedly assigned to the roles of yes-men...or, rather, yes-boys—looked every bit as difficult to impress.

But that was okay. Because what she and Turner had in their corner was sheer dynamite. Inhaling a deep breath and giving her jacket a good tug, she entered the boardroom with a cheery smile and got down to business.

TURNER SIGHED SILENTLY in relief as he took his seat beside Becca once the two of them had concluded their pitch to the Bluestocking people. It had gone even better than he'd thought it would. And they'd *loved* his new slogan, he thought smugly, which was, as Becca had suggested, short and memorable: Blue for You. Englund Advertising had even managed to secure the rights to an 80s pop song by that name to use in the TV spots, something that would hopefully make the women in Bluestocking's desired demographic of late thirties through late forties feel young and playful—and, with luck, horny as teenagers—again. He had only to look at the expression on Donetta Prizzi's face to know this account was in the bag.

"You've hit on exactly what we want to do with the new line of products," she said. "We want to take the company in a whole new direction. We want to show the women of today that Bluestocking Lingerie isn't their mothers' underwear of yesterday."

Turner gave himself a mental pat on the back. "I'm glad we were able to create a campaign that does that," he said. "Naturally, Becca and I are open to suggestions if you have any. Or if we've overlooked anything…"

"No, it's perfect exactly the way it is," Donetta said. "I wouldn't change a thing." She glanced at the two suits who had been sitting so obsequiously and obediently—and silently—on each side of her during the presentation, then back at Turner. "I think I speak for all of us when I say we'd be very comfortable going with the campaign you've presented. Naturally, though, I can only make the recommendation. The final decision will rest with others. In any event, we'll definitely get back to you early next week."

Each of the suits nodded once, wordlessly, and Turner's relief was complete.

Until he felt Becca's stocking foot nudging his under the table in a way that was infinitely more affectionate than he'd ever known her to be.

No, he told himself as a puddle of heat seeped into his belly. No, no, no, no, no. Nuh-uh. No way. No how. *La. Hayir. Oh-chee.* She was *not* coming on to him again. For God's sake, they were sitting in a room with a half-dozen other people! She was only giving him a little congratulations nudge under the table, since it was looking pretty obvious that they'd won the account. He was just jumpy because of what had happened Wednesday night. But Becca had explained all that—well, kind of—and they'd both agreed it wouldn't happen again. Or, at least, she had. Becca was only—

Rubbing her stocking foot up the length of his calf now. Slowly. Sensuously. Seductively.

No. *Mai chai. Bu. Bukan.* There was nothing sexual in what she was doing. She was just—

Putting her hand on his knee and giving it a little squeeze. She was only—

Inching her fingers up to his thigh.

She was just—

Moving her hand forward, between his legs.

She was—

Pushing her hand against his cock and palming it hard.

"Ms. Prizzi," Turner said suddenly, jumping up from his chair with enough force to send it scuttling backward, slamming into the wall behind him.

Every eye in the room fell on him, and, belatedly, Turner realized he had absolutely no idea what to say. Except for maybe "Becca, get your hand off my dick," which, just a shot in the dark here, probably wouldn't go over too well with the clients.

"Yes, Mr. McCloud?" Ms. Prizzi asked. And right when the word *dick* was going through his head, too, wouldn't you know it, which sorta threw Turner for a minute.

"I, um, I, uh, I'm glad you liked the presentation," he finally managed to stammer.

Fortunately—not to mention miraculously—Donetta Prizzi didn't even seem to notice he'd suddenly turned into a raging idiot. "Oh, I liked it very much indeed, Mr. McCloud."

She turned her attention to Becca then, obviously wanting to include her in the praise, but when she did her smile fell some. Turner told himself to look at Becca, but he honestly feared what he would see when he did.

Forcing his gaze in her direction, he saw that she had given him her full and undivided attention, and was completely ignoring the woman who was promising to be their newest—and most important—client. Worse than that, the look on Becca's face made clear what kind of mood she was in, and it was totally inappropriate for the workplace. Well, he amended, for any workplace that didn't involve the oldest profession, at any rate.

"Uh…" he began eloquently.

"Turner," Becca whispered. Loudly enough for everyone in the room to hear her. "I need to talk to you. Outside."

He closed his eyes, stole a few seconds to pretend he was in the Bahamas with a beautiful beach bunny named Mindy, then opened them again. Without looking at Becca, he said quietly, "Can't it wait?"

From the corner of his eye, he saw her shake her head. Vehemently. "No," she told him, still whispering. Loudly. "It's really, really important. I need you right *now*."

"Mercer," Robert Englund boomed, his tone of voice considerably less tolerant than Turner's had been. In fact, it was his don't-even-*think*-about-it voice, which no one in their right mind at Englund Advertising would mess around with. "It can wait."

"No, it can't," Becca immediately replied, her tone of voice, amazingly, even more terse than their employer's. "Excuse me, Mr. Englund, but you know, you don't always know everything, you know. You know?"

Englund's snowy eyebrows shot up nearly to his hairline at that, but he said nothing. Probably, Turner thought, he was too busy composing Becca's letter of dismissal in his head to be bothered with something so mundane as a reply to her suicidal comments.

She really wasn't long for this world, never mind this job, if she didn't shut up. So, not wanting her to risk her career any more than she already had—since, hey, it would be much better if *he* risked *both* their careers, right?— Turner murmured a hasty, "Excuse us for a minute," grabbed Becca by the hand and hurried them both out of the boardroom.

Not surprisingly, she followed him willingly, but Turner didn't want to take any chances, so he dragged her along as quickly as he could in an effort to put them into safer waters. Or, at least, into the corridor outside the main entrance to Englund Advertising, which was close enough. No sooner had the door closed behind them, though, than Becca dug in her heels and snapped to a halt. She yanked with all her might on Turner's hand, something that gave him no choice but to stumble backward, right into her. And then, faster than he could say, "What the hell is going on back there?" she had him pinned against the wall, was crowding her entire body into his and was covering his mouth with her own. And for one scant, scintillating second, Turner forgot all about—

Um, what was he supposed to be doing? He'd been so certain a second ago. It was right there at the very edge of his consciousness what he was sure he was supposed to be doing….

But then his consciousness went belly-up, shamelessly threatening to surrender, and Turner, even more shamelessly, let it. Because the sensation of Becca's tongue stabbing between his teeth and reaching for the back of his throat was simply too delicious to ignore. As was the press of her breasts against his chest, and the twining of her fingers in his hair, and the panting of her—

Oh, no, wait. The panting was coming from Turner. But it was no wonder, since she'd removed one hand from his hair to score it down his back and chest and ribs, then to cover his ass, giving it a good hard squeeze that ground his pelvis into hers, something that made Mr. Happy feel very happy indeed.

And that was when Turner remembered that their employer was anything *but* Mr. Happy right now, and that he or any number of other people might come striding through the door right next to them any minute, see them groping each other so enthusiastically, and conclude that their victory high five gave a whole 'nother meaning to that celebratory end-zone dance thing.

Turner tore his mouth away from hers, gasped for breath and said, "We can't do this here, Becca."

Hell, according to what she'd told him two mornings ago, they couldn't do it anywhere. But even Turner had to agree that the hallway outside the workplace probably wasn't a great venue for raw, unmitigated sex, regardless of…well, anything.

Becca didn't seem to share his opinion, however, because she launched herself up on tiptoe and tried to capture his mouth with hers again. But Turner was ready for her this time—well, okay, maybe not, but he wanted to delude himself into thinking he was—and managed to pull his head back, out of her reach, just in time. Unfortunately, that made him bang his head against the wall—hard—something that brought stars to his eyes and a frown to Mr. Happy.

Becca, too, pouted prettily in reply. "We can do this anywhere, Turner," she told him, her hands still roving freely over every inch of him she could reach. "That's the beauty of it. Our closet is right up the hall. No one will miss us."

"Becca, they've already missed us," he pointed out. "And if we don't get back in there soon, they're going to come looking for us."

She smiled seductively. "They won't be the only ones who are going to come."

"Becca," he interrupted as Mr. Happy began to smile again. Mostly because Turner knew that if she started talking to him like that, then Mr. Happy would get really, really happy, and neither Turner nor Becca was likely to go back into that room, and Mr. Happy was likely to go somewhere he shouldn't go, not when all three of them were standing—some more erect than others—in a public byway.

Which, strangely, when Turner thought more about it, actually gave him a good idea.

"Look," he said as he tried to detach himself from her.

But the moment he got her arms freed from around his neck, she was hooking her ankle around his calf. Then, when he managed to free his leg from hers, she had her hands tangled in his shirtfront. "Why don't you go home," he suggested as he did the disengagement shuffle again and stepped awkwardly to the side to sabotage her renewed efforts. "I think maybe you need to lie down."

She tittered at that. Honestly tittered. He didn't think he'd ever heard Becca titter before—he hadn't even realized she had titter capabilities. "I'm not the only one who needs to lie down," she said.

Then she wrapped an arm around his waist which Turner immediately grabbed and unwrapped again. Good God, what had gotten into her to be throwing herself at him like this?

"Becca," he repeated, still fighting off her maneuvers. Good God, what had gotten into him to be fighting her off again? Oh, yeah. The job. His career. His livelihood. Food on the table. Clothes on his back. A roof over his head during the cold winter months ahead.

She grabbed his cock, and all he could think was, *Who needs food and shelter?*

"Go home, Becca," he said again, more adamantly this time, dislodging her greedy fingers. "I really think it would be better if you took the afternoon off."

She smiled. "I'd rather take your clothes off."

Oh, he really should have seen that one coming. Turner squeezed his eyes shut tight. Damn. Did anything *not* have a sexual connotation when you were in a position like this? Dammit. *Position.* That was another one.

"Becca…" He tried again, using his cautionary tone of voice. He reflected for a minute. Nope. No double entendres in that. Now, had he said he was using his missionary tone of voice...?

"I don't want to go home alone," she cooed. "I want you to come with me."

"I have to go back into the meeting and try to explain why you and I left it, and then suck up and kiss ass until I've made it all better."

"I'd rather have you suck on me and kiss my ass."

Oh, he should have seen that one coming, too.

"Becca..." he murmured yet again. Finally, with a sigh of surrender, he told her, "Look. If you'll go home, I promise, after we're finished here, I'll come over, and then you and I can talk."

She smiled, a hot, aroused, predatory sort of smile. "Turner, in case you hadn't noticed, I'm not really interested in talking right now."

Maybe not, he thought. But they were going to do that, too. Either before or after—or, hell, even during—because he wanted to get to the bottom of this. Dammit. *Bottom.* There was another one. Somehow, he and Becca were going to come—dammit—to terms with this thing, whatever it was.

"Then I promise," he said, "that you and I can do whatever you want when I get to your place." *Provided I get to do a little of what I want, too,* he added to himself. And strangely, that meant talking. "Just go home now, and I'll see you later. Okay?"

She pouted again, clearly not happy about the state of affairs—dammit—but nodded reluctantly, anyway. "My coat's in my cubicle," she said.

"I'll get it for you," he told her, thinking it would probably be best if she just lay—dammit—low for now.

He hurried back into the office, and as he passed the glass-enclosed boardroom full of people gazing expectantly back at him, he held up one index finger in the internationally recognized sign language for "Hold that thought" and continued on to Becca's cubicle. There, he collected her coat, did the "Hold that thought" thing again when he passed the boardroom a second time—punctuating it with a flourish of Becca's coat in the internationally recognized sign language for "I'm taking a woman her coat"—and sped out into the hallway again.

He half expected to find her disrobing, but thankfully, she was leaning against the wall where he'd left her, looking agitated, irritated, exasperated, aggravated, frustrated and a bunch of other -ateds that hadn't even been invented yet. Very, very gingerly, Turner approached her, holding her coat at arm's length.

"Here," he said simply.

She took the coat from him and shrugged into it. "Remember. You promised to spend the afternoon with me at my place. You promised, Turner."

"I promise I'll come—" dammit "—over as soon as we're finished here," he assured her.

He thought she would turn away then and make her way toward the elevators at the end of the hall, but she hesitated, her eyes meeting his, her pupils growing dark.

"What?" he asked warily.

"I just need for you to touch me once," she told him. "That will get me through until you get to my place."

"Becca, there are people waiting for me," he reminded her.

"And I've been waiting for you a lot longer. Please," she begged. "Just once. Just touch me one time."

Knowing it was the only way he'd make—dammit—her

leave, Turner lifted a hand toward her face. But she lifted her own hand before he made contact, circling his wrist with sure fingers.

"Not there," she whispered, much more softly than she had earlier in the boardroom.

And as he watched, she drew both their hands downward, past her shoulder, past her breasts, past her waist. With her free hand, she hiked up her short skirt, until he saw that titillating flash of flesh between stocking and garter again. Pink this time. She took a step to the side, opening her legs, and moved their hands between her thighs. Turner swallowed hard, but did nothing to halt or slow the movement.

"There," she said with a sigh, her eyes fluttering closed as she pushed his fingers against her wet panties. Her mouth stayed open, even after she'd spoken the word, and her tongue came out to trace the line of her full lips. "Oh, Turner," she gasped as she moved his fingers harder against her. "Oh, that feels so good."

With her free hand, she pulled aside the scrap of silk and rubbed his fingers into her damp flesh, something that made Turner want to forget the job and everything else and just take her right here in the hallway, after all. But Becca withdrew his hand and shoved her skirt back down over her thighs, and the sensation ebbed. It exploded again, though, when she lifted his hand to her mouth and kissed each of the fingers that had touched her, one by leisurely one, sucking hard on his middle finger before finally releasing him. It was all Turner could do not to drop his trousers right there and turn her around and take her, up against the wall outside Englund Advertising, the rest of the world be damned.

As he visualized himself doing just that—and, ironically, trying to quell the erection pushing against his fly at the same time—Becca rose up on tiptoe again and pressed her mouth to his once, briefly, hotly, surely, long enough for him to taste a hint of her damp response on her own lips. Then she moved her mouth to his ear, murmured one word—"Hurry"—and turned toward the elevators at the end of the hall.

Turner watched her go, every nerve in his body screaming for him to follow her. But he forced himself to stay put, and thought about whatever he could to cool his aroused status. Glaciers crashing into the north Atlantic. A big bowl of slush. Hail the size of golf balls down his trousers. Salmon swimming up an icy stream. Ethel Merman in a thong bikini.

Oh, yeah. That did it.

Then he inhaled a few deep, fortifying breaths and returned to the scene of the crime.

When he arrived back in the boardroom, it was clear that the meeting was breaking up. Whatever Englund had done to mend the situation, it had worked, because Donetta Prizzi and her yes-boys were looking very happy and at ease, and there was much shaking of hands and patting on the backs going around for everyone. Even Turner's reappearance didn't put a damper on the mood.

His boss, however, was understandably curious about Becca's absence. "What happened to Mercer?" he asked when Turner rejoined the group.

"I, uh, I sent her home," he said. "She was burning up with fever, so I told her to go home and go to bed." And he congratulated himself for telling the truth. Becca had indeed been burning up with fever. And it was precisely the kind of fever that traditionally sent people to bed. Just, you know, not alone. And not to get any rest. "She wasn't feeling all that great this morning when she came in to work," he added, knowing he was skirting the truth now, but not much caring. "I think that's why she seemed a little, um, off."

"Off?" Donetta Prizzi echoed dubiously. Then she grinned, one of those knowing, woman grins that make men want to run screaming in the opposite direction with their hands cupped over their manhood. "When I was her age, we had a different word for it," she added smoothly. "I still don't think you can say it in polite company, though."

"No, no," Turner countered, shooting a nervous glance at his employer, who, thankfully, seemed not to be listening, because he was talking to one of Donetta's colleagues. "I'm sure it was just the flu. It's been going around, you know. That time of year and all that."

"Mmm," Donetta said noncommittally, still grinning. "Must be a new strain I haven't heard about."

"No doubt," Turner agreed. Kind of.

After one last, very brief, question-and-answer session, Donetta collared her boys and the trio took off. Before leaving, though, she all but confirmed Bluestocking's hiring of Englund Advertising, something that made Robert Englund very happy indeed. Maybe even happier than Mr. Happy had been earlier.

Nah, Turner thought. Nobody could be that happy. Except for Mr. Happy. Later. At Becca's place.

But what did he really want to have happen later at Becca's place? he asked himself not so much later, after he'd left the meeting and was heading down to the parking garage for his car. In spite of what he had promised her a little while ago in the hallway, he was still tempted to call her and tell her he wasn't coming—dammit—over to her place. That maybe what the two of them really needed was to spend a little time apart, since they'd obviously been spending way too much time together lately, under way too much pressure.

Because that really could be the only explanation for why Becca had been acting the way she had lately, he told himself, suddenly on, then suddenly off, then suddenly on again. Not that Turner wanted to look a gift horse in the mouth—though that probably wasn't an analogy Becca would appreciate, all things considered—but *she'd* always been the one insisting they were too good of friends to mess everything up by letting their relationship become sexual. Had it been up to Turner, they would have been doing the horizontal boogaloo together back in high school. And again in college. And again in the workplace. And then at his place. And at her place. And at some total stranger's place. Several public places. Water Tower Place, for instance. Or Place de la Concorde. Or Park Place, where he would pass Go over and over and over again. And in a million other places, too.

But he digressed.

He'd respected Becca's wishes, though, and he'd done what he had to do to keep his feelings for her from her, since her feelings for him had been platonic and in no way romantic. So what had suddenly changed in their relationship to make her want him so badly that she came on to him in the middle of a very important meeting with their very important boss and a very important—and as yet still potential—client? Especially after just reiterating that such a thing would never happen? Especially after such a thing had just happened a few days before?

But having it happen during the meeting this morning was the weirdest thing yet. That was much too stressful and pressure-filled a situation for Becca to be acting in such an unprofessional—never mind uncharacteristic—way.

Which was precisely his point, he supposed, in a long, roundabout way. Stress and pressure. They went together like peanut butter and jelly, only not so tasty. Becca's behavior had to be a result of how hard they'd both been working lately. That was the only explanation that made any sense. So that had to be it. It had to.

But what if it wasn't?

Turner had no choice but to consider that possibility. Because maybe, just maybe, Becca's sudden, vehement attraction to him wasn't the result of stress or pressure. Maybe, just maybe, it was the result of feelings she'd had for him for a long time that, for whatever reason, she'd finally decided to reveal. Maybe it was the stress and pressure bringing those feelings to the fore. It had happened twice now. And even though she was swearing it wasn't what she wanted, she was the one who kept doing it. And doing it *so well*.

Bottom line, he thought. What was the bottom line?

The bottom line was that Becca wanted to get sexual with him today. There wasn't any way he could deny that. And he wanted to get sexual with Becca, too. Today or any day. That was the bottom line.

Maybe the reasons didn't matter, he told himself. Maybe all that mattered was that they both wanted the same thing for a change. Why was he trying to fight it? This was what he'd wanted for as long as he could remember. And he knew Becca well enough to be certain that she only got sexual with a guy when she cared about him. Emotionally. So if she was coming on to Turner, it was because she had come to care for him in a way that went deeper than the way she'd cared for him before. And when all was said and done, what difference did it make what the reason for that was?

Becca wanted Turner. Turner wanted Becca. He didn't need to know any more than that.

He glanced up from his musings to see that he had driven halfway to Becca's apartment without even paying attention to where he was going. His subconscious, at least, knew what was what. Still, he was dressed in his work clothes, and he hadn't had lunch. Becca probably hadn't, either. So he decided that instead of going straight to her place, he'd go home first and change clothes. Maybe even pack a few things for the night. Then he'd stop by their favorite deli and grab some stuff to go. Becca had been awfully adamant earlier in voicing her needs. Turner's needs were no less demanding. What he had in mind for the rest of the day—and night—was going to require a lot of stamina. And that meant refueling. Once he entered Becca's apartment, he didn't want to leave again for a long, long time. So maybe a few provisions were in order before he arrived.

He smiled as he made an illegal U-turn to take him back to his place so he could change into something more comfortable. Something that would take less time for Becca to remove. Too bad Bluestocking didn't make underwear for men, since it might have been kind of fun to see where that led. Ah, well. Becca had taken all those samples home with her, so he'd still be able to enjoy their newest client's products. As long as it took for Becca to strip them off, anyway.

Oh, yeah, he thought as he pulled into his parking space

outside his apartment building. He had big plans for Becca's underthings once he got to Becca's house.

And he had even bigger plans for Becca.

7

BECCA AWOKE FEELING disoriented and confused, and wondering what the racket was that had caused her to wake up. Her bedroom wasn't fully dark the way it would be at night, but the blinds were drawn, and what little light did get through indicated it was late in the afternoon and not a sunny day. What was she doing sleeping in the afternoon? she wondered groggily as she pushed a long strand of hair out of her eyes. The last thing she remembered was—

Oh, God.

Her hand stilled in the process of nudging her hair over her shoulder, and she closed her eyes again—though not because she was sleepy this time. The pitch to the Bluestocking people. She remembered that she and Turner had given it that morning, and that it had gone extremely well. And then…

Oh, God.

And then Becca remembered being suddenly and inexplicably turned on. So turned on that she hadn't been able to stand it. And she hadn't wanted just anyone. She'd wanted Turner. The same way she had wanted him Wednesday night when they'd stayed late to work on the pitch: thoroughly. Completely. Obsessively. Immediately.

Oh, God…

What the hell was going on? she asked herself as the racket started up again, and she recognized it as someone pounding on her front door. Turner, she knew. Because she also remembered how he had dragged her out into the hallway, and how shamelessly she'd thrown herself at him, and how ruthlessly she'd pawed him and how adamantly she'd shoved her tongue into his mouth. And she remembered, too, how she had made him promise to come to her house after he'd finished the meeting, and how she'd compelled him to touch her so intimately before she would leave.

Oh, God...

Why had she done such a thing? How could she have behaved in such a way? Especially after just telling Turner something like that would never happen again? How could she have been so completely overcome by one emotion, to the utter exclusion of all others? And not just any emotion, either, but pure, unadulterated lust. For a man she'd always considered her best friend, the one man she had always vowed she would *not* have sex with. And not just once had this happened, but twice now. To the point where she had endangered not only her relationship with Turner, but her job—and his, too. How had such a thing happened?

Stress, she told herself instantly as she pushed herself to sitting and swung her feet over the side of the bed. Even as she uttered the explanation to herself, though, she knew it was pretty lame. But what else could it be? People reacted to stressful situations in different ways—often in ways that were so not beneficial, and sometimes in ways that were downright self-destructive. Some people drank. Some people smoked. Some overate. Some became irritable. Some bit their nails.

Some had sex?

Was that really possible? Becca wondered as she rose from her bed and made her way toward the front door, where Turner was still pounding away. Did people actually use sex as an outlet when they were under a lot of pressure? She'd always thought that was just some lame excuse used by arrogant, promiscuous politicians who got caught sleeping around. Male politicians, at that. Women seemed to be above that sort of thing. Whenever women got stressed out, they were supposed to eat chocolate and buy shoes, not throw themselves shamelessly at the nearest warm body. Women were the ones who were supposed to be in control of their baser instincts. It was just one of the many things to feel smug about when compared to men.

But Wednesday night, she'd been stressed-out trying to put the finishing touches on the pitch. This morning, she'd been stressed out because of having to give the pitch. Maybe on both occasions she'd just been on the verge of exploding—emotionally, she meant—because of the demands of her job. And because of that, she'd needed an outlet. In both situations she'd been unable to light up a cigarette because both times, she'd been in the office. And when her usual calming ritual had been denied her, she'd had to turn to another one. A sexual response to Turner.

In a weird way, it kind of made sense. Because Becca and Turner always smoked together, she must have decided on some subconscious level that being with him was a way to relieve tension. And since she hadn't been able to smoke with him on those two occasions, maybe on that same subconscious level, she'd decided that having sex with him would be the next best thing.

Hey, it could happen.

Because the minute she'd hit the street after leaving the

meeting this morning, she'd lit a cigarette. And she'd enjoyed another on the drive home. And by the time she'd arrived at her apartment, she'd felt a little better, a little calmer. But she'd still been turned on, she recalled, and she'd still been looking forward to Turner's arrival. So much so that she'd taken off her work clothes and replaced them with a lacy nightie and robe set that was virtually see-through. She glanced down at the set, which she still wore, and felt herself blush. She'd actually planned on answering the door to him wearing that and nothing else, and she'd fully intended to remove them again right after he walked in. But now…

Now, she didn't want to. Because she'd finished another cigarette when she got home, then had lain down to wait for Turner, and evidently fallen asleep. Between the cigarettes and the nap—not to mention the conclusion of the pitch to the Bluestocking people—her stress level had plummeted and the pressure had disappeared. And now that the pressure was off, so was her libido. The last thing she wanted to do at the moment was have sex with Turner.

That had to be it, she told herself again. It had to be the pressure and stress of the job. It had to be. Because if it wasn't…

How was she going to explain that to Turner, though? she asked herself without completing that last thought. Turner, who stood on the other side of the door whose knob she was holding and was about to turn? Uh, the door's knob, not Turner's, since turning his knob would totally negate everything she'd just said to herself. She'd had enough trouble trying to explain away her aberrant behavior of Wednesday night. She still wasn't sure he'd bought it. Now she'd have to do it a second time.

But then, he'd done his best to fight her off in the hallway, hadn't he? she recalled. And he'd done the same on Wednesday night. And Wednesday, he'd declined to come over to her condo when she'd called and asked him to. Today, too, he'd wanted to turn down her very blatant invitation.

Naturally, he hadn't wanted to get jiggy right there in the open, in front of Englund and everybody, but even at that, she'd had to practically beg him to promise her he would come over today. He honestly hadn't seemed to want to have sex with her today *or* Wednesday night. Both times, he'd been the one trying to put a stop to things. He had even told her that, although he'd come over after the meeting today, it would only be to talk. So it shouldn't be a problem telling him she couldn't go through with it now, right?

Right?

She glanced down at her attire again and thought, *Big problem*. Especially now that the pounding at her front door had grown more frantic and was being punctuated by Turner's voice calling out, "Becca! Are you home?"

Crap, she thought. The neighbors were going to wonder what was going on. She didn't have time to change. So she hastily ran back to the bathroom and grabbed her ratty chenille bathrobe from the hook inside the door, then jammed her arms through the sleeves and belted it as best she could before returning to answer the front door. She was a little breathless when she finally opened it, but the sight that greeted her completely took her breath away. Because Turner stood there looking freshly showered, shaved and dressed for a very nice evening.

A very nice evening *in*.

His charcoal corduroys were unrumpled and spotless beneath a heather-gray cashmere, V-neck sweater Becca had given him for Christmas the year before, with the compliment that it brought out his blue eyes and the complaint that he never had anything nice to wear for special casual occasions. So he must be wearing it now, she concluded, because he considered this a special occasion. Judging by the look on his face, however—among other things—he was thinking less in terms of *casual* and more in terms of *intimate*. Over the sweater, he had pulled on a black wool blazer that made the occasion seem even more special— if no less, ah, casual.

He was holding a dozen red, red roses wrapped in green waxed paper in one hand, and a dewy bottle of chilled champagne in the other—both items really sealing that "evening in" business—not to mention the *intimate* business. And even if they hadn't sealed the *in* part—as if— then the two items at Turner's feet would have. Because on the floor on each side of him sat a small shopping bag from his and Becca's favorite deli, and she could smell the aroma of her favorite menu items mingling with his.

All in all, he looked very, very handsome and very, very winsome. And he was smiling the sort of smile men smiled when they knew without a shadow of a doubt that they were going to get very, very lucky.

Oh. No.

But his smile fell some when he noticed her attire, the ragged bathrobe she usually only wore in front of him on those special occasions when she was puking her guts out because she had some heinous illness and he was at her place trying to nurse her back to health. Nevertheless, he rallied himself, and brought his head up again to meet her gaze, his blue, blue eyes earnest and eager and endearing.

And, alas, she had to admit, not a little excited.

Okay, so maybe they weren't quite on the same page yet, she realized, amending her earlier reassurances to herself. He *had* agreed to talk when they were in the hallway at work. Just because Becca had made it clear she wanted to, um, do other stuff first didn't mean they couldn't change their plans around a little bit.

"Turner," she said by way of a greeting, not sure what else to say.

"Becca," he replied. Earnestly. Eagerly. Endearingly. Excitedly.

Oh. Boy.

"I, um… Come in," she told him as she took a giant step backward into her living room.

He looked down at all the things he'd brought with him, then back at her, silently requesting a cue as to how he should proceed. So Becca stepped forward again and gathered the two deli bags from the floor and carried them in, once again stepping aside so Turner could enter, too.

There. Let him make what he would of that. That she went for the food instead of the flowers and champagne—or him. That was a pretty clear message, right? And one that shouldn't surprise him, either. At least, not under normal circumstances. Becca always went for the food first in any normal situation. Then again, their situation lately hadn't exactly been normal, had it?

When she looked at him again, she could tell by his expression that her reaction hadn't been what he'd expected. She could also tell that she'd hurt his feelings, and her heart turned over at that.

Oh, Turner, she thought. *Have I screwed this up so badly we'll never be able to straighten it out?*

It was a legitimate concern. On the few occasions in the

past when the two of them had come close to having sex, he'd always taken it badly when she'd backed off. He'd gone days without wanting to see her or talk to her, making up some excuse for why he didn't want to be around her that never made any sense. And even when he was around her again, he was moody and cranky for weeks. His reaction had only reinforced her determination not to get sexually involved with him. Because if that was how he acted after only getting close, then how would he act if they actually did have sex? Sure, it could be good for a while—it could be spectacular for a while—but once they got bored with each other, that would be the end of it. In every way. Turner wouldn't want to be around her at all after a sexual relationship. And she didn't want to lose him.

He followed her inside and kicked the door closed with his foot, but, like the big coward she was, Becca turned and fled to the kitchen with the food before he had a chance to say anything. Avoidance and denial had always worked great for her before. Why should she try something new now?

Gosh, Becca, maybe because Turner's not the kind of guy who will be avoided or denied?

Mmm, could be…

She sensed more than saw him follow her into the tiny galley kitchen, which suddenly seemed even tinier than before, something she wouldn't have thought possible. Without asking permission—probably because he knew he didn't need it—he opened the refrigerator and stowed the champagne on its side. Then he placed the roses carefully on the counter opposite the one where she was unpacking the food. And then he turned fully around and pinned her with his gaze.

Studiously avoiding it—hey, hadn't she just copped to

being a coward?—Becca dropped her eyes to the floor and said, "Thanks for bringing dinner. I'm starved." And then, because she was suddenly kind of curious as to whether or not she still had a job—and oh, all right, because she was still avoiding and denying…details, details, sheesh—she added, "How did the rest of the meeting go after I left?"

When Turner didn't reply right away, she dragged her gaze up to look at him. He was leaning against the opposite counter with his arms crossed over his chest and his ankles crossed over each other. His expression, she had to admit, was pretty cross, too.

Ironically, right next to his face, pinned to the refrigerator with a magnet, was a photograph of the two of them taken five years ago at the wedding reception of friends, where Becca had served as maid of honor and Turner as best man. She wore a surprisingly elegant bridesmaid dress of deep crimson, with tiny sweetheart roses twined in the dark blond hair braided around her head. He was dressed in a black tuxedo, and she was sitting in his lap. They were laughing uproariously about something—she couldn't remember now what it had been—as there were so many photographs of the two of them. It was a complete one-eighty from the way they were looking at each other right now.

"Turner?" she asked when he remained silent. "Is everything okay?" She tried to inject a lightness into her voice that she was nowhere close to feeling when she added, "Hey, do we still have jobs or what?"

He inhaled deeply and released the breath slowly, his blue eyes never straying from hers. "Our jobs are safe enough," he told her. "But there's a lot of other, nonjob-related stuff up in the air right now."

She dropped her gaze to the floor once again. "Yeah, about that…" she began.

"Becca, what the hell is going on?" he asked point-blank.

She didn't pretend to misunderstand. "I'm not sure," she told him honestly. But she had no idea what else to say.

Turner seemed not to suffer from the same problem, though. When she didn't elaborate, he continued, "I mean, twice now, you've made it clear you want us to get sexual, then you've immediately backed off in a big way. I was surprised that first time it happened—hell, I was surprised both times—but I wasn't sure I should question it. And when I thought more about it today, I decided I wasn't exactly averse to taking things to the next level myself."

The entire time he spoke, Becca couldn't bring herself to look at him. Probably because she couldn't disagree with anything he'd said. Not about her, and not about the two of them. Before, when they'd gotten physical, Turner had been the instigator, and Becca had gone along for a little while, because, at the time and under the conditions, it had felt nice to do so. But she'd only gone along with him long enough to decide that what they were doing was a mistake.

She'd never really let herself think too hard about *why* she was so certain it was a mistake, though. She *had* enjoyed herself on those occasions. In fact, she may have enjoyed herself too much, and that had been the problem. Because she knew neither of them had ever made much of a commitment to anyone they dated. Not one that lasted longer than a few months, anyway. For something to feel so good with Turner, she'd want it to go on forever. But she hadn't been able to convince herself that he would, too.

And as good as it had felt with Turner, there had still been something about getting physical that hadn't been quite right. She couldn't really describe or explain it to anyone, herself included. But *something* had made her stop them from having sex. Because somehow, she had known things between them weren't the way they should be for them to make their relationship sexual. And somehow, she'd known, too, that making it sexual when things weren't the way they should be would only mess up the great friendship that *did* feel right.

Oh, how did everything get so screwed up?

"Turner," she began cautiously, forcing her gaze up to meet his again, flinching a little when she saw how coolly he was looking at her. "I wish I could give you an answer that makes sense, but I'm not sure there is one."

He nodded slowly, but his expression changed not at all. "Okay, then tell me this. A few hours ago, you made me promise to come over here after the meeting, because you wanted us to have sex. Do you still want that?"

She owed him total honesty, Becca knew. But how could she be honest with him when she wasn't even sure she could be honest with herself? There was one thing she did know, though. She couldn't make love with Turner feeling the way she did right now. She was confused, uncertain and troubled. Although looking at him right now made her feel things she hadn't before, she couldn't imagine the two of them walking into her bedroom right now and falling into each other's arms. It would just be too weird. And it wouldn't feel right.

"No," she told him honestly. "I don't want that. Not now."

He closed his eyes and expelled a sound that was rife with frustration.

"I'm sorry, Turner," she exclaimed. "I know what I said… What I *did*…earlier," she added, blushing when she remembered the way she had taken his hand in hers and pushed it between her legs. Even the memory sent a wave of heat splashing through her midsection. "But I've had time to think since then, and now I'm just not sure it would be a good idea."

"And Wednesday night?" he asked, opening his eyes to meet her gaze levelly. "Is that what happened then? You came home and thought about it and decided we shouldn't go through with it?"

Actually, Becca couldn't remember doing much thinking about it Wednesday night. She recalled coming home and taking a bath and going to bed, feeling aroused and unsatisfied the whole time, and she recalled thinking extremely lusty and graphic thoughts about Turner, and she recalled a longer-than-usual session with her vibrator. Not once Wednesday evening had she had second thoughts about wanting him. It hadn't been until Thursday morning that she'd decided her behavior had been unwarranted and unwise—and that had come about after just one look at Turner, and very little thought. She honestly couldn't remember now what had made her change her mind.

"Yes," she told Turner. "That's what happened Wednesday, too."

"So what brought it on in the first place?" he asked.

She took a deep breath, sorted through her thoughts, then told him about everything she had decided upon waking a little while ago. Stress and pressure, pressure and stress, blah blah blah blah blah. And although she knew neither one of them was buying any of it anymore, Turner had the decency to nod when she was done.

"I'm sorry, Turner," she repeated lamely when she'd finished. "I really can't explain it any better than that. And I'm sorry if I led you to believe one thing and then pulled back and acted differently. I didn't mean for this to happen."

"Next time you get the urge," he said, "just light up a cigarette, for God's sake, okay?"

She nodded, but didn't feel good about the way they'd resolved things. Probably because they hadn't come close to resolving things. There was still a strange awkwardness between them that hadn't been there before, and she hoped she hadn't done irreparable damage to their friendship. Deep down, she didn't think she had. She just had to be careful not to send Turner any mixed signals in the future, even in jest. Their friendship was too precious for her to screw—ah, she meant *mess*—around with it.

He sighed again, uncrossed his arms and legs and pushed himself away from the counter. "Then I guess tonight we'll have dinner together as friends, if that's okay with you."

Becca smiled, relief winding through her. "That would be great," she said. "I'd like that a lot."

As he reached into one of the bags, he added, "Oh, I almost forgot. Englund has invited you and me to a party at his house next weekend. Though he didn't say so, I imagine it's part of our reward for landing the Bluestocking account."

"Then it's official?" Becca asked. She'd been reasonably sure, judging by Donetta Prizzi's face when they concluded the pitch, that the woman had been extremely impressed by the campaign. But no one had made a formal commitment by the time Becca left.

Turner shook his head back and forth. "Well, it's not quite official, but Donetta Prizzi made it pretty clear. We should know something for sure by midweek. She promised Englund a definitive answer by Wednesday. And, hey,

Englund is confident enough that we've won the account to invite us two peasants to the castle next weekend."

"That's good enough for me," Becca said. Robert Englund wasn't the type to take things for granted.

A party at the boss's mansion, she thought as she joined Turner in removing their meal from the bags. They were definitely coming up in the advertising world. It was just too bad they were doing it at a firm whose vision wasn't exactly their own. Still, she'd take what she could get at this point.

And hey, a party at the big house. How cool was that? Now all she had to do was figure out what to wear....

8

ROBERT ENGLUND'S SWEEPING estate in the Indianapolis suburb of Carmel was an exuberant Tudor mansion situated atop a high, regal hill, its unseasonably green lawn rolling down before it like a carpet of cold, hard cash. The house itself was a stunning bit of real estate, three stories of beautifully formed fieldstone and diamond-paned windows topped by a gray-blue slate roof. There was even a turret at one end. The double front doors, painted a rich patrician blue, formed a perfect arc at the house's center, and were outlined by beveled glass that glittered with the light shining from within.

As Turner rolled his Saturn to a halt in front of the valet—both behind and in front of expensive European sedans, Becca couldn't help noticing—she tried to quell the butterflies in her stomach. She'd visited her boss's home only one time before, and on that occasion, she'd been not a guest but a messenger girl, dropping off some work for her employer when he'd been at home feeling under the weather. She hadn't made it past the foyer that day, but even that small glimpse of the house had told her everything she needed to know. Specifically, that Mr. and Mrs. Robert Englund were rolling in dough. Of course, she'd already known that.

At any rate, it was a sure bet that tonight's glittering affair would be populated by the city's uppermost and crustiest upper crust, and Becca was more than a little nervous about having come from a solid middle-middle-class background. She hoped she didn't do or say something that would embarrass her or Turner or both of them. Like use her seafood fork to eat her salad. Or, worse, use her seafood fork to put someone's eye out. That could look really bad when it came time for her annual review at work.

And she had no idea how to strike up a conversation with a rich person. Unless it was to begin with something like, "Here are the papers you wanted from the office, Mr. Englund." Probably, she thought, it would be best to just avoid any subject that could lead to a vicious argument. Like politics, for instance. Or religion. Or personal wealth. Or fashion.

Oh, she was not looking forward to the evening ahead. She had a bad feeling about this....

She reminded herself that their boss had invited her and Turner to the party as a reward for their exceptionally good work. He'd reiterated the invitation, after all, on Thursday morning, right after the call from Donetta Prizzi saying Englund Advertising had, for sure, won the Bluestocking Lingerie account, as long as he could guarantee that that nice Turner McCloud and that, um, interesting Becca Mercer handled it. Becca was supposed to have a *good* time tonight. Nevertheless, she already felt out of place and was glad Turner was with her. At least she'd have someone to talk to who didn't make her feel nervous or poorly educated or plebeian.

Of course, he *did* make her feel really weird when she was around him now. Though that wasn't any of his doing, she knew. *She* was the one who kept coming on to him, not the other way around—though his reciprocation of her actions hadn't exactly helped her when she'd tried to figure things out. Not that she blamed him for that, either...

Oh, hell. She didn't know what to think lately. Really, she decided, she and Turner both needed to talk more about what was going on. Eventually. When they were both less edgy about what was going on. Which she figured they would be in, oh...twenty or thirty years. Fifty, tops.

The important thing was that there hadn't been a repeat of those two...bizarre incidents. She and Turner had passed the entire week without so much as a steamy look. Which, she had to admit, just went to reinforce that whole pressure-stress theory, making it seem a bit less lame. Once they'd landed the Bluestocking account, they'd turned their attention to other accounts that caused less tension. And they'd skipped their lunch hours so they could take shorter breaks during the day to go outside for an occasional smoke when they felt the need. This week had been a much calmer one, all things considered. And because of that, neither of them had felt the need to repeat their earlier sexual responses to each other. Becca was pretty confident that nothing like that was going to happen again.

No, she was *certain* it wouldn't happen again, she told herself adamantly. Now that things were settling down with her and Turner, and now that they had the Bluestocking account firmly in hand, and now that their boss had no choice but to realize how important they both were to the company, they could relax a little and sort out what was going on.

Eventually, she repeated to herself. But not tonight. Because everything between her and Turner was starting to go back to normal. Yes, there was still a certain amount of tension humming between them, but that wasn't exactly surprising. They were back to being friends again. And that, Becca was confident, was where they needed to stay.

"Nice digs," Turner said now from the driver's seat as he gazed through the passenger-side window at the Englund residence.

Becca nodded. Their boss's home was something right out of an estate magazine. But when she turned her gaze from the breathtaking house to the man seated beside her, she decided the view was even nicer. Under his dark overcoat, Turner wore a dark suit—an honest-to-God, exquisitely tailored suit, too, with pinstripes, no less—and a white dress shirt with a tastefully patterned silk tie. Clearly, he wanted to impress their employer with his appearance now that he had impressed their employer with his abilities.

As did Becca, since her own attire complemented his, and was equally conservative. Beneath her swingy black velvet jacket, she wore a little black dress that fell nearly to her knees, with long sleeves and a barely scooped neckline. To accessorize it, she'd added black sheer stockings, black heels that weren't *too* high, a strand of sedate pearls and pearl earrings. She was playing Robert Englund's game, too, for now, wanting to reassure her boss that she could play by the rules if it meant being compensated for it. He still hadn't said anything firm about a promotion or raise or bonus, even though she was confident all were forthcoming. And if she looked half as nice as Turner did tonight...

She let her thoughts stop there, because she didn't want to think about how nice Turner looked tonight. That way lay madness, she knew.

"You ready?" he asked as one valet came around to his side of the car and another tugged open Becca's door.

She nodded. "But I think I'm going to need a drink as soon as we get inside the door."

"Feeling like a commoner already, are we?" he asked with a smile.

She shrugged, but couldn't quite manage a smile in return. "Among other things," she told him softly.

She could tell her response puzzled him, and he opened his mouth as if he were going to say something else, but the valet on his side of the car opened his door, forcing him to exit and take a receipt from the young man instead. Becca climbed out, too, then used Turner's distraction to change the subject.

"Do you remember Mrs. Englund's name?" she quizzed him as he joined her on the steps leading up to the front door.

"Yes, I do," he told her. "It's Mrs. Englund."

This time Becca was able to smile. "Very good," she said.

She was about to make her way up the steps, but hesitated when Turner crooked his elbow and offered her his arm. Normally, she would have linked arms with him and not thought a thing about it. After the way things had been over the last couple of weeks, though, she wavered.

"Come on," he said quietly, obviously understanding her uncertainty. "If we still feel the need to, we'll talk more later, when we can both think a little more clearly. For tonight, though, we're just Turner and Becca, the way we've always been. Okay?"

She nodded, but wasn't sure she believed him. She wasn't sure he believed himself, truth be told. Because there was something in his eyes when he looked at her...

No, she told herself. It was just her imagination playing games. In spite of the positive way he'd responded to her overtures, when all was said and done, she didn't think he really wanted to take things to the next level any more than she did.

And she told herself she *wasn't* disheartened by that. She wasn't. And just to prove it, she wasn't going to think about it *at all* tonight.

So there.

The interior of the Englund home was as luxurious as Becca remembered, and then some. The foyer soared two stories above them and was paneled on all sides and the ceiling with a dark, rich wood she suspected was mahogany. A sweeping staircase rose before them, opening onto a second floor gallery that boasted a series of oil paintings of landscapes and still lifes. A thick Persian runner in variegated jewel tones covered the stairs, matching the carpet that spanned much of the foyer floor. To the left of the stairway and beyond it was a hall that led farther into the house, and on their immediate left was what appeared to be a roomy parlor. To the right was the living room, where much of the party seemed to have congregated for now, because the room was teeming with guests.

A liveried maid appeared out of nowhere to take Becca's and Turner's coats once they'd slipped out of them, then carried the garments off to the magical Kingdom of Infinite Coat Storage. Becca had no idea how the woman would keep track of who owned what coat, but she was confident Robert Englund would only hire the best coat-keeper-tracker-of that money could buy.

Turner threw her a reassuring smile as he gestured toward the hallway. "My tingling spider sense tells me the bar is thataway."

"Hmm," Becca replied as she followed him in the direction he'd indicated. "I think that's actually your bourbon sense that's tingling."

"Oh, right," he said. "I always get those two confused."

His bourbon sense was right on the mark, too, because they found the bar—at least one of them, since she suspected there would be more than one for a party this size—set up in the library. That room, too, was paneled in dark wood, but its walls were filled, floor to ceiling, with books, giving it far more color and character than the foyer. Turner deftly threaded his way through the crowd to the bar and, in addition to his own drink, returned with a Manhattan for Becca, since he knew that was what she always drank at parties and didn't even need to ask. He wasn't the only one whose bourbon sense was tingling.

"Thanks," she told him as she took the drink from him and enjoyed a fortifying sip.

"Anytime," he replied.

"You always know what I like," she added as she lifted the drink to her mouth again.

Belatedly, she realized how the statement could be misconstrued, and her gaze flew to his to see if he'd picked up on the double entendre. Of course, it went without saying that he had. She could tell by the way his blue eyes darkened, and how his pupils expanded briefly before returning to their normal size.

"I mean, uh…that is, um…what I meant to say is… I mean I *didn't* mean…" she backpedaled. Clumsily.

"Becca, don't," he said, his expression softening.

"Don't what?" she asked, feigning innocence. Badly.

He sighed softly. "Don't start worrying that every time you say something, I'm going to think you mean something else."

"I wasn't doing that," she stated. Futilely.

"The hell you weren't."

"Well, didn't you think—at least for a moment—that I did mean something else?" she asked. Suspiciously.

He lifted one shoulder and let it drop in what she supposed was meant to be a shrug. "Maybe."

"Then I should start worrying," she said. Worri—Oh, never mind.

"No, you shouldn't."

"Maybe we should talk more about what happened, sooner instead of later," she said.

Though, honestly, she didn't know what they could say that hadn't already been said. Okay, admittedly, she had some unresolved issues with Turner. But maybe what she needed was a little time—personal *alone* time—to figure out why she kept acting toward him the way she did.

"Look, let's just keep saying too much stress and too long between hookups, and leave it at that. And let's start moving forward again."

She met his gaze levelly. "*Can* you leave it at that?" she asked.

"Yes," he replied immediately.

Maybe a little too immediately, she thought. Because the look in his eyes when he answered her wasn't anywhere near as certain as his response had been.

In spite of that, she nodded. "Okay. I can leave it at that, too." Probably. Maybe. Possibly. Perhaps.

Um, what was the question again...?

"McCloud! Mercer!"

No, that wasn't it. That wasn't even a question. That was an exclamation. From her boss, she realized belatedly. And she didn't think he knew the question, either, never mind the answer. Of course, he did sign their paychecks, so maybe she should pay a little more attention to what he was saying.

What was it he had said?

She caught sight of Robert Englund picking his way through the crowded library toward them, and what little gaiety she'd managed to rouse fizzled out. She'd been hoping to come to the party and enjoy her employer's home and hospitality—not to mention his bourbon—without having to actually *see* her employer while she was enjoying it, since that would be in no way enjoyable. Alas, 'twas not to be.

"Mr. Englund," she said, conjuring a jovial smile as he joined them. "Thanks so much for inviting us tonight. Your home is lovely."

"Thank you," he said. "But I can't take credit. It's all my wife's doing. She hired the decorator."

"Great party, sir," Turner interjected for good measure.

"Can't take credit for that, either," their employer said with a smile. "My wife hired the caterer, too."

"Mrs. Englund sounds like quite a catch," Becca said. And she wasn't being sarcastic at all when she said it. Good delegators of responsibility were hard to find these days.

Interestingly, her boss made no comment one way or another in response. "I just wanted to congratulate the two of you again for a job well done, and a pitch well thrown," he said. "And to thank you again for landing us such a substantial account."

"Think nothing of it, Mr. Englund," Becca said modestly. "We were just doing the job you hired us to do." *And trying to get a long overdue promotion,* she added to herself less modestly. *Which you can give us anytime now, on account of, in case I didn't mention it, we're both* long *overdue.*

Turner nodded in agreement. "If there's anything Becca and I can do to further the good name of Englund Advertising, sir, we're always happy to do it."

Wow, Becca thought. That was good. He was an even better suck-up than she was.

"Well, the Bluestocking account is easily the biggest one our firm has ever landed," Englund told them, "and I can assure both of you that you'll be very pleased with the Christmas bonuses you'll find in your office stockings this year." He smiled. "In addition to all the free underwear you'll ever need, I mean."

He simultaneously clapped both Turner and Becca on the back and, with a smile of pure delight, strode off to greet some of the other partygoers. Becca barely noticed his departure, however, because she was too busy being suddenly overcome again by that strange urge she'd been having lately. That weird, unexplainable, uncontrollable urge to be close to Turner. Really close to Turner. Like naked close. Body-to-body close. Mouth-to-nipple and hand-to-cock close. Hand-to-nipple and mouth-to-cock close. Joined in a way where she wouldn't be able to tell where her body ended and his began.

She looked at him then, but his gaze had drifted away from hers, and he was scanning the crowded library as he lifted his drink to his mouth. In spite of the soft lighting in the room, his dark hair shone with silvery highlights, and his eyes seemed even bluer than usual. She loved it that he was so much taller than she—easily by eight or nine inches, a statistic she found interesting on more than one level. His shoulders were so broad, and his chest was so solid and well-formed, just perfect for laying one's head on after hours and hours of exhaustive sex.

He was just so incredibly handsome. Just so unbelievably sexy. And she just wanted him *so bad*.

What had she been thinking, to tell him she didn't want the two of them to get sexual? Why had she been so insistent over the years that they keep their relationship platonic? She obviously hadn't been in her right mind when she'd made such decisions. She'd been missing out on so much for so long. Sexual was *exactly* what she wanted to be with Turner. As often as possible. In as many ways as possible. As soon as possible. She should drop down on her knees and give thanks that he was up for getting sexual, too.

Or maybe she should drop down on her knees and get sexual. He'd be up for that, she was sure....

Man, it was hot in here. She lifted a hand to run her index finger under the scooped neck of her dress, pulling it lightly away from her skin. She gulped down another mouthful of her drink in the hope that it might cool her, but the cold bourbon seared her throat and her belly, spreading heat to every extremity.

All these people, she thought, looking around at the inconvenient crowd. There were too many people in here. It would be better if she and Turner were alone. No wonder she was so hot. She needed to get out of this crowd, someplace where she could breathe. And she needed to take Turner with her.

"Turner?" she said softly, scarcely recognizing her own voice. "I'm feeling a little, ah, warm. I think I'm going to take a walk outside. Would you come with me?"

He gave her a puzzled look and she could tell he was

trying to fabricate some excuse as to why he couldn't join her outside in the below-forty-degree evening. Of course, he didn't understand—yet—that they wouldn't be cold for long.

She hurried on. "Please? I'm just not sure I'll feel safe out there all by myself." Nor would she feel satisfied.

Now he started to look suspicious. "We're in Carmel, Becca," he reminded her unnecessarily. "The only crimes committed here are crimes of fashion. And even those only happen when it's discovered that someone bought something off-the-rack at Wal-Mart instead of in couture at Saks."

On any other occasion, Becca would have been wondering how Turner knew the difference between off-the-rack and couture—or even the difference between Wal-Mart and Saks, he was that backward when it came to fashion. Tonight, though, even her curiosity about that took a back seat to her...

Well.

She wasn't sure she could even put a name to what she felt at the moment. All she knew was what she had known before. On two befores, as a matter of fact: that day in her cubicle when she and Turner had been working on the Bluestocking account, and the morning of their pitch to the Bluestocking people. That she wanted...no, desired...no, needed...no, *hungered for*...Turner in a way she had never experienced before. And she hungered for him *now*. So she needed to be alone with him. *Now*. Because her hunger was so strong, she wasn't sure even the presence of scores of people in her employer's home would prevent her from having him. *Now*.

Having? she asked herself then. Hah. That sounded way too tame for what she intended to do to him. She felt downright predatory right now. If she didn't get Turner outside this minute, she'd be tearing off both their clothes and consuming him, the crowded room be damned.

"Please?" she heard herself say again, not even sure when she'd decided to speak. "Just for a quick stroll in the back." Or a long roll in the sack. "It's just so hot in here." And then, when he still looked uncooperative, she added the clincher. "You can have a cigarette."

Not surprisingly, that seemed to do the trick. Although Turner did continue to regard her with suspicion. Probably he was thinking about the last time she'd told him she was so hot, and then had proceeded to remove her shirt and climbed onto his lap. Well, she hadn't been able to help herself! There had just been something about him that night that made her want to be naked with him. Just like there was something about him this night that made her want to be naked with him.

This time, though, she intended to be naked with him someplace where they *wouldn't* be interrupted.

"Please, Turner?" she said again, moving her hand to the back of her neck, where perspiration made her flesh damp. It really was much too hot in here. Englund ought to look into his heating situation. "Just for a few minutes."

He nodded, but with clear reluctance. "Just a few minutes," he repeated. "It shouldn't take more than that to turn us both into Popsicles, anyway. Don't you want your coat first?"

Why? she wanted to ask. It would just be one more thing she'd have to take off.

"No, we won't need them," she told him. Boy, was that an understatement.

"If you're sure…" he said.

"Oh, I'm sure, Turner. I'm very, *very* sure." And not just about the coat, either.

Setting down their drinks, they maneuvered their way through the crowd, Becca's pace increasing with every step she took. Instead of heading for the hallway entrance through which they had originally entered, however, she made her way toward an exit she spotted on the other side of the room, through French doors that opened onto a patio on the side of the house. There were other people out there smoking, she saw, so she figured the doors must be unlocked. Strangely, however, in spite of her offer just now to Turner, she had no desire to go out there and join them for a puff.

And she didn't want Turner to join them, either. No, she had a different kind of smoking planned for him.

He, of course, didn't realize that yet, and the moment they passed through the French doors, he simultaneously closed them and withdrew a half-empty pack of cigarettes from inside his jacket pocket. Before he could shake one free, though, Becca circled his wrist with sure fingers and led him to a walkway that wound toward the back of the house.

Where it was dark.

And isolated.

And uninhabited.

"Becca, where are you going?" he asked as she led him in that direction. "The designated smoking section is back there."

That, she thought, depended on the kind of smoking one wanted to do. "It's too crowded," she said. "Too much secondhand smoke. And that stuff'll kill you."

"But—"

She halted and spun around to look at him, but didn't release his wrist. "Turner, if we stand there, we'll have to talk to those people," she pointed out. "And I don't feel like making small talk with people I don't know." No, she'd much rather be with someone she knew very well. Though, admittedly, she didn't want to talk then, either.

He nodded in understanding, but Becca suspected he didn't understand at all. However, he continued to follow her as she strode forward again. She didn't stop until they'd cleared the back corner of the house, where, as she had suspected, the valets had parked a good many of the cars. But not Turner's Saturn, unfortunately, which was what she had really been hoping to find. Because as hot as she was, she didn't relish the idea of being naked in nearly freezing temperatures.

"Whoa, will you look at that beauty?" she heard Turner say from behind her, his voice filled with awe, reverence and not a little affection.

When she turned around, she saw that he was looking *not* at her ass, as she had assumed, but at something beyond her ass, in front of both of them. She also saw that he had somehow single-handedly freed a cigarette from the pack before returning the latter to his jacket pocket, and that he had been about to tuck it between his lips when whatever it was that had caught his attention had, you know, caught his attention.

Following his gaze, Becca looked at the cars all crowded together on the lawn behind the Englund home, but she saw nothing out of the ordinary. "What?" she asked impatiently. She really didn't have time for this.

"Over there," Turner said, jerking his chin upward, toward the group of cars. Still not looking at her ass. Damn him.

Expelling a restless breath of air, and not bothering to turn around again, since she knew all she'd see would be a bunch of cars, she repeated brusquely, "What?"

Finally, finally, Turner looked at her, smiling when he did so in a way that made her think that maybe he was on the same wavelength as she, after all. Because the expression on his face then was borderline orgasmic, no two ways about it.

How very promising.

"Come here," he said softly, his voice filled once again with awe, reverence and not a little affection. "I want to show you something."

Well. That was more like it. She had something she wanted to show him, too, right after he showed her his.

This time Turner took the lead as they walked, and he wove his fingers with hers in a way she liked very much. But instead of glancing back at her, even occasionally, he kept his gaze trained forward. And he kept walking forward, too, and she kept following, farther from the house and deeper into the shadows until they were threading their way through the lines of cars. Finally, he drew them both to a halt, at the very farthest corner of the makeshift parking lot, next to a car unlike any she had ever seen.

"A 1957 Rolls Royce Silver Spirit," Turner said before she could even ask what it was. "Oh, man. This baby is unbelievable."

A car? Becca wanted to say. He'd been speaking with awe, reverence and not a little affection about a *car?* Instead of her ass, he'd been looking at a *car?* His borderline orgasm had been over a *car?*

Okay, so it was a *nice* car, she had to admit when she gave it a second look. It was big and elegant and excessive, gleaming silver in the scant moonlight overhead. The interior, she saw as she gazed through the driver's-side window, was as beautifully constructed as the exterior, with leather upholstery, finely crafted accessories and burled walnut on the dashboard.

And also a nice, big back seat.

Without thinking, she reached for the handle of the back door and jerked it upward, and was only marginally surprised when it sprang open and the interior light went on— but an alarm didn't go off.

"Becca!" Turner cried when he saw her do it. He slammed the door shut again. "What the hell do you think you're doing? Someone might see the light and think we're trying to jack this thing."

She ignored him, pulling on the handle again, opening the door wider this time. It wasn't the car she was looking to jack. "I'm getting in," she said as she did just that, as if the car belonged to her. "Come on. Let's see what it's like to ride in a Rolls." Especially the kind of riding she had in mind.

"Are you crazy?" he said. "Get out of there!"

"No," she told him, smiling. "You get in here."

"That car belongs to Englund's father!" he told her, clearly struggling to keep his voice down.

"Well, he'll never know," she pointed out. "Not unless you keep standing out there yelling at me."

"I'm not yelling!" he yelled.

When he realized how loudly he'd spoken, he quickly looked left, then right, then behind him to see if anyone had heard. But they were very much alone out here, and considering how loud the music and conversation had been inside, she figured they could detonate a ten-ton bomb before anyone would notice where they were.

"Come on, Turner," she said again, patting the seat beside her. "You know you want to."

"Becca…" he began, his voice edged with warning.

"What's the matter?" she prodded. "Are you chicken?"

"Becca…"

"Don't you want to see how the other half lives? Or at least drives?"

"Becca…"

She pointed at the overhead light. "That can be seen from the house, you know," she told him. "Unless you want someone to catch us out here, you better close the door."

"Then get out," he instructed her.

"You get in."

He was clearly torn. Part of him, she could see, just wanted to get the hell out of here and hope no one had seen them yet. But another part—a bigger part—obviously wanted to get into the car, too, to see what it was like to ride the way the big boys rode. He glanced over his shoulder again. He looked at Becca. Over his shoulder. Back at Becca. He smiled.

And slipped into the car beside her, closing the door behind himself.

"Wow," he said as he leaned back against the broad seat and took in his surroundings. "This is incredible. Now *this* is a car. Can you imagine sitting in the back of one of these babies?"

She smiled. "Um, we don't have to imagine it, Turner. We *are* sitting in the back seat of one of these babies."

"Oh. Yeah. Well, can you imagine sitting in the back of one of these babies while a gorgeous chauffeur takes care of your every need?"

Oh, yeah. That was just the opening she'd been waiting for.

"You don't have to imagine that, either, Turner," she said

softly, reaching toward him. "Because although I'm no chauffeur, I know how to drive a man. And I'm about to take care of your every need...."

9

TURNER JERKED HIS HEAD around to look at Becca, certain he must have misunderstood what she'd just said. Or, at least, what she meant by what she'd just said. Hell, he'd found a sexual innuendo in almost every word she'd spoken during the past week. But even in the scant light of the moon filtering through the car's windows, he could see that she looked very much the way she'd looked before, on those occasions when she'd gotten him all worked up just to tell him they'd be making a terrible mistake to take things where she'd so clearly intended to take them.

Not. Again.

"Becca, don't," he said adamantly, wanting to nip this thing in the bud—though, granted, that was kind of a painful metaphor to use, all things considered—before it even got started.

"Don't what?" she asked. "Don't take care of your every need?"

"Don't even *talk* about my needs," he said sternly. "We both agreed we're not going to go down this road again."

"What road?" she asked. "I don't know what you're talking about."

Turner eyed her warily. Okay, maybe he was jumping to conclusions here. Maybe she'd meant something else entirely. Maybe she'd been talking about different needs than the ones he thought she meant. Maybe she was talking about his automotive needs. Yeah, that was it. Things like good mileage, and decent shock absorbers, and the best steel-belted radials money could buy. But when he looked at her face again, he suspected it wasn't tire tread she was thinking about just then. And his suspicion only grew when she opened her hand over his cock and began rubbing it as she pressed her mouth to his.

Oh. Okay. So then it *wasn't* his automotive needs she was talking about.

For one scant, delirious moment, Turner eagerly returned her kiss, because he was just too surprised and stunned— and also interested—not to. He even went so far as to tangle his fingers in her hair and cup his hand over the back of her head to draw her closer, mindless of the fact that they were already about as close as two people could be. No, not yet, he thought as he looped an arm around her waist. There was still an inch or two separating their bodies.

But the moment he felt her breasts pressing into his chest, and realized he was the one who had closed the distance, he tried to pull away. But Becca followed, pushing herself forward to cover his mouth with hers once more. Then she anchored herself in place by roping one arm around his neck and palming his dick into fully erect status.

Oh, damn…

"Becca," he gasped as he tore his mouth from hers.

But she curved her fingers more possessively over him and rubbed him harder, and he knew there was no way he would try to stop her just yet. It had been too long since any woman had touched him there—well, before Becca last week, he meant. And any hope he might have for rational thought fled the minute she began to stroke him.

In spite of that, he managed to get out a halfhearted, "Don't do this to me again, Becca. Not unless you're planning to go through with it this time."

In response to his warning, she slowly, slowly…oh, so slowly, tugged down the zipper of his trousers and tucked her hand inside.

Okay, so that answered that question.

She found him immediately—which, he had to admit, couldn't have been all that difficult, since in his current state of arousal he practically ran out to meet her—and freed him through the opening in his boxers. Without hesitation, she fingered the head of his member, dampening her hand with the prelude of his release. Then she curled her fingers completely around his naked shaft and ran them slowly down to its base before slowly pulling them back up again. Unable to help himself, he hissed in pleasure.

Again and again, she moved her hand up and down his rock-hard rod, slowly at first, then gradually increasing both her pressure and her speed. Turner laid his head back on the leather headrest and closed his eyes, stretching one arm toward the car door and draping the other over Becca's shoulders. He wasn't sure how long they sat there, she kneading his flesh and he enjoying it, but after a while, he felt her hand come to a halt, and sensed her shoulders moving out of his grasp.

His disappointment was acute.

Until he brought his head forward again and looked down to see her bending over his lap. Until he felt her touching the tip of her tongue to the very sensitive head of his very aroused cock.

"Becca…" he said cautiously.

But as much as he wanted to voice his concern about the two of them being discovered out here like this, he couldn't push the words out of his mouth. Instead, he pushed his hand through Becca's hair, then along the back of her neck and over her shoulder, then down her spine to cup his fingers over the luscious curves of her ass. As she drew him more deeply into her mouth, he tugged on the fabric of her dress, and she shifted a little to aid him in his effort to drag the garment higher, until it was bunched up around her waist. As she drew him fully into her mouth, he pulled down her panties until her creamy flesh was bared to the scant moonlight. She was wearing those black garters again, and the sight of them striping her bare skin made Turner want to come right then and there. As she sucked him harder, he moved his hand again, pushing his fingers under the strip of black and spreading them wide on her sweet, naked ass.

She was so soft. So warm. So incredibly perfect. Again and again, he skimmed his hand over her tender flesh, at the same time reveling in the pleasure of having himself in her mouth.

As she gripped his cock at its base to hold him steady, Turner dropped his other hand to her hair, skimming his palm lightly over the silky tresses and curling errant strands around his fingers. She moaned in response to the movement of his hands on her, the vibration from the sound multiplying his enjoyment of her oral attentions. Her head moved slowly up and down in his lap as she took him deeper into her mouth, and the sight of that only excited him more. She squeezed his shaft lightly, then pushed her fingers deeper between his legs to incite him further, all the while wreaking havoc on him with her tongue and her teeth and her lips.

He'd never been more aroused in his life. But when his pleasure built to a point where he was about to come, he knew he had to slow both of them down. Or, at least, slow Becca down. He figured the best way to do that was to distract her, so he moved the hand on her fanny between her legs, dipping his middle finger deep into her hot, slick canal. She gasped at the unexpected penetration, thrusting her head upward, as he had planned. To keep her preoccupied—and to buy time to slow his own orgasm—he moved his finger inside her again, pushing even deeper this time, then bent to cover her mouth with his.

Gradually, she unfolded her body and sat up beside him, and Turner moved his hand to facilitate her action. He was still hard and unfulfilled, his dissatisfaction acute. But for them to carry this any further could get messy. In more ways than one. He still wasn't sure what was going on with Becca, and his own responses to her were anything but certain. Until they could put a name on whatever it was burning up the air between them, they needed to slow down.

"Turner, you can't leave me like this," Becca said when he pulled his head back from hers. "I need to feel you inside me."

He smiled. "I was inside you."

She smiled back. "You know what I mean."

He started to shake his head, wanted to hear her tell him exactly what she wanted from him. But they were sitting in a car that didn't belong to them—a car that cost more than the two of them made annually combined—and they were at a party hosted by their employer. This was the last place they needed to be getting down and dirty.

"Not here," he told her. "We need to get back to the party."

"You're going to do me in front of a hundred people?" she asked. Then she smiled. "Ooo. Kinky. I like it."

Hell, he wasn't going to *do* her at all, Turner thought. No, what he had in mind for her went way beyond simple *doing*.

"No, but we need to get back anyway," he told her, "at least for a few minutes, because if anyone misses us, they're going to come looking for us, and they're going to find us in a compromising position."

"Is that what that was?" she asked, her voice a soft purr cutting through the darkness. "I thought that was a totally different position."

He was about to tell her that as far as he was concerned, they could try every position in the *Kama Sutra* before the night was over, but feared that would only provoke her. So instead, he just repeated, "We need to get back to the party."

"And then?" she asked.

"And then we'll say our goodbyes to Mr. and Mrs. Englund, and thank them for a lovely time."

"And then?"

"And then we'll have the valet bring around my car."

"And then?"

"And then we'll go to your place."

"And then?"

He smiled. "And then, Becca, we're going to enjoy each other. In every way imaginable. All night long."

BY THE TIME THEY ARRIVED back at Becca's apartment, she was about to burst into flames, but she hesitated once Turner closed the front door behind them. He seemed hesitant, too, at first, because he stood there with his back against the door, his hands tucked behind him, as if he were trying to keep out whatever might be on the other side trying to keep them apart. But Becca knew now. Nothing was going to keep them apart. She wanted Turner in a way she'd never wanted anyone—anything—in her life. She didn't know why or where the need had come from, and she couldn't explain why she'd fought it so hard until now. But she wasn't fighting it anymore. She wanted him. Badly.

And tonight, finally, she was going to have him.

For long moments, they only stood gazing at each other, each seeming to wait for the other to make the first move. Becca had left on only one light earlier, an amber-glass desk lamp in the corner, so now the room was bathed in a lambent golden glow that gave their surroundings an almost too clear, somehow otherworldly quality. Turner's necktie was undone—Becca recalled untying it herself during the ride—and the top three buttons of his shirt were unfastened, again by her own hand. His dark hair was mussed from her eager fingers, and there were faint smudges of her lipstick on his chin and neck. Her breathing accelerated when she remembered how they'd gotten there.

Turner's eyes darkened when he heard her breath quicken, and he strode forward, stopping when scarcely a sliver of air lay between them. But he didn't reach for her, not yet. Becca didn't reach for him, either, and instead waited to see what he would do. She'd taken the initiative once tonight. Now she wanted to see if Turner was as eager as she was to get on with what she now realized was inevitable.

For one long moment, he only studied her face, starting with her eyes, then dropping his gaze to her mouth, then bringing his attention back to her eyes again. And then he was touching her, too, first cupping her jaw gently in his hand, then threading his fingers lightly through the hair at her temples. Then his other hand joined the first, dipping below her hair to curve possessively around her nape, the gentlest, most exquisite caress Becca had ever felt in her life. And then his mouth was on hers, coaxing and gentle, but with a promise of something more—something untamed, something unleashed, something she had never experienced with him before.

She melted into him instantly, curling the fingers of one hand into the fabric of his shirt, and threading the others through his hair. A soft sound of surrender—or maybe it was a sound of demand—escaped him as he intensified the kiss, wrapping his arms around her waist, splaying his hands over the small of her back. And the moment she heard that sound, the moment she felt his hands on her, the moment she understood the power of their bodies' responses to each other, she knew there would be no turning back. Not this time. Not ever again. She wanted Turner. Turner wanted her. There was nothing in this world that would keep them apart. Ever again.

So she pressed her body more urgently into his, wove her fingers more resolutely into his hair and cupped the crown of his head in her palm. And then she crowded against him—or maybe he was the one who crowded against her—so that she could savor him more thoroughly, and at her leisure. Not that she was feeling especially leisurely at the moment.

Turner seemed to want to take control of the kiss then, and Becca willingly let him. Again and again he pushed his tongue into her mouth, thrusting, parrying, tasting, testing. Sweet. He was so sweet. But his sweetness was mixed with something else, too, she thought vaguely, something sharp and spicy that was both unfamiliar and irresistible. It was something that made her hungry for things she'd never realized she needed before, made her long for things she'd never known she wanted. So she kissed Turner more deeply still, knowing he was everything she would ever need or want again.

Her hunger seemed to mirror his own, because his kisses deepened, kindling a fire low in her belly that threatened to burn out of control. She wanted him so much she was oblivious to everything else, only knew that she needed him closer, needed his body joined with hers in the most basic, most intimate way it could be. The fingers she had twisted in his shirt scooted lower, snaking around his waist, opening wide over his broad back. In response, Turner looped his arm around her waist, too, then jerked her body hard against him.

But counter to his actions, he tore his mouth away from hers. "Becca," he panted. "Are you absolutely, positively *sure* this is what you want?"

He still didn't believe her, she thought. He still didn't think she was going to go through with it. Even after what had happened at the party.

But then, why should he? she asked herself. She'd backed out every time she'd started this before. Though, at the moment, she couldn't begin to imagine why. She couldn't understand how she had ever had second thoughts about their having sex. What had she been thinking? Here with Turner, right now, the way they were, this felt so good. It felt so perfect. It felt so *right*. How could she have ever doubted that this was what she wanted?

"I'm absolutely, positively sure," she told him. "I've never been more certain about anything in my life."

"But those other times, you thought you wanted me then, too. What happens if you wake up in the morning and think you've made a mistake?"

There was no way Becca was going to wake up and think she'd made a mistake. Not unless she did something now to make Turner change his mind. "That's not going to happen," she told him.

He still didn't look convinced. So she spread the fingers of one hand between his shoulder blades and framed his jaw with the other.

"I want this, Turner," she told him with utter and complete confidence. "I want us to be together. I want to feel you inside me."

For a long time, he didn't respond, only gazed into her eyes as if he were searching there for the answer to a very important question. Which, she supposed, was exactly what he was doing. So she remained silent, knowing that he would find the truth in her eyes, and that then he would be reassured, once and for all. And after a moment, Turner smiled, the sort of smile that let her know he had indeed found the answer he had been seeking.

"Then take me, Becca," he told her, pulling her against him. "Take me every way you know how."

But it was Turner who did the taking after that, covering Becca's mouth with his once again. And as he thrust his tongue deep inside her, something hot and frantic splashed through her midsection. She moved her hand from his hair to curl her fingers over his warm nape, and lost herself in his kiss. He responded by pressing his hand more insistently against her back and moving his mouth from hers to brush his lips over her jaw and her cheek and her chin, then nuzzling the sensitive flesh where her throat joined her collarbone before skimming his lips along her shoulder.

"You taste sweet," he said as he pulled his head up and gazed down into her eyes, echoing her own earlier thoughts about him. He smiled. "But there's something kind of spicy in there, too."

She chuckled low. "I was just thinking the same thing about you," she said.

He stroked the pads of his fingers over her face, lightly tracing her lower lip and chin, then up along her jaw and cheekbone, then down again, over the sensitive skin of her throat. But his smile fell some as he moved his hand lower still, over the scooped neck of her dress, a caress that made her heart pound against her breastbone in anticipation. Instead of closing his hand over her breast, though, as she had expected he would do, he raised it back up to her face, as if he wanted to drag out the excitement for as long as he could. When he curled his fingers slightly and turned his hand to brush his knuckles tenderly across her cheek, Becca's eyes fluttered closed. A sharp heat sped through her with each gentle stroke, searing her to her very core.

More, she thought feverishly. She wanted—*needed*—more from him. More *of* him. His careful caresses somehow only enflamed her, sparking a hunger inside her she knew wouldn't easily be appeased. Touching him wasn't enough. But with Turner, she never would get enough.

She inhaled deeply, filling her lungs with the smoky, musky, masculine scent of him. No namby-pamby department store fragrances for Turner, no way. He smelled of pure, unadulterated man, and the woman inside Becca responded in kind. Instinctively, she arched her body against him to better experience his heat, and his desire, and his hunger and him. And still it wasn't close enough for her. She wanted—needed—so much more.

As if he'd read her mind, Turner leaned forward and kissed her, and Becca opened to him enthusiastically. She dipped the fingers of one hand inside the opening of his shirt, skimming her fingertips over the dark springy hair she encountered there. As he deepened the kiss, he pressed his body fully against hers, then began to move forward, urging her to move backward, in the direction of her bedroom.

As they completed their slow dance, they went to work on each other's clothes. Turner found the zipper of her dress and tugged it downward, past her waist and over her hips, pulling open the fabric when he finished the journey and splaying his warm hands over her bare flesh. Becca, in turn, freed his shirttail from his trousers and unfastened every button, opening her palms over the coarse hair on his chest and torso, raking her fingertips over the ridge of every muscle.

She wasn't sure how long it took them to reach her bedroom, but at some point, her legs connected with the edge of her bed. By that time, her bra was gone and her dress was down around her waist, and Turner's jacket and shirt had been discarded. Between kisses, they managed to pull the covers back, and then down, down, down Becca fell, until she felt the cool kiss of the cotton sheet against her naked back. Turner fell with her, and she looped one arm around his neck and the other across his back while he, in turn, arced one arm over her head and settled his body alongside her own. Then he bent his head and kissed her again, long and hard and deep.

She growled something needy and incoherent in reply, clinging to him, and he responded with a sound that echoed her own hunger, pushing himself half on top of her. Then he insinuated one leg between hers, jerking his thigh roughly into the juncture of her own. The slim cut of her dress prevented her from spreading her legs for him, but the pressure of his thigh against her excited core only enhanced the delicious friction. Heat pooled low in her abdomen, and she bucked her hips against him. Turner responded by dropping a hand to the hem of her dress and jerking the fabric upward, over her hips and around her waist. Then he spread her legs wide and shoved his thigh even harder against her, which made Becca lurch upward so she could rub herself against him again and again and again.

As she pleasured herself that way, she felt him tugging at her dress until he'd pulled the garment over her head to toss it aside. And then she lay beneath him in only her black panties, garter belt, stockings and heels.

Turner pushed himself up from the bed and stood beside it, gazing down at her. His chest rose and fell with his ragged respiration as he studied her, his expression revealing the extent of his passion—his eyes were dark, his cheeks were burnished and his mouth was swollen from her kisses. And seeing him that way made Becca burn for him even more. Because she knew she was the one who had roused him to such a state. And it would be she, and she alone, who brought him satisfaction.

"Becca," he whispered hoarsely, "you are such an unbelievably sexy woman."

The compliment made something primitive and satisfying purl through her, and she smiled. She threw one arm over her head and reached out to him with the other. "You're not so bad yourself," she murmured. "Now come and show me what a man like you does to a sexy woman."

"Gladly," he said without hesitation before returning to her.

As he stretched out alongside her again, he took her bare breast in his hand, covering the tender mound with sure fingers, squeezing it, palming it, fingering it, before raking his thumb over the stiffened nipple. And then his mouth was where his hand had been, wet and greedy and deliberate, soaking her warm flesh as he tried to suck as much of her into his mouth as he could.

Becca gasped, but her breath got stuck in her throat when he moved his other hand between her legs, pressing his three middle fingers over the silk of her panties, wet now with her body's response to him. She opened her legs wider, and Turner spread his fingers wide, too, moving them in slow circles over her sensitive flesh to pleasure her even more. Never had she felt more reckless, more ravenous, more *aroused* than she did in that moment. Her breathing had become shallow to the point of making her dizzy, and her thoughts were chaotic and indistinct. All she registered were the dual sensations of Turner's mouth consuming her breast and his diligent fingers wreaking havoc between her legs.

More, she thought again. She needed more of him. She needed *all* of him.

Impulsively, she reached for the waistband of her panties, then lifted her hips from the mattress and shoved the garment down. Once Turner understood what she wanted, he helped her in her efforts, until her panties had joined her dress on the floor. Becca reached for one of her garters, intending to remove that and her stockings, too, but Turner covered her hand with his and halted her efforts. When she glanced up in curiosity, he was smiling.

"Don't," he told her. "Leave them on. The shoes, too. It'll be incredibly erotic."

She arched her eyebrows in surprise.

"That first time in your cubicle," he said, his voice hoarse and breathless, "when you climbed into my lap and your was skirt hiked up and I saw what you were wearing…" He closed his eyes for a moment, as if remembering. "I couldn't believe you'd been wearing stuff like that and I never knew it." He grinned wickedly. "Turn over a minute," he told her.

"Why?"

"I want to see what they look like from the back," he said. *Oh, boy…*

"Come on, Becca," he cajoled. "Just show me."

She felt herself grow warmer and damper just hearing the timbre of his voice as he spoke the request. She sat up on the bed, then turned around and rose up on her knees to give him a full view of her from behind. She'd heard, of course, that men found garter belts on women to be very sexy. But surprisingly, although she'd always liked wearing such undergarments herself, Becca had never made love in them. They'd always come off with the rest of her clothes. No man had ever asked her to leave them on. And the fact that Turner did now…

Well. She found it to be very sexy, too.

He must have liked what he saw, because she heard a sound, low and feral, from behind her. When she turned to look over her shoulder, she saw that he was staring at her ass. Feeling playful—or something—Becca bent forward until her hands were flat against the mattress. She was about to say something—something flip and flirtatious that would make them both laugh—but before she could get the words out, Turner had a hand on each buttock, and he was bending forward, too, pressing his mouth to one sensitive cheek.

The sensation was quite exquisite.

So exquisite, in fact, that Becca pretty much forgot what she had intended to say. Especially when Turner dipped a hand between her legs again and slipped one long finger into her slick, heated channel.

"Oh," she cried out at the deep penetration. "Oh, Turner. Oh. Oh, that's so—"

Her words halted there, however, because he brought another finger into the action, and nipped her fanny lightly with his teeth as he drove into her. He kept tasting her as he continued to penetrate her, his fingers moving slowly at first, then quickening, until she was right at the edge of an orgasm. But he seemed to sense her nearness and pulled back again, just when she would have lost herself to the ecstasy.

The big brute.

When she turned around to call him that, she saw him smiling, and realized he had left her that way on purpose because he wasn't finished with her yet. Pouting in frustration, she lay on her back once more. But as Turner gazed down at her, she saw the fire burning in his eyes and realized he was even further gone than she was.

"Don't worry," he told her. "We're not even close to being finished. Right now, I just want to look at you. All of you. And then I want to touch you. All of you. And then I want to taste you, and smell you, and listen to every little sound you make while I do all the things to you that I want to do to you."

"Oh, Turner…" She was close to climaxing, just listening to his roughly uttered promises. Somehow, though, she found the strength to ask him, "And what are all the things you want to do to me?"

Slowly, he lay down beside her again. He curled his fingers over one bare shoulder, then skimmed his hand downward, over one breast. "I want to suck you here," he said, circling his thumb over her nipple. Then he moved his hand lower, over her flat belly. "And I want to suck you here." He moved his hand lower still, into her tawny curls. "And I want to finger you here." He brushed a fingertip lower still, over her tender clitoris, but only long enough to rouse a hiss of wanting from her. "And I want to lick you here." A shudder of heat racked her as he completed his to-do list, and she wished he would hurry up and get to it.

"And then," he said softly, "I want to bury my cock inside you, and I want to watch you come apart at the seams."

Oh, dear…

He rolled over on top of her, settling himself between her legs, and she groaned in frustration that he was still dressed—or at least halfway. She flattened her palms against his hard chest, loving his strength and the density of each elegant muscle she encountered. Her fingertips skimmed over ridges and sinew, tripped along ribs, dipped into the hollow at the base of his throat. Turner closed his eyes as she explored him, as if he wanted to relish each brush of her fingers. When he opened his eyes again, they seemed darker than before somehow, and a thrill of anticipation shot through her when she realized what that meant.

He scooped his hands beneath her hips and pulled her toward him, rubbing his body urgently against hers, and she felt how full he was, how heavy, how hard. Before she realized his intention, he'd circled her wrist with strong fingers and pushed it between their bodies, flattening her palm over his stiff erection. Eagerly, Becca curled her fingers over him and stroked him through his trousers, loving the frantic sound that erupted from somewhere deep inside him.

And she smiled, thinking it was nice to know he wasn't the only one who could wreak sexual havoc.

"Oh, Becca," he gasped against her neck as he buried his face there. "Do that again."

Becca threw her head back to grant him better access, then rubbed her hand against him again. And then she did it again. And again. And again.

"Don't stop," he commanded when she slowed her hand.

She raked her fingers obediently—and none too gently this time—over him.

"Again," he whispered coarsely.

Once more she palmed and possessed him.

"Again, Becca, again."

She fumbled with his belt and fly, then tucked her hand inside his pants to take his hot, naked shaft in her hand. She palmed the damp head, her actions made easier by the dampness of his early response, then curled her fingers completely around his arrogant staff. Leisurely, methodically, she pumped her hand up and down.

He went still as she slid her fingers along his cock, bracing himself on his elbows, which he'd anchored on each side of her head. He threw his own head back as she increased her pace, his eyes shut tight, his lips parting slightly as he struggled to take one ragged breath after another. So overwhelmed was she by his barely restrained passion that Becca lifted herself up from the mattress to press a frantic kiss against his throat. And then suddenly, without warning, Turner reached between their bodies to clamp his hand over her wrist to halt her.

"That was way too close," he growled before she could

even ask him why he'd done it. "And you haven't had your turn yet."

That's what he thought.

"Lie still, Becca," he said, before she could assure him otherwise.

Well, no need to be hasty, she thought as he moved away from her.

"If you can…" he further challenged with a knowing smile as he knelt on the floor beside the bed…and between her legs.

Well, gee, that sounded promising….

Happy to accommodate his request, she lay back on the bed, arcing her arms over her head in silent challenge. Turner grinned as he dipped his head between her legs, curving his hands over the insides of her thighs to push her legs apart. He skimmed his hands down to the undersides of her knees, folding them until her legs were bent and her feet were planted firmly on the edge of the bed. Then he pushed his hands under her bare bottom and lifted her up, moving her to his waiting mouth.

Becca gasped at the first flick of his tongue against her, a keen shot of heat firing through her at the contact. With soft, butterfly strokes, he enflamed her, flicking the tip of his tongue over her sensitive flesh, tasting, teasing, tempting, drawing slow circles around her clitoris before lapping the flat of his tongue gently over it. Gradually, though, his hunger mounted, and the wispy touches became eager, insatiable tastes of her. And then the eager tastes grew bolder, and he slipped a long finger inside her as he ate. Writhing and groaning, on the brink of orgasm, Becca tangled the fingers of both hands tightly in his hair, begging him by turns to end his voracious onslaught and to promise that it would never, ever stop.

And it didn't stop for a very long time. Turner, she soon realized, was a very hungry man. And he took his time feeding that hunger.

Eventually, though, he did satisfy himself—leaving Becca feeling decidedly less so—because he pulled his head back and climbed up alongside her in bed again. By then she was only half-coherent, on the brink of her third orgasm. He smiled at her with what she could only liken to smugness, then shifted his body over hers once more. And then he kissed her, long and slow and deep, and she savored the taste of herself on his tongue and the play of his hands as they explored every inch of her body.

As he kissed her, he curved his fingers over one breast, rolling his thumb insistently over the sensitive nipple before catching it in the V of his index and middle fingers. Then his mouth was where his hand had been, his tongue laving her, loving her, circling her nipple before tracing first the underside of her breast and then the top. He rolled her nipple between his fingers, flicking the tip of his tongue against it, again and again and again. Then he moved his hand and sucked her breast deep into his mouth, the hot, wet pressure sparking heat through her entire body.

And as he sucked her, Becca went back to work on his trousers, pushing the garment down to bare his taut buttocks, and gripping them with both hands. He finally got the message and moved away from her long enough to shed them and his boxers and socks, then returned to her, nestling his pelvis against hers and bracing himself on arms he folded onto the mattress on each side of her head. She felt him start to push inside her, and she bent her knees again, bracing them on the bed once more to facilitate his entry, because he was more man than she was accustomed to.

But she was so ready for him after everything they'd already done that he slipped inside fairly easily. He filled her to the brink, though, in a way she'd never felt full before, and she squeezed her eyes shut tight at the sense of completion that flooded her. Having Turner inside her made her feel whole in a way she hadn't felt before. His body fit hers so perfectly, as if the two of them had been one all along, two pieces of a whole that had somehow been split apart. Now they were back together again. And she found herself wishing they'd never be apart again.

And then they were moving as one, Turner withdrawing from her and ramming forward again, Becca launching her body up to greet him every time. With every penetration they joined more completely, until one final, hurtling thrust incited their completion.

Becca cried out at the intensity of her orgasm, her entire body shuddering as Turner spilled himself hotly inside her. His exclamation was equally savage, and his body went rigid against hers for the long moment it took him to empty himself. With a ragged groan, he collapsed beside her and gathered her close, burying his face in the tender curve where her shoulder met her neck. She felt his warm breath dampen her flesh, registered the wild beating of his heart against her own.

And she knew things between them would never be the same again.

10

BECCA AWOKE SLOWLY, gradually registering the things she usually did upon waking on this, her favorite day of the week. She loved, loved, loved Sunday mornings, because they heralded such a lazy, obligation- and stress-free day. She sighed with satisfaction as, still half-asleep, she luxuriated in her surroundings.

Her bed was warm and cozy, the sheets piled around her smelling like a tropical breeze, courtesy of her tropical breeze scented—new and improved fragrance!—laundry detergent. Soft classical music drifted from the clock radio beside her bed, a lovely, lilting piano piece, the composer of which she couldn't possibly identify, but she'd bet good money he was Italian. When she opened her eyes to half-mast she saw that gauzy, golden, late morning sunlight filtered through the closed blinds, striping the flowered walls and hardwood floor beneath. Outside that window, she could just make out the sounds of birds singing, children laughing and a soft breeze tinkling the wind chimes on her deck.

What a glorious morning, she thought, smiling as her eyes fluttered lazily shut again. Outside, the weather was sunny and clear. Inside, her bed was snug and toasty. Her entire day lay before her, blissfully agenda-free, and, at the moment, she felt as if she had all the time in the world to enjoy the lack of a schedule. Everything in her world was perfect. The Earth was spinning in its orbit, the planets were aligned, all was well in the universe and—

And she'd had relentless sex with Turner, *all night long*.

Her eyes snapped open when she remembered what had happened only hours before. Then they closed again when those memories became clearer. And more graphic. And more erotic. And more arousing.

Oh, Turner...

As if she'd spoken that last thought aloud, she felt him stirring beside her in the bed, and only then did she finally register the nearness of his body. He was spooned behind her, his broad—naked—chest pressed to her own—naked—back, his powerful—naked—thighs resting against her own—naked—thighs. One of his—naked—arms was slung up over her head, and the other—naked—arm was folded over her—naked—waist. Most obvious, though, in more ways than one, was how his full, rock-hard—and had she mentioned he was naked? And so was she?—erection was pushing against her fanny.

Her eyes fluttered closed again at the realization that he was waking up so ready for her, and she went wet, just like that, at the recognition of her own readiness for him. The hand at her waist crept higher, closing over her breast, and he nuzzled her neck from behind. Instinctively, Becca turned her head on the pillow to grant him freer access, and he brought his mouth into the action, dragging soft butterfly kisses along her throat and shoulder and back. Reaching behind herself, she tangled her fingers in his hair, her other hand covering the one splayed open now over her belly.

She felt him shift behind her, and without preliminaries, he slipped easily into her from behind. He pushed his hips forward slowly, languidly, so much less fiercely than he had during the night. This was obviously meant to be a slow, leisurely, good-morning coupling, and she couldn't help thinking it was a much better way to ease into her Sunday.

His hand massaged her breast while the other pressed into her belly, and he gently nipped her shoulder as he bucked his hips less gently against her. Becca pushed herself back to greet him as he thrust deeper inside her, and he dropped his hand from her breast to anchor it to her waist. Holding her still with both hands, he jerked his hips forward, slamming against her ass. Becca moved her own hand between her legs to seek the wet, stiff little button of her clitoris. She gasped when she found it, then drew little circles on it with the pad of her middle finger, keeping time with Turner's thrusting, until she felt the first waves of her climax rising.

He came more quickly than he had during the night, as did she, both of them crying out softly as the ongoing tremors of their orgasms shuddered through them. Launching his body into hers one final time, Turner spent himself inside her, then collapsed against her, burying his face in her hair.

Becca lay still as she waited for her body to calm, loving how the heat and dampness of Turner's skin mingled with her own. For long moments the two of them rested in silence, their bodies still joined as one, their respiration united in uneven, irregular breaths. Eventually, she found herself wondering if their thoughts, too, were shared. Somehow, though, she suspected that their thinking might be the only place they *weren't* currently connected.

Finally, Turner rolled onto his back, bringing Becca with him. She landed with her head on his shoulder, her fingers tangled in the dark hair spanning his chest. He looped an arm around her shoulders and held her close, capturing a strand of her hair and wrapping it idly around his index finger as he gazed up at the ceiling.

And Becca couldn't help noting that not only had neither of them said a word to the other, but also they couldn't seem to look each other in the eye.

She surprised herself by being the one to break what threatened to become an awkward silence. "Gee, I guess that sort of answers my first question," she said as she snuggled closer to him and opened her hand over his heart. She took comfort in the way his heartbeat buffeted her palm. She wasn't positive, but she thought his heart rate was in sync with her own. So maybe there was hope they could be in sync with other things that mattered more.

For a moment, he didn't say anything and, she sensed, continued to gaze up at the ceiling. Then he turned his head toward hers—not looking her in the eye, she couldn't help noticing—and murmured against her hair, "What question?" He punctuated the query by brushing his lips lightly over her temple, but he still didn't look at her.

Quietly, she said, "Last night did we really do what I thought we did, or was it just a dream?"

He chuckled low and nuzzled her hair affectionately again. "Ain't no way that was a dream," he told her. "Because whenever I have dreams like that, they always end way before I'm satisfied."

As strange as Becca felt, she couldn't help but smile at that. "Judging by what just happened, you still weren't satisfied by what happened last night." Less happily, she added, "So maybe it was a dream, after all."

"It wasn't a dream," he repeated. "And believe me, Becca, I am satisfied."

He rolled to his side and bent his head to kiss her, and when he finally pulled back, he met her gaze. Better than that, he smiled at her. "At least I am for a little while."

Somehow, she was able to smile, too, but it didn't quite feel genuine. Turner seemed to realize it, because his own smile faded.

"Is everything okay?" he asked, his voice edged with concern.

She nodded, but said nothing.

Now his smile disappeared completely. But he didn't withdraw from her, only skimmed her cheek with his thumb and then turned his hand to repeat the action with the back of his knuckles. "'Cause, you know, Becca, as nice as last night was, right now, you kind of look like you're having second thoughts about what happened."

"No, I'm not," she lied.

He said nothing for a moment, his fingers still caressing her cheek. Then, very quietly, he said, "Yeah, I think you are."

She sighed softly. "Okay, maybe I am. But not the way you think."

"No?"

She shook her head. "I'm not having second thoughts about what we did last night."

"You sure?"

She nodded, for the first time feeling certain about her reply. And about her feelings, too. "I'm not sorry we made love," she told him. "I'm just not sure I understand how it happened, that's all."

His smile was back, but there was something melancholy about it this time. "That makes two of us," he told her.

She hesitated for a moment, then said, "I know I'm the

one who started things last night. And the other times, too. And I know that, before last night, I was always the one to stop them before we had a chance to finish."

"But last night you didn't," he added unnecessarily.

"I know," she said. "That's what has me so confused."

"You don't understand why you didn't put a stop to things last night?"

She shook her head. "No. I don't understand why I *did* put a stop to them *before*."

He propped himself up on one elbow to look at her, clearly very interested in what she was saying. "So then why was last night different from the other times?"

Becca thought about that before answering. She hadn't felt any different, she realized. Last night her feelings had been identical to the first two times she'd wanted to have sex with Turner. But the first two times, those feelings had subsided. Last night, they'd just kept growing fiercer and fiercer. And last night, she couldn't put her reaction down to stress or pressure. Because last night, the two of them hadn't been under any stress or pressure. And even if they had, she could have eased the tension by going outside to smoke a cigarette, the way so many other people were. Instead, she'd bypassed the smoking area and had gone straight into the shadows with Turner. Because she hadn't wanted a cigarette. She'd wanted him. Powerfully. Intensely. Immediately.

But why had last night been different? she asked herself. Why had she finally gone through with it, and taken what she so desperately wanted? And why had she denied herself what she so desperately wanted before last night?

"I don't know," she finally said, not just in reply to Turner's questions, but to her own, as well.

He said nothing for several moments, his expression offering not a clue about his thoughts. Ultimately—and, she had to admit, surprisingly—he seemed okay with her answer.

"Maybe it really doesn't matter why," he told her. "Maybe we shouldn't question it. Maybe it's something really simple that we're just trying to make too complicated." He shrugged. "Maybe it's like in the song."

"What song?" she asked.

He smiled. "You know. It's that crazy little thing called—"

Love, she finished silently for him when he stopped himself before saying the word out loud. And also when his expression changed from one of fond affection to one of stark-raving terror.

"Lust," he finished then. "That crazy little thing called lust."

Becca nodded. In a way, she even believed it. For some reason, though, she didn't much like it.

But what else could it be but lust? she asked herself. What they'd done last night certainly hadn't been generated by love. It had been too powerful, too hot, too raw, too extreme. It had been much too intense to be anything but a purely physical response to a purely physical feeling. Love was founded on the emotional, not the physical. Love was tender. Love was gentle. Love was sweet. What she and Turner had done last night had been—

Well. Something she wasn't likely to find with anyone else, that was for sure. But it hadn't been love. It couldn't have been. It had been way too potent for that.

"Lust," she repeated, thinking maybe it made sense, after all. Certainly more sense than that other *L*-word.

"Lust," he echoed.

She nodded, still thinking about it. "We have both been a long time without dates," she pointed out.

"Too long," he said.

"Maybe we both just had an itch we needed to scratch," she offered further, warming now to the idea.

"You got that right," he agreed.

"And since there wasn't anyone else available, we turned to each other," she finished.

"That has to be it," he stated.

"Has to be," she concurred.

When she looked at Turner's face again, though, he didn't seem to be buying it, either. Still, it was the only explanation that made any sense.

"So then, now that we've scratched that itch," she said slowly, still trying to work things out in her brain, "do you think we'll do this again?"

He eyed her intently. "Do you want to do this again?"

She thought about that before answering. What had happened last night had been amazing. Incredible. Phenomenal. She'd never had a sexual encounter that even came close to how it had been with Turner. And this morning, they were still speaking to each other, and although she felt a little weird, there was none of the awkwardness or embarrassment she might have thought would result from such a thing. She had slept with her best friend last night, something she'd always sworn she would never do. *Slept?* she repeated dubiously to herself. Hah. They'd done a lot more than sleeping. They'd explored every sexual avenue they could think of during the long night.

But did she want to do it again? she asked herself.

Her baser self, the part that was spontaneous and irresponsible and hedonistic, replied with a resounding "You bet your ass I want to do it again!"

But her more lucid self, the part that was honest and rational and far-thinking, piped up with a "Not so fast there, girlfriend…"

It had been wonderful with Turner, she thought. But how long would it stay wonderful?

Ultimately, the only answer that came to her was the one she'd had to accept for so many other things this morning. "I don't know," she told him.

And she watched Turner's face carefully as she replied, trying to discern even the smallest clue as to what he might be thinking, how he was reacting. But his face changed not at all, and his gaze remained steady and unwavering.

So Becca said, "Let's just take this one step at a time for now, okay? Because I just…" She sighed heavily and met his eyes again. "I don't know, Turner. I just don't know."

And what bothered her more than anything was that she was being honest again. Even after everything that had happened last night, she truly didn't know how she felt about Turner this morning.

TURNER STOOD NAKED under the hot spray of Becca's shower, letting the water blast his face full-force, and hoping it would pound some sense into his idiot brain.

Lust, he repeated to himself distastefully. That crazy little thing called lust. Why the hell had he said that? Why couldn't he have just called it what it was? Why couldn't he have told Becca how he felt about her? That he loved her? That the reason last night had happened—at least on his side of things—was because of the way he felt about her? Emotionally as well as physically? He'd had the perfect opportunity. Instead he'd forced himself to retreat before he could make himself get the word out. Because he'd watched her face carefully as she'd sorted out her thoughts and feelings, and he'd noted the confusion and the uncertainty and the fear that had been so unmistakable. And he'd stopped himself from saying that one little word that would have changed everything. Because he'd known then that, even after last night, Becca still didn't feel the same way about him that he felt about her. And he hadn't wanted to bare himself—well, not *that* part of himself—to her unless he could be certain she loved him, too. But she didn't.

She didn't love him.

He had no choice but to make himself accept that now. Because if she loved him, she would have told him so. At some point during the night, she would have revealed it, because Becca wasn't a woman to keep something like that to herself, especially during a time when she was letting down so many barriers. And the fact that she hadn't voiced her love for him—or *any* feelings for him, short of *Oh, baby, do that again, it feels so good*—could only mean one thing. What had happened last night hadn't happened because she loved him.

Dammit.

He turned until the shower was pounding his shoulders and back, pushed his troubling thoughts to the back of his brain, and reached for the shampoo. He wrinkled his nose in distaste at the words *passionfruit fragrance*. Then he tipped the bottle sideways to pour as little as he thought he could get away with into his palm, and scrubbed it vigorously into his wet hair.

Hey, that actually didn't smell too bad. In fact, he kind of liked it….

Then he realized the real reason he liked the fragrance was because it reminded him of Becca, and he ducked his head under the stream of water again to rinse it out. The soap, too, something pinkish-orange and citrusy smelling, roused more reminders of Becca, so he hurried through the rest of his shower and stepped out, reaching for the clean towel she had handed him on his way to the bathroom.

But it smelled like the sheets on her bed, and that, naturally, just brought back all the memories of the night before, not that his memory needed jogging there, thankyouverymuch, but there it was all the same, and he wondered if he would ever be able to do anything again for the rest of his life that didn't remind him of Becca, and his night with Becca and his feelings for Becca.

Doubtful, he thought as he knotted the towel around his waist, since so much of his life involved Becca. He worked with her every day. He lived within three miles of her place, so they often ran into each other, even when they didn't plan to, at the grocery store or Starbucks or the park in between their apartments. And they liked a lot of the same things, too, so they went out together regularly, to movies, or concerts, or restaurants, or whatever caught their fancy. And, hell, he'd grown up with her, so he couldn't even claim any memories from childhood or adolescence that didn't include her in some way, too.

So that kind of sucked.

Maybe that was the problem, he thought as he searched through the bathroom closet for a comb and hair dryer, feeling in no way hesitant about rifling through her things, since that was what friends did—they felt comfortable enough together that they didn't need to always ask permission or worry about the repercussions of their actions.

Maybe he and Becca had spent too much time together over the years, and they continued to spend too much time together now. No wonder he'd never formed a long-term attachment to another woman, and no wonder Becca had never formed a long-term attachment to another man. They'd scarcely given themselves a chance to do that, because they always hung out together.

Of course, the fact that Turner had been in love with Becca since junior high school may have kind of hampered him with regard to that long-term commitment business, too....

But Becca hadn't been in love with him ever, he reminded himself as he thumbed on the hair dryer, and she'd never kept a boyfriend for more than a year. Usually, she called it quits with a guy after a few months. And that—

His thoughts stopped right there. As did his hand, so that the hair dryer was blowing one section of his hair straight up toward the ceiling. But Turner didn't care, because he suddenly realized that since Becca never stayed with a guy for more than a few months, then that meant he might not have more than a few more months with her, either. Because he'd witnessed for himself how she tended to lose interest in guys not long after getting sexually involved with them. Not that Turner had ever paid that close of attention to her sexual liaisons with other men over the years, but...

Oh, all right. So he'd watched her sexual liaisons with other men over the years like a hawk and analyzed them to death to see what those guys had going for them that he didn't. And not only had he come to the conclusion that none of them was in any way good enough for her—in fact, the majority of them were bums, but who knew what attracted women to jerks like that?—but he'd also noticed that Becca's feelings for them cooled not long after the initial launch stage.

So to speak.

And now that Turner had fully launched himself—yeah, baby, he'd launched himself like a surface-to-Becca missile—and was orbiting her like a satellite, his days might very well be numbered.

But maybe that was good, he told himself, grimacing when he realized how one side of his hair was sticking straight up in the air, making him look like a dog with one ear perked in curiosity—or stupidity. He wet his hand under the faucet and flattened the hair again, then moved the hair dryer to the other side of his head. Maybe it was good that Becca would soon grow tired of him, because then he'd have to accept once and for all that there was no future for the two of them the way he'd always hoped for, and fantasized about a future for the two of them. And then he could get on with his life. A life where he might have the chance to build a loving, lasting, sexual relationship with someone else.

Hey, it could happen.

He looked at his reflection in the mirror as he tried to convince himself that such a thing was possible. That they'd both enjoy this new sex thing for as long as it took to run its course, and that Becca would ultimately tire of Turner the way she had all the other men in her life. That they'd talk it over and agree to remain friends, and just put down that brief sexual dimension as an aberration, however amazing and satisfying and incredible and erotic and licentious and hot and sweaty and tasty and zesty and arousing and raw and—

And where was he?

Oh, yeah. That they'd talk it over and decide they could still be friends, and both would move on to other people. And then, armed with his newfound resolution about not spending the rest of his life in a man-woman thing with Becca, Turner would finally be forced to look elsewhere for the man-woman thing with someone else. And he would find someone else. And fall in love with someone else. And the sex thing with the new woman would be even better than the sex thing with Becca had been. He and his new woman could invite Becca and her new man to their new home for cocktails and cards, the way his folks and Becca's folks had spent a couple of nights a month together when they were kids, playing cards and filling the family room with the sound of laughter and the haze of blue cigarette smoke and the sharp scent of bourbon.

Yeah, they could do that, he told himself. Sure they could.

Except that Becca's guy would no doubt be some bum who wasn't nearly good enough for her, and all Turner would be able to do was sit across the card table from her, shaking his head and wondering what she saw in some schmuck when she could have had him, because not only had the sex thing been phenomenal between the two of them, but also he loved her more than any guy ever could or would, even if he did have a new wife and a new house and a family room for entertaining.

"Idiot," Turner said to the guy in the mirror. "You're a first class, see-exhibit-A idiot."

"What was that?" he heard Becca call through the door. "Did you say something, Turner?"

He closed his eyes tight and felt like the biggest fool who ever had the misfortune to be born. "Nothing," he called back through the bathroom door. "I was just talking to myself."

Idiot, he berated himself silently now. He should have told Becca how he felt this morning when he'd had the chance, no matter how she felt about him. Because he might never have the chance to do it again. She hadn't exactly said she wanted them to continue on this newly discovered path of sexual enlightenment. For all Turner knew, last night might end up being a one-night stand. The best damn one-night stand he'd ever had, but a one-night stand nonetheless. What if he never had the chance to be skin-to-skin and heart-to-heart with her again? What would he do then?

Suffer, he told himself. *A lot.*

Because now that he'd been with Becca the way he'd always fantasized about being with her, he knew the reality was even better. Because what had happened last night had been incredible.

And it might never happen again.

11

IN THE TWO WEEKS that followed Becca and Turner's excellent adventure, neither said another word about it. There were days, honestly, when she wondered if maybe she'd dreamed the whole thing. Some weird, oversexed fever dream unlike any she'd ever dreamed before, the result of simply going too long without the sort of basic skin-to-skin contact with another human being that every normal, red-blooded adult demanded. But then she'd remember some of the things they'd done that night, things she'd never even dreamed about before—because, quite frankly, some of it was stuff she hadn't even known was physically possible—and she'd had no choice but to admit that what had happened had been very, very real.

And very, very amazing.

And very, very surprising.

And very, very satisfying.

And very, very odd.

Which maybe was why neither of them talked about it afterward. Because it had just been so out of character for either of them, so outside the normal boundaries of their friendship. Once they'd cleared the air that morning after waking, they'd taken separate showers and dressed in separate rooms, then had walked together—but not hand-in-hand—to a nearby café where they often went for coffee. They'd seated themselves at their usual table near the window and had chatted the way they normally did, about work and people they knew and books and movies and all the other usual things. Then they'd taken in a movie and dinner, as they so often did on the weekend, and then Turner had walked her home, as he always did after such a day.

But there had been a moment of awkwardness at her front door, when neither of them seemed to know what to do or say, or what the other expected. Finally, though, Turner had smiled and bent forward to brush a kiss over Becca's cheek, something he'd never done before, but which for some reason didn't feel awkward at all. And then he'd left, and she'd gone inside, and she'd wondered if things would ever feel normal between them again.

And although things hadn't quite felt normal over the last two weeks, they hadn't been as uncomfortable as Becca had feared they might. Gradually, she and Turner had fallen back into their usual routine, both at work and when they saw each other socially, and little by little, things had started to feel, if not normal, then at least okay. Like maybe they'd be normal again eventually. Just…not yet. In any event, neither of them had said another word about…

That Night.

Oh, certainly over the two weeks that followed That Night they both thought about That Night—at least, Becca thought about it, and she was reasonably certain Turner did, too, on account of that statistic about men not being able to go longer than a nanosecond without thinking about sex, and since That Night had consisted of some of the most amazing sex Becca had ever had, and since *any* sex is the best sex men have ever had, then Turner must have considered the sex of That Night to have been pretty freakin' phenomenal, which, of course, the sex of That Night *had* been—pretty freakin' phenomenal—and not just from a physical standpoint, either, so—

Where was she?

Oh, yeah. She'd been thinking about how neither of them had talked about That Night over the past two weeks, but both had probably thought about That Night over the past two weeks. A lot.

And neither of them had tried to initiate an encore performance. They seemed to be in a constant state of anticipation, as if each was waiting for a cue from the other, but neither seemed to want to be the one to offer the other a cue. It was almost as if they were afraid to. Though whether that fear was of rejection or the consequences of a repeat performance, both of which weighed heavily on Becca's mind, she couldn't rightly say.

There had been one definitively good thing to happen since That Night, though it had nothing to do with That Night. She and Turner both had been promoted to managers, effective the first of the year, and each would move into new offices at Englund Advertising. Naturally, they were delighted by the news, but Becca, for one, knew she would miss being able to glance up from her desk and see Turner sitting scarcely ten feet away from her, behind his own desk. They'd be in two different parts of the business now, he on one side of the building, she on another. So those shared smiles and the simple pleasure of his company during the day would be a thing of the past.

The thought of being so far away from him felt weird. As did the prospect of not working closely together anymore. As managers, they'd be making more money and have more benefits, but they wouldn't participate as much in the creative side of their work, where the two of them had been so good together. And although they'd be performing the same job, they'd each oversee different projects now. They wouldn't see nearly as much of each other at work as they used to.

Still, it *was* good news, Becca reminded herself. Right?

Now, as she stayed late at work on a snowy Friday evening two weeks after That Night, sitting alone in the boardroom of Englund Advertising and gazing out the windows that surrounded her on two sides at the rapidly falling snow outside, she was thinking about That Night again.

And she still didn't quite know what to make of it.

She should be working on the Bluestocking account, she told herself. Turner had offered to stay late with her, but she'd made him promise to go home. There was no reason they both needed to be here. She was just going over sales figures and projections that he'd already gone over himself, and tomorrow they were going to compare notes on the company's demographics and how they seemed to be affected from one area of the country to another. It was a one-person job, for the person who hadn't done it yet, and that person was Becca.

Besides, she'd kind of looked forward to being here by herself after hours. She was perfectly safe in the office this time of night, not to mention the place was quiet and peaceful and all hers. And the weather outside *was* frightful. The roads would be clear enough to travel later, when she was ready to go home, after the salt trucks had made their rounds, and she didn't relish driving while the snow was falling so thickly. As beautiful as it was out there, she'd just as soon wait until the storm had passed.

Still, she sighed with something akin to longing as she looked out the windows at the high-rise across the way, its offices lit up here and there from one floor to the next with the late-burning lamps of other late-working people. All around her, the Indianapolis skyline sparkled amid the fat, furiously falling flakes, as if some snow fairy jacked up on Ritalin had cast down fistfuls of diamonds along with the frantic flurries. Becca might as well have been the only human being allowed into this magical winter wonderland.

Suddenly, for no reason she could name, she felt very, very lonely.

She pushed the strange sensation away and went back to the figures that lay before her on the table. She wasn't sure how long she'd sat there studying them when she heard the buzzer that heralded the arrival of someone in the outer office. She wasn't alarmed by the sound, however, since the only people who had access this time of night were the security guards and a handful of other employees who had keys to the place. But when she heard Turner's voice greeting her softly from the boardroom door behind her, she smiled.

"Hi," she said as she turned in her chair.

He still wore his work clothes of earlier in the day, but they were rumpled and disarrayed, his white shirttail spilling free from the waistband of his dark blue corduroys, his necktie completely undone and hanging unfettered from a collar unbuttoned to the third button. But then, Becca's work clothes weren't any tidier than his were. Her slim, tobacco-colored skirt was wrinkled, her cream-colored blouse was unbuttoned at the cuffs and neck, not to mention untucked. She'd also discarded her jacket a long time ago and kicked off her shoes, as well, to get more comfortable.

Turner looked comfortable, too, she thought. And also pretty sexy.

And he was holding a bottle of scotch in one hand, two highball glasses in the other. Since she recognized the cobalt color of the latter from the bar on the first floor of the building they frequented, she assumed he'd acquired the scotch there, too. Which was some feat, since the bar didn't have a package license. He must have sweet-talked one of the bartenders into turning a blind eye.

Probably that bottle blonde named Jessica, Becca thought uncharitably. That tramp. She'd always made it clear she'd do anything for Turner. That tramp. She'd even crashed the office Christmas party last year with a sprig of mistletoe, Becca remembered, and she'd deliberately sought out Turner to corner him with it. That tramp.

Had she mentioned Jessica was a tramp?

But then, Turner wasn't with Jessica right now, was he? Becca reminded herself smugly. No, he was here with her.

"Thought you might like a nightcap, since you're going to be working late," he said. But he remained framed by the doorway, as if he were hesitant about entering the boardroom without her okay.

She smiled. "That would be great. Thank you."

With that, he smiled back, but his entry still seemed a little tentative. Nevertheless, he set the bottle and glasses down on the table and shrugged out of his jacket, tossing it over the back of a chair at the end.

"You always seem able to read my mind," Becca said as she watched him complete the action. "I was just thinking I should have taken this stuff home with me, so that I could at least relax in my jammies with a drink while I went over everything."

"And why didn't you take it home?" he asked as he unscrewed the cap of the bottle and poured a generous two fingers of the amber liquid into each glass.

She shrugged. "I didn't think I'd really go over them at home. I thought I'd probably turn on the TV or open a book instead. And I really need to get this stuff studied."

"Yes, you do," Turner agreed. "But there's no reason why you can't take a little break."

She nodded. "You're right. I've earned it."

She didn't mention that, so far tonight, she'd spent the bulk of her time staring out the window at the snow and thinking about him instead. A break was a break.

Turner extended a glass toward her, which she took gratefully, sipping the potent spirits carefully. She didn't usually drink her scotch straight up, so wasn't used to the heat of the liquor as it warmed her mouth and tongue and throat. She liked it, though. It reminded her of Turner's heat, when he'd set her on fire That Night. Which made it an even more welcome diversion.

"How come you're not at home?" she asked him.

He lifted one shoulder and let it drop, then gazed at the scotch as he swirled it around in his glass. "It was snowing when I got downstairs, so I went into the bar to have a drink and wait for it to ease up some. It never did, so I ordered something to eat, to wait for it to ease up some." He looked up at her and smiled. "It never did."

"I know," she told him. "I've been watching it for the last hour and a half, and it hasn't let up once."

Turner sipped his drink and lowered the glass to the table. "I knew you were still up here, so I thought, since we were both probably going to wait it out, we might as well wait together."

"Thanks," she told him. And she hoped he realized she was thanking him for a lot more than just the scotch and the company.

"You're welcome," he told her. "How much more do you have to go?" he asked, dipping his head toward the paperwork before her.

She sighed heavily. "Not too much," she hedged. She'd gone through more than half of it. "It's just not organized very well. Bluestocking should hire a new company to do their next demographic analysis."

"I thought it was a mess, too," he said. "So I broke it down myself, according to each product group."

Becca arrowed her eyebrows down in confusion. "What do you mean?" she asked.

He set his glass on the table and stood to move behind her, reaching past her to fan the papers out and rearrange them. And as he did, Becca became more aware of him, of his physical presence and the effect it had on her. As he moved in a thoroughly benign, completely nonsexual way, she couldn't help but be reminded of how he'd moved That Night—in an aggressive, totally sexual way. And something inside her kindled at the memory, the flames flickering higher with each passing second. She started noticing more about Turner—how he smelled and sounded—and when his arm accidentally brushed her shoulder, the heat inside her leaped higher.

"Here," he said as he finally finished his reorganization of the papers. He pointed at the first one, an action that left his chest pressing against her shoulder, and she swallowed hard as the heat inside her multiplied. "This is a list of all of Bluestocking's product categories," he continued, his voice and posture nothing but professional, his effect on Becca anything but. "Hosiery, bras, panties, yada yada yada."

He dropped his hand from the paper and straightened, which moved his body away from hers. But her awareness of him remained just as acute. She could still smell him and hear him and sense him, and she found herself wanting to reach behind herself to grab his hand and pull him forward again, so that his body was pressed to hers once more.

That she wanted him closer, she realized then, told her a lot. Maybe she did know how things stood between them. Or, at least, she knew how things stood with her. And maybe it was time for her to start thinking about that. To start focusing on what she *wanted*. Maybe she should stop fighting this thing and just *do* what she wanted to do. Right now. In this moment. And what she wanted to do, right now, in this moment, was stand up, turn around and drape her arms over Turner's shoulders, then cover his mouth with hers and see what developed. She'd worry about the rest of it later.

Without a word, she pushed her chair back from the table, an action that made Turner step backward to make room. Then she stood and pivoted, and silently met his gaze. He gazed back at her, his expression reflecting confusion mixed with…something else. Curiosity, maybe. Or anticipation. Or hopefulness. She wasn't sure.

"Is something wrong?" he asked. "Am I not explaining this well? Am I not making it clear?"

Well, no, actually, Becca thought, he wasn't being clear. But then, she hadn't been clear on too many things herself lately. Now, however, she had a chance to set that to rights.

Before she could say anything, though, Turner pointed to the papers he had taken such care to arrange, and continued as if she'd never moved.

"What I was going to add," he said, "and this will help it all make sense, I think, is that Bluestocking could have made it a lot easier on themselves and us if they'd just grouped all those foundation products together and headed it 'underwear' or something."

The fire that had been sizzling inside Becca suddenly exploded, heating her entire body, creating a sensation unlike anything she had ever felt before. Oh, no. Wait. She had felt it before. It was just like it had been That Night two weeks ago. And again at the meeting with the Bluestocking people before that. And again that night in her cubicle with Turner, when she'd suddenly wanted him—needed him—as she never had before.

"Kiss me," she told him. "Forget about the account and just…" She expelled a restless, needy sound. "I want you so bad, Turner. Right here. Right now. I'm tired of fighting it. Let's do it right here."

His eyes went wide. "Here?" he echoed. "Now?"

She nodded, curling the fingers of both hands over his shoulders, then added, "Fast. Hard."

He hesitated, opening his mouth as if he wanted to tell her something, then closed it again. Evidently making up his mind, though, he looped one arm around her waist to jerk her body against his, and cupped his other hand under her jaw, splaying his fingers wide. His forcefulness surprised her for a moment, sending a thrill of something dangerous and exciting shuddering through her. Then she smiled when she realized she felt kind of forceful, too. Gripping the front of his shirt with both hands, she yanked the fabric hard enough to tear the garment open wide. Then she buried her fingers in the dark hair on his chest, raking her nails lightly down his muscular torso.

· The fierceness of her response surprised him, too, she saw, but he grinned. "What if someone sees us?" he murmured as he dipped his head to press his forehead to hers. He dragged his fingers through her hair, anchoring his hands at the back of her head. "We're surrounded by windows on two sides. And there are still lights on in some of the offices across the street. There's still a light on in here."

"It's snowing too heavily," Becca countered, feeling a little breathless. "No one can see us through the windows."

"How do you know?" he challenged. "What if they can?"

She dropped her hand to his already hardening cock, rubbing her fingers shamelessly along the heavy length of him. "Then they're about to get a real show," she said.

And why did that make her feel even more aroused? she wondered. Ah, well. No matter. She had other things on her mind right now.

Turner evidently did, too, because he placed both of his hands on her shoulders and spun her slowly around, to face those very windows he had said he was so concerned about. Then he moved his hand to the back zipper of her skirt and tugged it slowly, slowly, oh, too slowly, down. As she flattened her palms against the big table that bisected the boardroom, she felt her skirt slide down over her hips and realized Turner wanted to move things along even faster than she did. When the tiny garment pooled at her feet, she kicked it aside, only to feel him press his entire body against hers. He snaked his arms around her waist and moved his hands to the buttons of her blouse, unfastening each in another leisurely, maddeningly slow motion. She shrugged her shoulders to discard it even as he was tugging it down her arms. Her bra disappeared next, then his hands were on her breasts, palming her sensitive flesh, cupping, weighing, squeezing, kneading, flicking the pads of his thumbs over her swollen nipples.

His hands moved lower, and he hooked his thumbs into the waistband of her panties, urging them down, and baring her ass completely. But he left the scrap of silk at her knees in a way that made her feel almost bound by it. When he began to rake his hands over the smooth skin of her bottom, Becca leaned forward, bending at the waist, gasping when her hot breasts came into contact with the cool surface of the table beneath her. She gasped again when Turner moved his thumbs to the elegant line bisecting her ass. Grasping her firmly in both hands, he opened her, then penetrated her shallowly with one thumb before scooting his other hand to her front to dip it between her legs. He furrowed one finger into the damp folds of flesh there, drawing a few slow circles before inserting his middle finger deep inside her. Then he pushed his body forward again, pressing his pelvis to her bottom, rubbing himself against her as he drove his thumb deeper inside her, too.

Becca cried out at the exquisiteness of the double penetration, instinctively pushing herself backward as she pressed against the table. She stretched her arms across its slick surface, reaching toward the other side, hoping to find purchase that would help her hang on. But she couldn't quite reach the edge, so she stretched her arms wide on each side, closing her eyes to enhance the sensation of Turner moving his finger and thumb inside her, and the friction of the table against her agitated breasts.

For a long time, he penetrated her that way, his breathing becoming as ragged and irregular as her own. Then, with agonizing slowness, he withdrew his thumb, and she heard the soft metallic sound of his belt unbuckling. With his other hand, he continued to finger her between her legs, penetrating her with a second digit, then a third, spreading them to increase the friction. She heard the rasp of his zipper, the soft whisper of fabric, and then he moved both of his hands to her waist as he buried his stiff cock deep, *deep* inside her.

Again, Becca cried out at the roughness of his thrust, at the way he filled her so thoroughly from behind. She was so wet and ready for him by the time he entered her that the size of him proved no problem at all. On the contrary, the size of him only enhanced the experience, because she felt parts of herself come alive she hadn't realized could feel. He stretched so deep into her that he seemed to become one with her, until she couldn't tell where her body ended and his began.

And as he pumped inside her, he moved both hands to her ass again, kneading the tender flesh, spreading it, closing it, opening it wide once more for an even deeper exploration than before. Again and again, Turner thrust into her with both his hard rod and his tireless thumb, until Becca feared she would shatter from the exquisite sensations pounding through her. She curled her hands into fists, cried out again and again as he claimed her, wondered deliriously how long the two of them could make this last.

Not long enough, she soon discovered. Because with each new thrust, Turner brought her closer to orgasm, and when he hurried his rhythm, he hurried her response, too. As one, both of them cried out at their climax, and he spilled himself hotly inside her.

For one long moment they both stilled, waiting for the tremors of their shared orgasm to subside, both of them struggling for breath and grappling for coherent thought.

Little by little, though, they remembered where they were, what they had been doing before they both succumbed to the fire burning inside them, and how they were supposed to be behaving. Becca felt Turner's hands open over her bare back, urging her to rise and turn around to face him. When she did, she found that he was only half-dressed, and that they were standing in the boardroom of their workplace, and that it was still snowing quite heavily outside.

Oh, yeah, she thought. She knew exactly how she was supposed to behave in a situation like this. Smiling, and still facing Turner, she sat down, bare-assed, on the table, gasping at the cold surface against her heated flesh. She placed her hands on his shoulders and pushed downward, and smart guy that he was, he knew to seat himself in the chair immediately behind him. Then he rolled it forward and curved his hands over her thighs, bending at the waist to lower his head as he settled her legs where her hands had been—on his shoulders. Without a word, without a glance, without a care, he moved his mouth to her inner thigh, to draw a long, slow, easy line there with his tongue.

Becca placed her hands behind herself on the table and threw her head backward, groaning when Turner finally, finally centered his attentions where she wanted them. Again and again he licked her wet flesh with the tip of his tongue, then flattened it for long, broad strokes of her. She felt the ripples of a second orgasm trembling low in her belly, and she closed her eyes to allow them their freedom. Turner sensed her readiness and increased his attentions, lapping her, sucking her and penetrating her as deeply as he could with his tongue. She tangled the fingers of one hand in his hair as her climax multiplied, and when he brought his hand into the action to finger her sensitive little clit, she cried out in its completion.

When she opened her eyes, she saw him watching her, smiling a salacious little smile.

"You are *so* sexy," he said.

She smiled back. "You make me sexy," she told him.

He shook his head. "No way. It's all from you, Becca. All of it."

"No one else has ever made me feel this way, Turner. Only you," she said. "Only you."

His expression changed at her declaration, but before Becca could identify quite how, he was reaching out to her with both hands, silently offering to help her down from the table. So she placed her hands in his and let him help her down, until her feet were on the floor again. But instead of moving to pick up her clothes, she leaned into Turner and covered his mouth with hers. He kissed her back, dropping his hands to her bottom and pushing her pelvis into his.

He was still hard as a rock, she noted. But he ended the kiss and said, "I imagine you'd like to get dressed and get back to work, otherwise we'll be here all night."

She smiled and said, "You're partly right."

He eyed her curiously. "What do you mean?"

"I'll get dressed," she told him. "But only because it's getting kind of cold in here."

"And work?" he asked.

She smiled again and tucked her hand inside his trousers, curling her fingers snugly over his staff. "What I have in mind won't be work for me at all," she told him. "And I think *you're* going to enjoy it a lot." She moved her hand up and down his cock, palming the ripe head with much affection. "And, although we might indeed be here all night, if you promise to help me with those Bluestocking figures," she said, "I promise I'll make it worth your while…."

IN THE WEEK THAT FOLLOWED, what Turner came to think of as The Great Boardroom Caper, he and Becca were scarcely out of each other's sight. Their days consisted of being at work and wanting to be at home, and their nights consisted of being at home and not wanting to go to work the next day. Because what they had discovered together at night made everything else seem inconsequential. Even the Bluestocking account, which they'd been so proud of themselves for winning, took a back seat to their newly discovered passion for each other. A distant back seat. Like in another car back seat. Another car in another city back seat. Another car in another city in another country back seat.

Um, what was in the back seat?

Well, Turner and Becca, at one point. And they'd also done it in the front seat. Not to mention their closet at work. And the park between their homes. And the ladies' room at the café where they enjoyed lunch—among other things. And once, in the laundry room of Turner's apartment building, where Becca experienced the pleasures of the spin cycle while sitting on the wildly vibrating washing machine, and then provided Turner with a new meaning for the words *rinse cycle*. Not to mention the words *permanent press*. And also *hand wash*. And *lay flat to dry*.

And not once did Becca express any regrets or misgivings about what they were doing. Whatever had confused her about this new aspect of their relationship, it was gone after that night in the boardroom. Neither of them questioned it. Both of them enjoyed it. They were insatiable after that night.

It was as if some monster had been unleashed in both of them that had to rampage all over town, setting fire to everything it encountered, before being satisfied. And speaking for himself, *everything* caught fire, and *nothing* was satisfied. Turner began to think maybe he and Becca were making up for lost time, that they should have become sexually involved in college that first time they'd had the chance, and that the fierceness of their responses to each other must be due to their denying themselves for so many years.

But it wasn't just Turner's physical desire and need for Becca that grew. His love for her grew, too, every time they made love. And he couldn't help thinking her feelings for him changed, too, during that time. They must have. Because no two people could respond to each other the way he and Becca did unless there was a deep, abiding affection underneath it all. And thinking, feeling, as he did, even if he never put voice to those thoughts and feelings, only made sex with her even better.

He was never happier to see the end of a Friday workday than he was that Friday after the boardroom incident. Where he and Becca normally worked a little past their five-thirty quitting time, that day they snuck out early, so eager were they to get home to an entire weekend together. And no sooner were they through Turner's front door than they went to work on each other's clothes, their mouths desperately exploring whatever part of each other they could reach, their hands and fingers tangling together as they tried to remove their own and each other's clothing.

Finally, though, Becca fell back onto his couch, completely naked, opening her legs in silent invitation. And when Turner made no move to join her, because he was still trying to undress, she smiled that seductive little smile that had driven him mad on so many occasions. As he watched her, she moved her hand between her legs, threading her fingers through the dark blond curls at their apex, until the middle one disappeared into the soft thatch. Then she inhaled a sharp gasp as she touched herself, closing her eyes at how good she made herself feel. She moved her other hand to her breast, circling her nipple with her index finger, and it was all Turner could do not to come right there, seeing what she was doing.

For long moments, he just watched her caress herself, becoming aroused as much by her facial expressions as by the movements of her hand. Because with each new stroke of her fingers against her pink, wet flesh, her face changed, color blooming on her cheeks, her teeth nipping at her lower lip, her tongue darting out to touch one corner of her mouth before disappearing again. And the sounds she made…

No longer able to tolerate even the small distance separating them, Turner knelt on the floor in front of her and gently pulled her hand away, kissing each fingertip in turn, sucking the middle one deep into his mouth to savor the taste of her that lingered there. She smiled as she watched him settle her hand to the side, then place both of his, palm out, against the insides of her thighs. And then he dipped his head toward the place she had just been touching, pushing her legs wider, opening his mouth against the melting core of her.

Again and again he licked her, laved her, loved her, teasing her first with the tip of his tongue, then tasting her with broad, flat strokes. Becca sighed and groaned with each new caress, tangling her fingers in his hair and pulling him closer still.

"Oh," she whispered. "Oh, Turner. Don't stop. I'm so close. Please. Don't stop."

He hurried the motions of his tongue then, his head nodding as he took the strokes high and low, growing more and more intoxicated on the scent and sound and taste of her. Her hips bucked against him, and he shoved his hands beneath the lower curves of her firm ass, lifting her closer to his mouth so that he could penetrate her now with his tongue. Over and over, he pleasured her that way, feeling the muscles in her buttocks tightening and straining as her need for satisfaction grew more intolerable. And then, suddenly, with a cry of outrageous exhilaration, she pushed herself upward one final time, her orgasm complete.

Turner moved his mouth to the insides of her thighs, kissing the hot, silky flesh there, dragging his tongue down to her knee and back again. The fingers tangled in his hair relaxed some, but her breathing came in ragged, irregular gasps for some moments more. Then she moved her hands to his shoulders, pulling him forward, a silent invitation to join her on the couch.

Just as he sat beside her, though, she dropped down to the floor, situating herself between his legs. She reached for his stiff rod, closing her fingers over the base of him, and bent her head to draw him toward her mouth. Just the sight of her slight fingers over his aroused flesh made him want to topple her flat on the floor and bury himself inside her. Before he had the chance, though, she touched the head of his shaft to her lower lip and darted her tongue out to taste him, and he stilled.

She was tentative at first, circling the head of his cock with the flat of her tongue, her fingers scooting up and down his shaft as if she wanted to explore every inch of him. Then she ducked her head lower, drawing him completely into her mouth, sucking him as she circled the sensitive hood with her tongue again.

"Oh, Becca," he half said, half groaned. "Oh, yeah…"

Emboldened by his reaction, she moved her fingers up and down him again, a delicious sort of friction that sent shock waves through his entire system. She bobbed her head slowly up and down, consuming more of him with each motion, until he felt the head of his shaft pressed hotly against the roof of her mouth. The pressure of her suction was agonizingly sweet, and her fingers wreaked havoc as they dipped between his legs to cup the rest of him in her palm. When she pulled his rod slowly from her mouth, he started to object, but the words were halted when she nipped the head lightly with her teeth, then laved the scant wound with her tongue.

She repeated the action a dozen more times, and each time, Turner cried out at the keen sensations that knifed through him. Finally, when he knew he was close to coming, he threaded his fingers into her hair and gently pulled her head away. And when she looked up at him, puzzled, her eyes so dark, so full of passion, he was very nearly overcome.

"I want to be inside you," he told her. "I don't think I'm going to last much longer."

She nodded silently and rose, but where he had been ready to move from the sofa and lay her on her back, she instead hooked one leg over both of his, straddling him. Gripping his shoulders, she moved herself over his straining shaft, then eased down slowly until he was deep inside her. Her position brought her breasts conveniently to the level of his face, and he eagerly leaned forward, sucking one rosy nipple deep into his mouth.

She began to move then, so he settled his hands on her waist to help her along, thrusting deeply into her, filling his mouth with her breast. As their pace quickened, so did Becca's cries, until with one final outburst, she settled herself hard in his lap. At the same time, Turner exploded inside her, filling her with his hot response as she spilled her own over him.

But their satisfaction was short-lived, because less than an hour later, Becca was at the center of the bed again, positioned on all fours at Turner's request, and he was kneeling behind her.

"Spread your legs more," he said roughly.

Becca did as he instructed, planting her knees farther apart on the bed, glancing back to watch him as he knelt between her legs.

"That's good," he said as he leaned over her.

He pressed his mouth to her ass, brushing his parted lips over the sensitive flesh, palming her, squeezing her, nipping her gently with his teeth. He cupped both hands over the breasts swinging beneath her, lifting them, separating them, squeezing them. Then he dipped his head between her legs and tongued her wet flesh, tracing with his finger the line bisecting her ass from where it began at the small of her back, down to that part of her that was so wet and ready for him.

Oh, Becca thought as he completed the action. Oh, it felt so good. The slow circular motion of his tongue against her clitoris was exquisite. She closed her eyes and let herself enjoy the languid, liquid sensations pouring through her, held her body completely still to let Turner go wherever he wanted to go next.

Where he wanted to go was inside her. Because he slid

his tongue into the damp, heated opening between her legs and pushed it inside her, moving it in and out in a slow, methodical fashion that left her feeling anything but slow or methodical.

"Oh," she said aloud this time. "Oh, that feels so good...."

"It's about to get better," he told her.

And before she could ask why, he was working his body under hers, positioning it in the opposite direction, so that his head was still between her legs, and her head...

Oh, my. What a prize she saw beneath her, situated perfectly for her to enjoy. Still bracing herself on all fours, she dipped her head down and covered Turner's shaft with her mouth, circling its tip with her tongue, exerting varying amounts of pressure as she drew him in and out. Vaguely, she heard him groan, the sound vibrating his tongue against her overly sensitized flesh, something that made her moan in response, inadvertently increasing his pleasure, too.

For long moments, they pleasured each other that way, their bodies jerking in time with their mouths, their passion rising with each new touch. But when Becca felt close to coming, she lifted her head from him and scooted forward, straddling Turner's middle, positioning herself over his thrusting rod. Her back to him, she lowered herself over him just as he settled his hands on her hips, and he filled her so full, he nearly split her in two. She bent forward a little to ease the pressure some, then decided she liked the pressure and straightened her body again. His hands on her hips clenched tighter and he bucked his hips upward, embedding himself even deeper inside her. Becca cried out, moving her hands to the twin spheres between his legs, something that made him buck upward again.

"Oh, yes," she whispered. "Do that again."

With great enthusiasm, he did as she told him, jerking his body upward again and again. Never in her life had Becca felt so complete. Never had she joined herself so completely to a man. In that moment, she could almost believe that she and Turner had fused into one being and that they would never be separated again. And then that keen, familiar sensation of pleasure began to coil tighter inside her, and she ceased thinking at all. After that, she could only feel. Turner inside her. Turner beneath her. Turner filling her hands, her body, her heart, and so much more.

With one final upward thrust, he felt as if he was deeper inside her than he had ever been before—physically, emotionally, in every way he could be—and he filled her up as he came. But after a moment, she felt him relax, and he withdrew from her—physically, at least. She turned and collapsed alongside him, opening her hand on his chest, loving the way his ragged heartbeat buffeted her palm.

She wanted to tell him something very important, but a deep, narcotic fatigue was trying to overtake her. It was right there at the very fringe of her brain, though, what she wanted to say, right there at the edge of her soul, pushing out of her heart. She wanted, no, needed, for him to know it. It was absolutely essential that he know how she felt.

"Turner..." she began softly. But her eyelids fluttered closed, and she gave in to the liquid, languid satisfaction purling through her body.

"What?" she heard him say, as if from a very great distance.

"Turner..." She tried again. "I think I..."

But that was as far as she got. She never quite made the

words leave her mouth, never quite said them aloud. So she never quite told him she was pretty sure she'd fallen in love with him.

12

As Turner exited the jeweler's shop on Main Street, he was clutching a little red bag that held a ring of which he was confident Becca would approve. He had looked at it before—several times, in fact—and had fantasized often about coming back to buy it for her. Now, like so many of his other fantasies of late, this one was a reality, too.

The ring was perfect for her. A single, flawless, square-cut white diamond—one carat, since she would consider anything larger than that too ostentatious—nestled in a filigreed white-gold setting. It was at once modern and old-fashioned, splashy and elegant, familiar and extraordinary. Just like Becca. Turner was thinking as he left the shop how much she was going to love the ring.

And he was thinking, too, about how much he loved Becca.

He had left her sleeping in his bed an hour ago, had snuck out without waking her, because he didn't want her to know where he was going. He'd stolen a moment to watch her sleep, and to think about how much—and how often—they'd enjoyed each other in the week following The Great Boardroom Caper. And even before that. The other times they'd made love, when they'd been so uncertain about the way their relationship had changed.

And even before *that*. Back before they'd become sexually involved. When they'd still been friends—but not. Because thinking back, Turner realized they'd always been a bit more than friends, even if they hadn't quite been lovers. They'd meant more to each other than most friends did, even friends who'd grown up together. They had a connection unlike any other, and it spanned decades.

Love, he realized now. That was what it was. That was what it had always been. Because he did love Becca. He had always loved Becca. He'd probably fallen in love with her in the first grade, before he'd even really understood what love was. Then again, maybe at that age kids had an even better understanding of love than grown-ups did—it was something pure and simple, something given without conditions or limits, something that would last forever. That would explain a lot about why Turner had never been able to love anyone except Becca.

But it was different now. It had changed in the last few weeks. Because now he understood that Becca loved him, too.

Oh, maybe neither one of them had said those three little words to each other yet. But they'd shown each other how they felt in infinite ways over the past month, many times. Nobody could make love with the abandon and abundance that they did unless there were some serious feelings involved. And nobody could enjoy it as much as they had unless the feelings involved were love. On both sides. Given and received. And last night, as she'd fallen asleep in his arms, she'd started to tell him something, something she'd seemed to be trying very hard to get out. And somehow Turner knew—he wasn't sure how he knew it, but he *knew*—she had been about to tell him she loved him.

Everything was perfect now. Everything was exactly as it should be. Or, at least, it would be. Today. After he got home. After he asked her what he wanted to ask her. And after she said yes.

He couldn't wait to tell her—and *show* her—how much he loved her. And he couldn't wait for them to start planning the rest of their lives together.

A consummate, absolute happiness wound through him as he thought about that. And so warm did his thoughts make him that he barely noticed the wicked wintry day into which he had walked. In response to the cold wind that whipped around him, he only jerked up the collar of his black wool coat and tugged on his black leather gloves. Below-freezing temperatures were nothing to him in his current state. He had thoughts of Becca and the life he wanted to build with her to keep him nice and toasty. He even smiled at the big, fat, furiously falling snowflakes, and silently bade them to continue, until they piled so high in the city that he and Becca would have an excuse to blow off work next week and spend it together in bed.

Naked, save for the square-cut, one-carat, filigreed-set diamond on her left ring finger.

Tonight, he thought. He would pop the question tonight. First he'd cook for her. Steaks, since he did those better than anyone in Indianapolis. Filet mignon, yeah. And he had a really nice bottle of pinot noir he'd been hoarding for a while now, waiting for a special occasion. What could be more special than asking the woman you loved to join her life to yours forever and ever and ever?

Man, he'd turned into a romantic sap over the last month, he thought, his smile feeling goofy as it curled his lips. And damned if he wasn't enjoying every minute of it.

Still thinking about Becca and the way she looked and sounded and smelled, and the way she was going to light up all over when she saw the ring, he almost didn't hear the feminine cries of "Turner! Oh, Turner! Hello! Turner!" until he had almost stumbled right over a slender woman in a gray wool coat, with a black beret perched atop her head.

It took him a moment to identify her, so wrapped up was he in his thoughts of—and plans for—Becca. But eventually, the woman's face registered in his muddled brain and he recognized her as the Amazing Dorcaso...uh, he meant Dorcas Upton, of course. The hypnotherapist he and Becca had seen weeks earlier.

"Oh, hi," he said as he reached out a hand to steady her. "Dorcas, right? How are you doing?"

"I was just going to ask you the same question," she told him.

She met Turner's gaze levelly and smiled what he could only call a "knowing" smile. What she might know that he didn't, however, he couldn't have said.

"How are you and Becca doing?" she asked.

He shrugged philosophically. "Actually, Dorcas, I have to be honest with you. The session Becca and I had with you didn't work for us at all."

The hypnotherapist's smile fell. "Oh, dear. The two of you still aren't making love?"

"Oh, we're making love," he said enthusiastically, without thinking. "All the time, in fact. We just never quit smoking." Then the gist of her question hit him, and he frowned. "Wait a minute. Why did you ask me that? That was a really personal question."

She eyed him with confusion. "Turner, why did you and your wife make an appointment with me?"

"Becca's not my wife," he said, feeling even more puzzled. *Well, not yet, anyway,* he added to himself. But he didn't want to break the news to anyone just yet. In spite of the humongous strides forward his relationship with Becca had made, the two of them would probably need some time to get used to the idea of being married themselves before revealing their intentions to anyone else.

Now Dorcas eyed him with something akin to horror, and Turner grew downright bewildered. He was about to ask her if there was something wrong, but she spoke again before he could put voice to the question, asking him a question of her own. But it didn't make any more sense than the one about Becca being his wife did.

"Turner, what's your last name?"

She should already know that, he thought. And even if she didn't remember it, what difference did it make now? In spite of his confusion, however, he told her, "McCloud. Why?"

"And Becca's last name?" she asked without answering.

"Mercer."

The color went right out of Dorcas's face then, and her eyes fluttered closed and stayed that way for a moment. Turner honestly feared she was about to faint, and was relieved when she opened her eyes again. But her color was still off, as if she were becoming gravely ill about something.

"And why did the two of you make an appointment with me?" she asked again.

Oh, now, she really ought to know that, he thought. It couldn't have been more than a month ago that he and Becca had gone to see her. If she recognized him in a crowded street and remembered his first name, she should certainly recall the circumstances of their initial meeting.

"To quit smoking," he told her.

Her mouth fell open, but no words emerged.

Turner's puzzlement turned into something else then, something he didn't want to put a name to, but something that felt very much like fear. "Why are you asking me this stuff?" he asked. "What the hell is going on?"

Instead of answering him, though, she only muttered, very softly, "Oh, dear."

"Dorcas?" Turner prodded.

"Tell me something, Turner," she began again, still offering him no explanation for her line of questioning.

"I've already told you a lot of somethings," he pointed out, biting back his irritation. He didn't like it when people played games with him. Especially when he didn't know the rules they were playing by. "But you're not telling me what *I* want to know."

She ignored his comment. "Were you and Becca sexually involved before coming to see me?"

"No," he answered without thinking. "We were just friends." Well, Becca was just friends, he amended to himself. Dorcas didn't have to know anything more about that. She didn't have to know about any of this. None of this was her business. So why was she going on about it?

"But you are sexually involved now," she said.

He nodded, still not sure why he was continuing with the conversation.

"And when did that begin?" she asked.

He thought back. That first time Becca had tried to get jiggy with him had been during the week before they made their pitch to win the Bluestocking Lingerie account, he recalled. Which had also been the week they saw Dorcas. Yeah, that was right. In fact, that first time happened the day after their session with Dorcas. Hmm. How about that? What a coinci—

No. No, no, no, no, no, he thought. *Nein. Nyet.* No way, José. The two events couldn't possibly be related. That was just nuts.

In spite of that, he told her, "The first time happened the day after our session with you."

She closed her eyes again, but this time color flooded her face.

"Dorcas?" Turner asked warily. "Is there something wrong?"

She sighed and opened her eyes again. "I'm afraid so."

And there was something about a hypnotherapist one hadn't quite trusted, but whom one had seen reluctantly anyway, telling one there was something wrong that sent a cold shiver down one's spine.

"Dorcas," he said softly, making himself voice the question to which he was pretty sure he didn't want to know the answer, "did you try to help me and Becca quit smoking?"

After a moment's hesitation, she shook her head. "No. I mistook you for an earlier appointment who I now realize never showed up. At the time, I thought my quit-smoking appointment was the no-show. Now, however, I realize that was you and Becca. You arrived early for your appointment, didn't you?"

Wordlessly, Turner nodded.

In response, Dorcas only looked more concerned.

He eyed her warily. "And this earlier appointment you mistook us for," he said. "What was it they wanted to be hypnotized for?"

Dorcas hesitated again, then, very softly, very slowly, she told him, "They were a newlywed couple. And they were having problems with…" She inhaled a deep breath and released it slowly. "They were having problems with…consummating their marriage."

"Meaning?" Turner asked, a sick feeling rolling into his belly.

"They were having trouble getting over their shyness and inhibitions about making love. Three weeks after their wedding, they still hadn't had sex. They wanted me to hypnotize them and help them get over their inhibitions."

Turner was certain he must have misunderstood. How could anyone need to be hypnotized for something so lame? "I'm sorry?" he said. "Could you say that again?"

"Although this couple had been married for weeks," Dorcas repeated, "they weren't able to have sex because they were both too modest and fearful about the sex act."

Turner let that sink in for a minute, then said, "And you helped them—or, at least the people you thought were them, which were actually me and Becca—get over that modesty and fear?"

"Yes," she said.

"And how did you do that, Dorcas?"

She inhaled another one of those deep breaths, again exhaling it slowly. "By planting a posthypnotic suggestion in both of you that every time you heard a certain word, you would be overcome with sexual desire for each other, and that you would have no fears or inhibitions about the frequency or adventurousness of sex."

This time it was Turner's eyes that fluttered closed, as he was hit by a barrage of realizations he really didn't want to face. "And what word was that?" he asked.

"Underwear," Dorcas told him.

"Underwear," he repeated. A word that had come up

often once he and Becca had landed the Bluestocking Lingerie account. Right after seeing Dorcas Upton.

Oh, God...

"Are you telling me," he said, amazed he could even find his voice, let alone string words together, "that the only reason Becca and I have been making love this past month is because we both keep hearing the word *underwear*?"

It was a dumb question. Turner knew the answer before Dorcas even gave it to him. Or, at least, part of the answer. *He* hadn't been making love to Becca because of any word he heard. *He'd* been making love with Becca because he loved her. Completely and irrevocably. Till death do him part. But Becca...

He tried to remember what was going on that first time she'd come on to him with such surprising enthusiasm. It had been that evening in her cubicle, when they were working on the pitch for Bluestocking. What had he said just before she unbuttoned her blouse and dumped herself into his lap? What had they been talking about?

Think, Turner, think...

The slogan, he remembered. They'd been trying to come up with a slogan, and they hadn't been having any luck. And he'd been tired and irritable, and he'd been about to give up. And then he'd said... What had he said...? Something about how he couldn't believe they were going to so much trouble just to sell some dumb lingerie. No, wait. Not *dumb*. He'd used the word *stupid*. And not *lingerie*, either. He'd said he couldn't believe they were going to so much trouble just to sell some stupid *underwear*.

Oh, God...

But the second time, he hurried on, not wanting to accept anything at face value. What had happened then? It had been right after the presentation of their pitch to the Bluestocking people. Oh, man, no way could he remember what had been said then. There had been a lot of people in the room, and they'd all been talking at once. Still, it was a good bet the word *underwear* had come up in discussion at least once.

Oh, God...

But that third time, he hurried himself forward again, had been at their boss's house the following weekend. And that had been a high-society party. Ain't no way anyone could have been talking about underwear there, he tried to reassure himself. And just before Becca had come on to him that night, they'd both been talking to their boss. And Englund had said... *What?* Turner thought, trying to remember. Something about the presentation the week before, and something about his and Becca's bonuses, and how they'd be pleased with what they found in their Christmas stockings this year, in addition to—

All the free underwear either of them could ever use.

Oh, God...

He thought about all the other times he and Becca had been together. And just about every time, the Bluestocking Lingerie account came into play. Even if he couldn't remember exactly what was said, it was a safe bet that the word *underwear* had come up prior to Becca's sudden interest in having sex.

It was true. Becca had been coming on to him not because she cared about him that way or because she was turned on by him. And not because the two of them had been working on a racy-lingerie campaign. It hadn't even been because she was stressed out and working under pressure and not thinking straight. It was because she'd been told by a hypnotist that when she heard a certain word, she'd want to have sex. Hell, for all Turner knew, she would have responded to Robert Englund himself if it had been their employer with her on those occasions instead of Turner.

She hadn't been making love to him because she loved him, he realized. She'd been making love to him because a certain word made her horny. That was all.

But if they'd both been hypnotized, which Dorcas had insisted they were at the time, then why hadn't he responded to the word, too? Turner asked himself. That first time with Becca, he'd been turned on, sure, but he was in a perpetual state of arousal around her. When she'd initially come on to him that first time, he'd thought she was joking, and he'd done his best to tamp *down* his desire for her. If he'd been affected by the posthypnotic suggestion, then he would have been all over her, wouldn't he? But there had been a lot of hesitation on his part, and not just that first time, either. Why hadn't he been as turned on by the word *underwear* as she had been?

Not all people are able to be hypnotized. And of those who are able to be hypnotized, not all respond to hypnotherapy.

Dorcas's disclaimer from that day in her office came back to him then, and Turner understood. She may have put him under, but the posthypnotic suggestion hadn't taken for him. It had worked for Becca, but it hadn't for him. So *his* response to *her,* at least, had been genuine. Not that he needed reassurance about that. He already knew he'd been making love to Becca because he loved her. She just hadn't been making love to him for the same reason.

"Turner?" he heard Dorcas ask now.

But her voice seemed to be coming from a million miles

away. And he had no idea how to respond to her. Too many thoughts were whizzing through his head at the moment, ricocheting off each other and crashing into each other, and mixing with each other, until he couldn't begin to figure out what he was thinking. What he was feeling.

Oh, wait. Yes, he could, too, figure out what he was feeling. Bad. Really, really, really *bad*.

"Turner?" he heard Dorcas say again.

But he only shook his head numbly and told her, "I gotta go."

"Turner, wait," she said, curling her fingers over his forearm. "There's something you need to know."

"No, I gotta go, Dorcas," he repeated, gently shaking her off. He took a few steps backward. "I'm late for… something."

"But—"

"Really late," he assured her, completing a few more steps.

"But, Turner—"

"Later than I realized," he said. "I really gotta go."

And without awaiting a reply from her, not that any reply was necessary—or even forthcoming, because all Dorcas kept saying was his name over and over again—Turner pivoted around and made his way down the street in the snow, the red jeweler's bag still dangling from his fingertips. The bag that held the ring that was so perfect for Becca.

Too bad the guy carrying it couldn't say the same thing about himself.

WHEN HE ARRIVED BACK at his apartment, Becca wasn't there, but he found a note on the table telling him she'd gone to her own place to take care of a few things, and that she'd be back by dinnertime. So Turner put the little red bag holding the ring on a shelf in his bedroom closet—way in the back, where he wouldn't have to look at it until it was time to return it, and flopped onto the bed that Becca hadn't bothered to make. The bed that still smelled like her and their recent coupling. The bed he would never be able to sleep in again without thinking of her and all the things they'd shared together.

And not just the sex things, either. Everything else, too. The fun they always had together. The way they were so comfortable together. How they could say anything to each other without fear that the things said would be misconstrued or used as a weapon.

And he thought about what Dorcas had said, too, and tried to make better sense of it. Not that the sense he made was better in any way. He'd liked it more when he was confused and befuddled and none too sure about what was going on. Now that he was mulling things over and figuring out what was what, he felt like crap.

Becca didn't love him. Becca had never loved him. If Dorcas had never planted that posthypnotic suggestion in Becca's brain, she and Turner never would have created the sparks they'd been creating together. They'd still be just friends. Well, Becca would still be just friends. And Turner would still be carrying a torch for her that was in no danger of ever going out.

Now they might not even be friends again, he realized. Once Becca knew what was going on, once she realized the real reason she'd been behaving the way she'd been behaving, she was going to feel pretty embarrassed. Worse than embarrassed. Horrified. She might never want to see him again once she knew the truth. He might lose her for good.

How was he going to explain this to her? Because he *was* going to have to explain this to her. She'd have to go back to see Dorcas so that the hypnotherapist could rehypnotize her and excise the posthypnotic suggestion that had her jumping into his arms every time she heard the word *underwear*. Right? He had to tell Becca the truth because that would be the moral, ethical, decent thing to do. Right? That's what a friend would do. Right?

He actually had to pause a minute to think about that. Maybe…

Maybe nothing, he told himself. What the hell was he thinking, wanting to keep Becca under the influence just so she'd keep making love with him? Had he really sunk so low?

We-ell…

He had to tell her, he insisted to himself again. And he had to do it as soon as possible. Tonight. He had to tell her tonight. Instead of proposing to her, he'd tell her what had really happened in the hypnotherapist's office that day. That had they not seen Dorcas, they'd still be going along with their usual lives, being friends, not lovers. It was only through hypnotherapy that she'd found something more in him to respond to than she had before. It certainly hadn't been because she was in love with him.

Oh, but, hey, on the upside, maybe they could try hypnotherapy with Dorcas again to quit smoking and have it work this time….

Small comfort, he thought. Hell, no comfort. All that mattered was that he and Becca wouldn't be making love anymore. And once she realized what had been going on, she'd probably never want to see Turner again. It would be too awkward. Too weird. This was going to ruin their friendship for good. But then, after having experienced with Becca what he had over the past month, he didn't think he could go back to being friends again, either. Not the way it had been with them before. Now that he knew what he'd be missing, now that he'd experienced for himself just how amazingly good it could be with her, it would be impossible for him to be around her for any length of time and not start wanting her—badly—again.

She wouldn't want to be his friend, because she'd be too embarrassed. And he wouldn't want to be hers, because he was too much in love.

Damn, he thought as he stared blindly up at the ceiling and saw nothing. Damn, damn, damn, damn, damn.

BECCA WAS FRESH OUT OF the shower, wrapped in a flowered silk robe and towel-drying her hair when she heard her doorbell ring. She smiled. Turner. She just knew it was him. It was weird, but lately, she felt as though she could sense him whenever he came within fifty feet of her. She'd become that in tune with him.

She still marveled at how their friendship had slipped into so much more over the past few weeks, but she couldn't help wondering now why she had resisted him for so long. She'd been so afraid sex would complicate everything in their friendship and mess it all up, but sex had just made everything even better. It was amazing how much better. She and Turner together were like magic. When they made love, it was as if someone had choreographed the act for them, as if they were performing an intimate duet the steps of which they knew by heart. There was no awkwardness, no fear, no worry. They were just naturals together.

Which wasn't to say that the sex had been predictable or unvarying or overly comfortable. On the contrary, she'd never realized how adventurous and insatiable she could be when it came to sex. But whenever she was around Turner for any length of time, she just couldn't resist him.

Resist him? she echoed to herself, biting back a chuckle. Man, she was all over him. Never in her life had she been so eager to initiate sex with a man the way she was with Turner. She wasn't sure what had finally opened her eyes, but she never wanted to go back to being just friends with him again. Because now she realized what she felt for him was so much more than friendship. What she felt for him was—

Well. Too new for her to really voice it just yet, even to herself. But it was something special. And it was something that would last forever. For now, though, she would keep it to herself.

This new direction into which their relationship had moved felt too right, too perfect to mess with it. She was even beginning to think in terms of making it permanent, it was that good. The thought of spending the rest of her life with Turner seemed so obvious, so logical. Not that she hadn't planned to spend the rest of her life with him in the first place, but she'd always figured that someday the two of them would meet people and marry and go their separate ways in that regard. They could still see each other with their spouses. Maybe even someday their kids would be friends. Now, though, she saw how ridiculous such an idea was. How she and Turner could ever commit to anyone besides each other was laughable in the extreme. The two of them were too great together, in every way that mattered, for them to be apart. Weird how it had taken her so long to realize that.

Out of habit, she peered through the peephole before opening the door, and saw Turner standing on the other side. Evidently he was too impatient to wait for her to come back to his place, impetuous boy that he was. Though the fish-eye lens distorted his appearance, she could make out his attire of blue jeans, hooded black sweatshirt and the disreputable-looking denim jacket he often wore. Clearly, he was planning for an evening in. Which, of course, was fine with Becca. She didn't have any big desire to go out anywhere. And not just because of the weather, either, she realized with a smile. Staying in on a snowy night with Turner sounded like quite a delectable way to pass the time. Maybe they'd get lucky and the power would go out, and they'd have to stay very, very close in order to keep warm.

As if they needed a power outage to do that.

She slung her towel over her shoulder with one hand as she opened the door with the other. She was smiling, leaning forward to give him a kiss hello, but the expression on his face stopped her before she even got started. He looked like a man who'd just lost his best friend.

"What's wrong?" she asked, her smile falling.

"We need to talk," he said without preamble. Or without greeting, for that matter.

She stepped to the side in a silent invitation for him to enter, but he didn't move an inch from where he stood. He only continued to stand with his hands stuffed deep in the pockets of his jeans, scowling. Unbidden, an eerie chill seeped into Becca's belly.

"Aren't you going to come in?" she asked.

For a moment, he continued to just stand there, gazing at her in a way that only compounded the chilliness inside her. Finally, though, he shook his head. "I can't stay," he replied quietly.

"Why not?" she demanded. Not that they'd made any firm plans for the evening, but it was pretty much a given that they'd spend the weekend together. And if he couldn't stay, then why had he come in the first place? Especially in weather like this? If he needed to tell her something, he could have picked up the phone and called her.

Instead of answering her question, Turner asked one of his own. "Remember when we went to see the hypnotherapist? Dorcas Upton?"

Becca nodded. "Sure. It was only a few weeks ago."

"Well, I ran into her today downtown," he stated.

"So that's where you ran off to," Becca said. "Why did you need to go downtown?"

Instead of answering that question, either, Turner continued. "Dorcas asked me something really weird, and I couldn't figure out why, and then one thing led to another, and—" He halted abruptly, his gaze glancing off of Becca's face now to focus on something over her left shoulder. "And she told me something that you need to know about, too."

Becca frowned in confusion, wondering what Dorcas Upton had to do with anything. "Turner, what are you talking about?" she asked.

He inhaled a deep breath and released it slowly, still looking over her shoulder instead of at her face. "Becca, when she put us under, she thought we were other people."

"Other people?" she echoed. "But why?"

"Because we were so early for our appointment," he told her. "She thought we were *late* for an *earlier* appointment, one she had with a married couple who never showed up. So when she hypnotized us and gave us a posthypnotic suggestion, it wasn't to quit smoking, the way we wanted, it was to help this other couple—this married couple—she thought we were instead."

"But that's great," Becca said. "That explains why we're still smoking. We can go back and try again." And then the rest of Turner's admission hit her. "Wait a minute, though. If she didn't hypnotize us to quit smoking, then what did she hypnotize us for?"

Turner's gaze darted back to Becca's again, long enough for two bright spots of color to blossom on his cheeks, then flickered away again. "Like I said, she thought we were a married couple," he said, though what difference that should make, she couldn't imagine. "A *newly* married couple who were having trouble, um, consummating their marriage."

Becca narrowed her eyes at him. "Meaning?"

He sighed heavily again, and what he said next came out in a rush of words so hurried that it took a couple of minutes for them to register. "Dorcas thought you and I were newlyweds who wanted to have wild, passionate sex, but we were too shy and inhibited and scared to do it, and we needed to get past our shyness, inhibitions and fear so we could do it, so she gave us both a posthypnotic suggestion that whenever we heard the word *underwear* we'd be overcome with desire for each other, and jump into each other's arms and have wild, passionate sex, so the only reason you've been having sex with me lately is because of some subconscious trigger Dorcas planted in your brain, and it isn't because you…" He paused for just a moment, then concluded, "It isn't because of anything else."

Slowly, understanding crept up on Becca until it dawned like a good solid blow to the back of her head. Dorcas hadn't hypnotized them to quit smoking, she repeated to herself, which would explain why the two of them were still smoking. But she *had* hypnotized them to be turned on by each other, which would explain why—

No, she immediately told herself. That didn't explain anything. How could she have been hypnotized to behave the way she had, to react to Turner as strongly as she had been reacting to him? Yes, her response to him had been sudden, and yes, it had been surprisingly strong. But that was just the point. Her emotions and responses to Turner had felt so real. Had *been* so real. How could they have been created by a posthypnotic suggestion?

For the past couple of weeks, she'd begun to suspect she was falling in love with him, and *that* was why she'd been behaving the way she had been. That somehow, she'd loved him for years, but for some reason had only just recently allowed herself to accept it. Who knew what caused people to finally understand something they should have comprehended all along?

Well, in this case, she thought, evidently it was a post-hypnotic suggestion that did it. Which meant her feelings for Turner couldn't be genuine at all. Was that possible, though? Could it really all have been nothing but a ruse? Surely not….

"But that's…" she began. Unfortunately, she had no idea what to say after that. It was crazy. It was nuts. It made no sense.

But the more she thought about it, the more sense it began to make. The first time she'd felt so drawn to Turner, that night when the two of them had been working late in her cubicle, she'd been puzzled to no end about what had made her come on to him the way she had. One minute she'd been frustrated by the Bluestocking pitch, and sex had been the last thing on her mind. The next minute, she'd looked up at Turner and wanted nothing more than to be naked with him, writhing on top of her desk, with him buried deep inside her. What could have caused such an immediate and unexplainable change in her? Had he uttered the word *underwear*? Had she? She couldn't remember now. But it was certainly likely, considering the campaign the two of them had been working on.

Was it really possible? she asked herself again, still unable to quite believe it. Could that be why it had happened? Because Dorcas had given her a subconscious desire for Turner that only came to the fore under the right stimulus?

Then something else hit her. Turner had been there in the hypnotherapist's office that day, too. He'd been put under the influence the same way Becca had been. He'd heard the same things coming from Dorcas's mouth that she had. So he must have been making love to her for all the same reasons she had been making love to him, right? He'd only been responding to her because of that same posthypnotic suggestion, right? He'd heard the word *underwear* whenever she had, and he'd reacted to that and not to Becca, right? So he couldn't be any more in love with her than she was with him, right?

Right?

"But, Turner," she said, still trying to make sense of everything and not having much success. "You've been operating under the same conditions, haven't you? I mean, we were both under that day, and Dorcas gave us both the same posthypnotic suggestion. So you've been making love to me for the same reason, haven't you?"

In response to her question, Turner did look at her again,

full on. But it was in a way she'd never seen him look at her before, with an expression that was all wistful and poignant and melancholy. And only then did Becca begin to fully understand what was inherent in that look.

Oh, no, she thought. He couldn't be. Not Turner. It wasn't possible. He couldn't be in love with her. Not in some un-posthypnotic way. Could he?

"Turner?" she prodded again.

This time, in response to her question, he nodded. And, his gaze still fixed on hers, he confirmed, "Yeah, I love you, Becca. Honestly. Truly. I always have. Even before we went to see Dorcas. Back in college. Back in high school. Hell, back in second grade. I've always loved you. And I always will."

His declaration left her speechless. She had no idea what to say.

So Turner continued, "Even though Dorcas did hypnotize me that day, for some reason, the suggestion didn't take for me. It doesn't matter what word I hear when I'm around you. I want you. In the most basic, most intimate, most loving way there is. I always have. I just never told you how I feel, because I was afraid you wouldn't want to be around me if you knew. You always said you wanted us to be friends and nothing more. But, then, over the past few weeks, with all the time we spent together, and the way we—"

He halted, closed his eyes for a minute, took another deep breath and tried again. "I started to think that maybe you loved me, too," he told her, opening his eyes once more to study her. "But it's all been a Vegas lounge act. It's all been a big joke. A big, fat, stupid joke. And the joke's on me. Pretty funny, huh?"

Becca had no idea what to say to that, either. No idea

what to do. No idea what to feel. This was just too much. Too much for her to take in at once. In a few minutes' time, she'd lost Turner, the love she had for him and any future she'd been thinking might lie ahead for the two of them. All because of something she still wasn't sure she understood.

When she said nothing in response to his confession, only continued to gaze dumbly back, he nodded slowly, silently, and turned to walk away. Becca told herself to call him back, to tell him that they needed to talk more about this, but at that point, she truly had no idea what to say to him.

So she let him go, watching helplessly as he made his way down the hallway toward the elevator at the end. And she watched, too, as he extended a lethargic hand to push the button that would summon the elevator. And she watched as he stepped aboard when the metal doors slid open. Never once did he turn around, however. Not even to push the button so the elevator would take him down to the first floor. He waited until the doors closed on his rigid figure, because he obviously didn't want to have to look at Becca again.

Ever? she wondered. Would he never want to see her again after today?

And although she wanted answers to all the questions zinging through her brain, the answer for that last one was the one she feared the most.

13

BECCA SKIPPED OUT ON WORK the following Monday. She called the office to tell them she'd come down with a bug, completely unconcerned about the lie. Some things were more important than work, after all. And when the receptionist at Englund Advertising told Becca that Turner was out, too, in a tone of voice that more than hinted at her belief that the two absences were connected, it was all Becca could do not to agree with the woman. She just wished the reason really was what the receptionist suspected. That Becca and Turner were together, taking the day off so that they could steam up the sheets and thumb their noses at the rest of the world, including their employer.

She'd spent Sunday trying to sort everything out, had looked at the situation from every way she could think to look at it. And although a lot of stuff still didn't make sense, there were two things she knew unequivocally. Number one, the feelings she'd discovered for Turner couldn't possibly be the result of any posthypnotic suggestion. And number two, the feelings she'd discovered for Turner were indeed love. The kind of love that bound two people together forever. As for the rest of it…

Well. That was why she'd taken the day off.

She made it to Dorcas Upton's office downtown in even

better time than she had on her first visit with Turner, not caring that she didn't have an appointment. She'd camp out in the hypnotherapist's office all day if the woman was booked solid. Becca wasn't leaving until she had some answers. But when she told the receptionist to ask Dorcas if she could fit her in, the hypnotherapist herself came into the outer office to usher Becca inside.

She still looked like a school librarian, Becca thought as she followed Dorcas to her office. Today, though, the other woman was a study in gray, her slim wool skirt stopping at her knees, under a charcoal tweed blazer donned over a pale gray blouse. Her hair was wound atop her head in the same sort of knot she'd worn before, and the black half-glasses sat perched on her nose. Her professional attire was at odds with Becca's casual dress. She herself had thrown on the first pair of jeans she found in the drawer, along with a slouchy blue sweater and her battered bomber jacket.

"I am so glad to see you, Becca," Dorcas said as she closed her office door behind them. "I was going to call you myself this morning as soon as I had a free moment. I'm so sorry about what happened with you and Turner."

"Just what did happen, anyway?" Becca asked.

The hypnotherapist explained exactly what Turner had already told her, but with more detail—and more apology—until Becca had no choice but to accept that her worst suspicions were confirmed. She really had only responded to Turner sexually because of the instructions Dorcas had fed to her while she was in an altered state. Her reaction to him hadn't been genuine at all. She hadn't been making love with him because of any honest emotional response, but because she'd heard a word spoken aloud. And it had been a silly word, at that.

So that kinda sucked.

"But, Becca," Dorcas added quickly after concluding her explanation, "there's something very, very important that you need to know about hypnosis."

"What's that?" Becca asked halfheartedly. Frankly, she didn't want to know anything more about hypnosis. What she did know had already bummed her out really badly.

Dorcas leaned forward, folding her elbows carefully on her desk and weaving her fingers together. "Whatever has happened between you and Turner since our session," she said, "it was bound to happen eventually, with or without hypnosis."

Becca studied her through narrowed eyes. "What makes you say that? Turner and I were just friends before we came to see you."

"Were you?"

There was something about the way Dorcas voiced the question that put Becca on the defensive. "Yes," she said tersely. "We were just friends. We'd been friends since elementary school. Nothing more."

Then she remembered what Turner had told her Saturday, and realized that wasn't true. Not for him, anyway. For herself, though, it was. Wasn't it?

"You'd never been attracted to each other before coming to see me?" Dorcas asked. "Sexually, I mean?"

Becca opened her mouth to say of course not, but hesitated. There had been those few—very few—occasions when the two of them had gotten a little closer than "just friends" normally did. But on those occasions, there had been other factors at play. Overactive teenage hormones, for instance. Or too much spiked eggnog. Things that messed with an otherwise rational mind. Had they been thinking clearly, Becca and Turner never would have fooled around the way they did. And besides, they'd always stopped before they went all the way.

"Well, there were a couple of times when maybe we were attracted to each other," she told Dorcas reluctantly. "Sexually, I mean. But we never actually had sex. It was just a few kisses. A little groping. It didn't last long."

Dorcas nodded slowly, seeming to find this information a lot more interesting than Becca did. "And what made the two of you stop before actually having sex?" she asked.

"I made it stop," Becca told her. "Because I came to my senses and realized what a bad idea it would be."

Now Dorcas smiled. The sort of smile, Becca couldn't help thinking, that indicated she was very pleased with Becca's answer. All she said, though, was, "I see."

"No, I don't think you do," Becca told her, feeling defensive again for some reason. "What's been happening between me and Turner the past few weeks never would have happened if I'd been in my right mind."

Dorcas studied her thoughtfully, long enough that it began to make Becca feel a little edgy. Finally, though, she started talking again. "Just because someone is hypnotized, Becca, doesn't mean they can be made to do—or feel—something they wouldn't otherwise do—or feel—if they *weren't* hypnotized."

Now Becca studied the hypnotherapist thoughtfully right back. "What do you mean?"

Dorcas leaned back in her chair, obviously feeling more relaxed about matters now. "I mean that the greatest hypnotist in the world can't make someone do something or behave in a manner that that person wouldn't normally do or behave in while *not* hypnotized. While in their right mind, you might say."

"Go on," Becca said softly.

"It's impossible," Dorcas said, "to coerce someone hypnotically to behave in a way they would find morally, ethically or personally offensive when *not* hypnotized. Which is why a hypnotist can't *make* someone rob a bank, say, or commit a murder, or be a traitor to one's country. If the person under hypnosis is a moral person, he or she can't be made to do any of those things." She met Becca's gaze pointedly as she added, "So a woman under hypnosis could never be compelled to have sex with a man whom she had no desire to have sex with in what you call her 'right' mind."

"Which means…" Becca began, feeling both hopeful and fearful. Not to mention more than a little creeped out.

"Which means," Dorcas finished for her, "if you've been having sex with Turner, it's not because you were hypnotized into doing it. It's because on some level, you've wanted—very much—to have sex with him, anyway. Otherwise, the posthypnotic suggestion wouldn't have worked for you. All the hypnosis did was help you move past whatever fears and inhibitions have been holding you back. For the past few weeks, all you've been doing is something you've been wanting to do all along on some subconscious level. If you're having sex with Turner, Becca, it's because you *want* to. And you probably have for some time now. You were just too scared to act on your desires."

Becca thought about what Dorcas said for a long time without speaking, and suddenly, it was as if a little light went on in the back of her brain. Actually, she realized, she *hadn't* been making love with Turner because she wanted him. Well, not *just* because of that. It was more because she *loved* him. And she probably had for a long time now. She had just been too scared to acknowledge it.

Her feelings *were* genuine, just as she'd told herself they were. And if her feelings were genuine, then her love for Turner must be genuine, too.

Holy moly, she thought. All this time, she'd been in love with him and had never even realized it. She'd been too afraid to accept it. Too afraid of its strength. Too afraid maybe he didn't love her back. But she *had* always loved him. Just as he had always loved her. That was why the two of them had ended up horizontal at the office Christmas party two years ago. It was why they'd come close to having sex in college. It was why they'd fooled around when they were teenagers. Even then, they must have been falling in love. And even then, they'd been too half-witted to realize it.

Or at least Becca had been too half-witted to realize it. Turner, she thought, recalling the look on his face the Saturday before, had known all along. But he hadn't told her, because he'd been afraid he would lose her. She, who had always said sex would mess things up in their friendship.

She was such an idiot. She should have realized that, with Turner, sex would be infinitely more than just sex. It would be love, too. And it would only make what the two of them already shared better. Better than better. Perfect. Because that was how she'd felt over the past few weeks with him. As if nothing in her life would ever be wrong again.

"But the posthypnotic suggestion didn't work for Turner," Becca objected. Though why she was objecting when it looked like things were going to be okay, was beyond her. "He told me the other night. And I remember that first time, when I came on to him, he did his best to put me off. I mean, he did put me off. It wasn't until later that we actually made love. And even then, he resisted me for as long as he could. So he couldn't have been responding to the word *underwear* the same way I was. Otherwise, that first time, he would have been all over me the same way I was all over him."

"If the posthypnotic suggestion didn't work for Turner," Dorcas said, "it was only because Turner obviously didn't *need* a posthypnotic suggestion to put aside any inhibitions he might have. He would have made love with you no matter what the circumstances. All he needed was to know that you wanted it, too. Once he did know that…"

Wow, Becca thought. Dorcas was good. Forget the hypno part. This was therapy, plain and simple. Becca should have been on a couch a long time ago.

Except it should have been on a couch with Turner.

"Dorcas," she said, "I don't know how to thank you."

"Well, a good start might be not reporting me to the hypnotherapist watchdogs," she said nervously.

Becca smiled. "Throw in a free quit-smoking session for me and Turner—once we get this straightened out, I mean—and we'll call it even."

"Done," Dorcas said with a smile that showed obvious relief.

Because she and Turner *would* get this straightened out, Becca promised herself. Today. Hey, he was home from work, right? She just needed to stop by her place first to change clothes and pick up a few things. She'd be spending the night with him, after all. The first of many, if she had anything to say about it. And she'd show up unannounced, of course, since that would give him no choice but to open the door to her. And then she'd tell him…

Well. She'd tell him how much she loved him.

No. Better than that. She'd *show* him.

But there was something else she had to do first. "Dorcas?" she said. "I need one more favor from you."

"Anything," Dorcas told her.

"I need for you to take away that posthypnotic suggestion about the word *underwear*," Becca told her. "Because I don't need it anymore. And I need for you to do it as soon as possible. I need for you to hypnotize me again, right here and now, and clear all the cobwebs out of my brain. Because the next time I make love to Turner, I don't want there to be anything between us." She smiled a little tentatively. "No fears, no worries, no inhibitions, no posthypnotic suggestions."

No underwear, she added to herself with a smile.

Dorcas nodded. "No problem."

Good, Becca thought. That was good. And soon, it would be good between her and Turner again, too. Better than ever, she promised herself. Because the next time she and Turner got together, it would be for the rest of their lives.

EVEN THOUGH IT WASN'T a Friday or Saturday night, Turner was lying on his couch staring at the TV—wow, he'd never realized how *Night of the Living Dead* was such a perfect metaphor for romance in the twenty-first century—when he heard the knock on his front door. But he didn't feel like answering it. Even though it was early afternoon, he'd left the blinds closed throughout his apartment. The bright, cheerful, sunny day outside would have ruined the lousy mood he wanted so badly to nurture. Whoever was at his front door was sure to offer a diversion, and he didn't want one of those, either.

No, he just wanted to lie here comatose and watch while Duane Jones beaned the undead right and left with a variety of household objects, because it made Turner feel so much better about the way he'd left things between himself and Becca. Hey, maybe he'd lost the love of his life, but at least he wouldn't be eaten by zombies.

So that was a definite bonus.

Unfortunately, whoever had come calling evidently didn't appreciate the undead's influence on cuisine the way Turner did. The banging continued until he figured the only way to shut the person up would be to answer the door, tell whoever it was to shove it, then slam the door in the idiot's face and return to his couch and his undead.

Grumble, grumble, grumble.

Jackknifing up from his prone position, Turner grabbed the remote and thumbed the button that paused the DVD, then felt enormous gratification that the halted picture was a close-up of one of the odious, rotting, putrid zombies. It captured so perfectly the way Turner felt about himself at the moment. Then he shuffled slowly to the front door, caring not one whit that he was dressed in nothing but boxer shorts decorated with chili peppers, and a T-shirt bearing the logo for a notoriously bad brand of beer. But when he pressed his eye to the peephole and saw who stood on the other side, he—

Oh, hell. He still didn't care how he looked.

He did, however, unlock and open the door to Becca, whose appearance was infinitely more attractive than his own. Her tawny hair hung loose past her shoulders beneath a cuffed knit cap the color of a ripe apple. A matching scarf was wound around her neck what appeared to be two or three times, disappearing into a halfway zipped leather bomber jacket. Her blue jeans, as always, were snug and faded, ending in hiking boots that should have looked incongruous on her, because they were so masculine, but instead just made her seem that much more feminine.

"Hi," she said, smiling.

Turner tried to smile back, but couldn't quite manage it. "Hi," he said quietly.

"We need to talk," she told him, echoing his words of two days before.

Frankly, Turner was of the opinion that they'd said more than enough on Saturday, and, speaking for himself, he had nothing left to say. Except maybe a few words that weren't fit to see light anywhere but the men's room at the bus station.

"So talk," he told her, hoping his gruff delivery would make her go away.

Instead, she only smiled more. "What a lovely invitation," she said. "I think I will come in and stay for dinner. Thank you so much for asking me."

Before Turner could stop her, she was pushing past him, much the same way she had that night she'd spent at his place a month ago, when she'd wanted to make sure he stuck to the terms of their bet, and she'd come out of his room wearing his football jersey and knee socks, and he hadn't been able to help smoking, and then he'd lost the bet and had to go with her to see a hypnotherapist.

And, hell, look how that had turned out.

"Becca, what are you doing here?" he asked defeatedly as he closed the door behind her.

His gaze dropped to her hand, though, when he saw that she was carrying the same oversize bag she'd been carrying that other night, when she'd had it filled with enough stuff to last the entire weekend.

And, hell, look how that had turned out.

"We need to talk," she said again. "Or, at least, I need to talk. I need to tell you something very interesting that Dorcas told me about hypnosis."

Turner held up a hand in a silent plea for her to go no further. "Don't," he told her. "I don't want to hear another word about hypnosis, or hypnotherapy, or barking like a dog, or flapping my arms like a chicken, or Vegas lounge acts, or red crushed velvet. I don't want to ever hear another word for the rest of my life about any of that stuff."

"Okay," Becca said agreeably. "Then I'll just tell you this. I love you, Turner McCloud. And I have for a long, long time. And if you don't make love to me soon, I'm going to have to wrestle you to the ground and have my way with you."

Okay, since that wasn't exactly what he'd expected Becca to say, then maybe he should let her clarify herself. Even if it meant bringing hypnosis into the conversation.

"Come again?" he said.

She smiled. "I thought you'd never ask."

She dropped her bag onto the floor, tugged off her cap, unwound her scarf and started to unzip her jacket. But even after she'd tossed the jacket onto a chair, she didn't stop. Instead, she went to work on the buttons of the flannel shirt she wore beneath it, tugging it free from the waistband of her jeans to finish the job, then tossing it, too, onto the chair. Beneath it, she wore a long-sleeved T-shirt, so Turner figured she just must have been overwarm with the flannel one, too, and now she would sit down.

But she didn't sit down.

Instead, she pulled the T-shirt free of her jeans, too, crossing her arms over her midsection to grab the hem on each side, then pulled the shirt up over her head to reveal a rather ravishing bit of black lace beneath. It was one of those bras whose cups came to a stop when fully half of a woman's breasts were still showing, the kind that was worn not for support—about which he'd learned more than he cared to know, working on the Bluestocking account—but for seduction.

Then she went to work on the fly of her blue jeans.

Turner watched her activity with much puzzlement. Well, not *just* puzzlement, of course, but he was definitely baffled by her behavior. Had he said the word *underwear* since she'd arrived? He thought back. Nope. Not even a variation thereof. Had Becca used the word *underwear*? he wondered. But nope, she hadn't, either. So why was she taking her clothes off, as if she intended to engage—right away, by the looks of it, since she'd dropped to the couch to wrangle off her boots—in some wild monkey lovin'?

"Becca?" he said. "What are you doing?"

"What does it look like I'm doing, Turner?"

He took a moment more to watch her, just in case, you know, maybe he had the wrong idea. She pulled off one boot and tossed it aside, then bent over to unlace the second. When she did, her breasts spilled a little more out of the black lacy bra, pushing against her thighs in a way that made him want to walk to where she was sitting and stoop between her legs and run his mouth over all those body parts that had so conveniently moved into such close quarters. Before he could take a step toward her, however, she was plucking off the other boot and pitching it to the side, then standing again to peel off the blue jeans that had gotten caught around her ankles.

Yeah, he was pretty sure now that she was getting undressed.

"It, um, it looks like you're taking your clothes off."

She beamed at him as she stomped out of her jeans and kicked them away, too. "Oh, I do so love a man who's got smarts."

Turner suddenly had something else, too, when she straightened and he saw the black lace panties that matched the bra and which were—almost—there. His mouth went dry as other parts of him started to catch fire.

"Becca?"

"Do you like it?" she asked when she saw where his gaze had fallen. Then, before he had a chance to reply, she added, "Look, it's a thong." And she spun around to give him a rear view. In more ways than one.

"Becca…"

"I never wore one before today," she continued blithely, her back still turned to him, as if she were talking about something as harmless as a Scooby-Doo Band-Aid. "It's a Bluestocking product. It's amazing how comfortable it is. I think we should make it a focal point of the campaign. What do you think?"

What Turner thought, he should probably keep to himself. Because it mostly involved, um, focaling Becca's, uh, point. And bluestocking her product. That kind of thing.

"Turner?" she asked, looking over her shoulder.

But still not turning around. And the sight of her bare ass beckoning to him that way just made him want to walk over there and cover it with both hands. Among other things.

"Don't you like it?" she asked.

It occurred to Turner then that he had no idea what she was talking about, whether it was the garment she was—almost—wearing or the body part she was—almost—wearing it on. No matter. He knew the answer.

"Yeah, I like them... I mean it...a lot," he said. And then some semblance of reason returned to his fuzzy brain—dammit—and he remembered that he was supposed to be objecting to what she was doing because...

Well, he couldn't remember why at the moment, because she moved her own hand to her backside, splaying it over one ivory cheek. But he did know he was supposed to be objecting to...something.

Wasn't he?

Becca sighed impatiently as she looked over her shoulder again at Turner and wondered what the hell was taking him so long. She'd gone so far as to reach out and grab it herself. How much more incentive did a man need? Fine. Then she'd just go over there and give him a helping hand. Literally.

Straightening, she turned around and covered the short distance between them in three easy strides. Dropping her gaze to his shorts, she saw significant—very significant—evidence of his interest. In fact, that evidence was *so* significant, it was going to become documentation if it got any bigger, because it would be right out there in the open where no one could deny it.

Not that Becca wanted to deny it. No, she had other plans for Turner's evidence, if he'd just get with the program.

Dropping her hands to the hem of his T-shirt, she tugged upward very insistently, so insistently that he had no choice but to raise his arms over his head so that she could strip the garment off of him completely. She then hooked her thumbs into the waistband of his boxers. But she paused before jerking those down.

She met his gaze intently. "Have either of us used that word that was causing me to behave like a shameless hussy around you?" she asked him.

He shook his head, but said nothing.

"And yet, here I am, behaving like a shameless hussy around you," she told him.

This time he nodded, but he still said nothing.

"Why would I do that, do you think?" she asked.

He shrugged, then said, "Have you been under a lot of stress and pressure lately?"

This time Becca was the one to shake her head.

"Been working on any racy lingerie accounts?"

"No more than usual," she told him.

He looked thoughtful for a moment. "And I know you haven't gone too long without sex."

Well, that was debatable, she thought. It had been *hours* since the two of them were last together.

"Then I'm stumped," he said.

She looked down at the documentation between his legs. "Oh, I don't know about that…."

"I mean I'm out of ideas," he said, his documentation growing larger at her compliment. "I don't know why you're behaving this way," he added.

Becca smiled and looked at his face again. "I do," she said. "It's because you turn me on. And it's because I love you. And it's because I want to spend the rest of my life loving you and being turned on by you."

He narrowed his eyes at her. "Come again?"

She expelled an exasperated sound. "I'm *trying* to."

"No, I mean… How can you know that?" he asked. "Dorcas hypnotized you and—"

"She did," Becca agreed. "This morning, in fact. And she took away the posthypnotic suggestion about that word, which I don't want to say, because I don't want you to think I'm responding to that, when what I'm really responding to is you, and when what I've been responding to all along is you."

Before he could ask more about that, Becca told him about her exchange with Dorcas, and how the hypnotherapist had told her it was impossible for anyone to be hypnotized into doing something they didn't want to do in the first place. And with every new word she spoke, Turner's expression changed, going from wary to cautious to hopeful to ecstatic to totally and completely aroused. And then to something else, something Becca recognized, because she felt it, too: love.

"Dorcas took the suggestion away?" he echoed when she was finished talking.

"Yup."

"You're not responding to…that word…right now?"

"Nuh-uh."

"You're responding to me?"

"Yah-huh."

"You've always been responding to me?"

"Yepper." Becca pressed a quick kiss to his mouth, then added, "And I'm responding to my love for you, too."

She started to tug down his boxers, but he pulled away from her, saying, "Hold that thought."

His retreat caught her off guard, but the next thing she knew he was disappearing into his bedroom. "But it's not the thought I want to hold!" she called after him.

With a sigh of frustration, she followed him, halting in the bedroom doorway when she saw him turn away from the closet holding a little red bag that she recognized from a downtown jeweler.

"What's that?" she asked.

He withdrew a little red box from the little red bag and

opened it, then crossed the room to show it to Becca. Nestled in a crush of red velvet was the most beautiful diamond ring she'd ever seen in her life. She gasped with delight when she realized what it meant.

"I bought it just before running into Dorcas," he said. "That's why I went downtown Saturday. I wanted to give it to you Saturday night. But then—" He halted, because they both knew what had happened to prevent him from going through with the plan. "You like?" he asked.

She shook her head, happiness welling inside her to near overflowing. "I love," she told him.

His relief was almost palpable. "Then you'll wear it?" he asked.

"Only if it means what it traditionally means to wear a ring like that," she told him.

He smiled. "It means that sixty years from now, you'll still be putting on stuff like that and we'll still be smoking up the sheets together. Only we'll be doing it as randy old married people instead of randy young single people." He thought for a moment before adding, "And when we come home from work at night, it won't be Englund Advertising. It'll be Mercer-McCloud Advertising. A Fortune 500 company we started up shortly after our wedding."

Becca plucked the ring from the box and put it on her left ring finger. It fit perfectly. "A Fortune 100 company," she corrected. "Mercer-McCloud," she murmured as she turned the ring one way, then another, admiring the sparkle. "I like the way those two names go together. A lot." She looked at Turner again and grinned. "And I like how those two people come together even better. So I'll wear this ring for the rest of my life," she promised. "Now let's get smokin'."

He pulled her to himself and kissed her deeply, lifting his hands to palm her breasts as she moved hers to the opening in the front of his shorts. Each of them growled in satisfaction at the touches, and for a long moment, they only stood there, kissing and caressing each other.

Becca pulled away first, pushing down Turner's boxers as she sank to her knees. When she knelt before him, she curled her fingers around his cock and guided it to her mouth. First, she only teased him with the tip of her tongue, gliding it down one side and up the other, circling the taut head with hasty, butterfly touches. Turner groaned aloud and wove his fingers into her hair, lightly nudging her head forward, silently urging her to take him more deeply. So Becca did, sucking him into her mouth with gentle pressure, pulling him back as far as she could. He moved his pelvis forward, propelling himself deeper still, and she opened her mouth wider to accommodate him, loving the way he filled her.

She reached up with one hand to flatten it over his torso, reveling in the feel of his contracting muscles as she pleasured him. Eventually, though, he pulled away from her, then dropped to the floor to join her, moving behind her. Becca bent forward, bracing her hands on the rug as he situated himself between her legs, his stiff rod pressed into the cleft of her ass. He leaned over her, cupping a breast in one hand as he drove the other into the hot wet flesh between her legs, and Becca moved one knee to the side to better accommodate his exploration.

She sighed in delight when he inserted his middle finger deep inside her. As he caught her nipple between his thumb and forefinger, he fingered her slick canal, knuckling her sensitive flesh with the others. Again and again, he penetrated her that way, and with every new foray, her legs grew weaker and her breathing grew shallower. Gradually, a second finger joined the first, then a third, until he was stretching her wide and driving her crazy. And all the while, he rolled and taunted her nipple, until Becca could scarcely remember her name or where she was.

He must have sensed when she was close to coming, because he withdrew from her and turned her body again, until she lay on her back on the floor beneath him. Then he knelt in front of her and gripped an ankle in each hand to spread her legs wide. Moving his entire body forward, he thrust himself inside her to the hilt, filling her in that way she loved so much, the way that made her feel as if the two of them were one. Still holding her legs apart, he withdrew and thrust forward again, their bodies joining with a fierceness unlike anything she'd felt before. Again and again he took her that way, utterly controlling the action. Finally, though, he released her legs and withdrew from her, then took both of her hands in his and helped her to a sitting position.

But Becca already knew what he wanted, so in tune was she now with what he liked. With what they both liked. He placed his hands on her waist and guided her over, turning and positioning her body so that she was on all fours again. Then he moved behind her once more, placing his hands on her ass and spreading her, to insert his thumb inside her, shallowly at first, then penetrating her deeper. And as she gasped at the depth of his intrusion, he thrust his body forward again, filling her once more from behind, this time with his hard, heavy cock.

They coupled that way for a long time, Turner pummeling her from behind and penetrating her with his thumb.

And then, with one final thrust forward, he came inside her, their essences mingling as their bodies and their spirits and their hearts already had.

A long time later, they lay in Turner's bed, naked and satisfied—for now. In the velvet light of the twilight filtering through the blinds, Becca turned her left hand one way, then another, catching the scant light in a way that made her ring glisten.

"You're sure you like it?" Turner asked.

"I'm sure I love it," she corrected him. She dropped her hand to her side and snuggled against him. "Just like I'm sure I love you, too."

"Forever?" he asked.

She pushed herself up on one elbow and met his gaze levelly. "I can't believe you're still uncertain about that," she said.

He lifted a hand to push her hair over her shoulder, then cupped her jaw gently in his fingers. "I'm not uncertain anymore," he told her. "I just like to hear you say it, that's all."

She smiled. "I love you, Turner McCloud. *Je t'aime. Ich leibe dich. Te amo. Ik houd van u.*"

He gaped at her, then laughed. "Hey, you've been reading my *How to Talk to a Girl in Any Language* books, haven't you?"

"Well, *you're* not going to need them anymore," she pointed out.

He pulled her close, tucking her head beneath his chin. "No, I'm not," he agreed. "Because we speak the same language, and we speak it fluently."

"But can I make a suggestion?" she asked.

"As long as it isn't posthypnotic," he told her.

She chuckled, but wisely made no comment on that.

"From now on," she said, "let's talk to each other in the universal language of love."

"You talk," he told her as he scooted down on the mattress beside her. "Me, I'm going to rely on the sign language of love…."

And as the night grew darker around them, Becca got a crash course in the sign language of love, no textbook required. And she discovered that it was a *very* demonstrative language indeed.

* * * * *

Look for Elizabeth Bevarly's new title
YOU'VE GOT MALE
coming in October 2005
from HQN Books

If you enjoyed what you just read,
then we've got an offer you can't resist!

Take 2 bestselling love stories FREE!

Plus get a FREE surprise gift!

eHARLEQUIN.com

The Ultimate Destination for Women's Fiction

Becoming an eHarlequin.com member is easy, fun and **FREE!** Join today to enjoy great benefits:

- **Super savings** on all our books, including members-only discounts and offers!

- Enjoy **exclusive online reads**—FREE!

- Info, tips and **expert advice** on writing your own romance novel.

- FREE romance **newsletters,** customized by you!

- Find out the latest on your **favorite authors.**

- Enter to win exciting **contests and promotions!**

- Chat with other members in our **community message boards!**

To become a member, visit www.eHarlequin.com today!

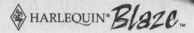

HARLEQUIN®

Blaze™

COMING NEXT MONTH

www.eHarlequin.com